Sophie

William Wheaton
Paul Armstrong

1st WORLD
PUBLISHING

SOPHIE

William Wheaton

© William Wheaton 2009

Published by 1stWorld Publishing
1100 North 4th St., Fairfield, Iowa 52556
tel: 641-209-5000 • fax: 641-209-3001
web: www.1stworldpublishing.com

First Edition

LCCN: 2009927407
SoftCover ISBN: 978-1-4218-9088-3
HardCover ISBN: 978-1-4218-9087-6
eBook ISBN: 978-1-4218-9089-0

This material has been written and published solely for educational purposes. The author and the publisher shall have neither liability or responsibility to any person or entity with respect to any loss, damage or injury caused or alleged to be caused directly or indirectly by the information contained in this book.

The characters and events described in this text are intended to entertain and teach rather than present an exact factual history of real people or events.

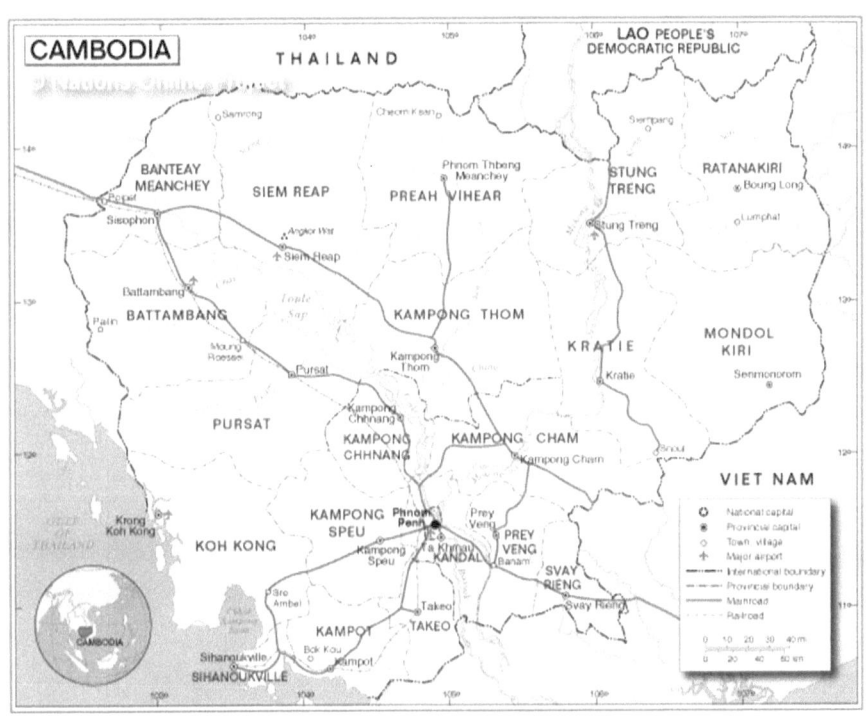

Acknowledgments

I want to thank Paul Armstrong and Sonja Tanaka, who contributed their talents and time in assisting me to bring to the world, through this book, my childhood experience and the story of my escape from Cambodia in 1975; it was the time when the Communists took over my country and killed nearly 2 million people.

A lot of thanks to my editor Christine Schrum. She worked hard to ensure that every sentence of the book was clear and precise. Christine is the true master of communication. I also take this opportunity to thank all of the staff at 1st World Publishing who worked on this book.

Thanks to Mr. Douglas MacPhail, who reviewed my final draft, gave *Sophie* two thumbs up, and offered some additional suggestions, making the book even better. Mr. MacPhail was a lawyer in the U.S. Navy in his early career. He was truly one of a few good men in those days.

Thanks to my friends at work who encouraged me throughout the process of writing this book and offered me valuable suggestions to improve the quality of my writing and thought. I also have many friends outside of work who showed me support and encouragement. My thanks go to them as well.

And last but not least, special thanks go to my family, Vicki Yeb, Cathy Yeb, my mother, my two brothers and my sister, who give me all their love and support.

Author's Note

Sophie is a book about my adventure, escaping to freedom, first to Thailand and then immigrating to the United States, when the Communists took over Cambodia in 1975. Communism is no longer a threat to our free world, and means nothing for our young generation today.

Sophie takes you back to the era of Communist expansion in Asia, from 1954 to 1975. The final French defeat on the battlefield of Dien Bien Phu, the region in the northwestern Vietnam, on May 7, 1954, was the beginning of French withdrawal of their troops from Indochina (Vietnam, Cambodia and Laos). The French left the area in 1954, during the period of the Cold War, while the Soviet Union dominated Eastern Europe. Asia might have fallen into Communist hands if the United States had not been present in South Vietnam at the time.

This is a quote from The New York Times published on July 7, 2009: "In retirement, he (Robert McNamara) listed reasons: a failure to understand the enemy, a failure to see the limits of high-tech weapons, a failure to tell the truth to the American people and a failure to grasp the nature of the threat of Communism." We failed because we did not understand our enemy, who had chosen every means to defeat us. Psychologically, our enemy was successful in convincing the American people that The Vietnam War was futile. I believe wholeheartedly that the American men and women who served in Vietnam sacrificed their life to stop Communist expansion in Asia and to protect freedom and liberty of the human race.

Saigon (South Vietnam) fell on April 30, 1975. That day, millions of Vietnamese left their country, for fear of Communist prosecution. They left on small boats heading to China Sea, where they were picked up by the American 7th fleet. The Americans rescued everyone, gave them new homes and a new country.

In Cambodia, there were 1.7 million people killed by the hands of Communists in 1975 alone. We owe our life to America, and to the men and women who served in Vietnam. Withdrawal of American troops from Vietnam in 1975 was not our defeat in the war against Communism, but a setback; fourteen years later the Berlin wall came down; the Cold War ended in 1990 and the Soviet Union collapsed one year later. Today we face a new enemy of the same kind: they want to take away our freedom, liberty, and our ways of life.

Sophie takes you one step further, looking at corruption in Cambodia. Corruption alone is the cause of poverty and disgrace, and led to the defeat in the war against Communism. The character flaw of our King, Prince Norodom Sihanouk, is mentioned in the book. He repeatedly lied to his people, executed anyone who was against his politics and agenda. His soldiers tied victims against poles, covered their eyes with black cloaks, and shot them in cold blood. The scenes were filmed and shown on TV and movie theaters before shows started or during intermissions. The images of these executions are vivid in my mind today. All dictators' minds work alike: they lie, manipulate the people who give them their trust, and silence anyone against them.

The power of a country should belong to the people, not to the government!

William Wheaton
The Author

Chapter One

On the morning of April 3, 1975, I said goodbye to my mother, two brothers, and sister and walked out from the Phnom Penh airport terminal to the airfield toward the DC-3 plane. I walked in line with the other passengers, and as we approached the plane a missile flew over our heads like a hissing snake, followed by a thunderous explosion. Black smoke rose from the ground at the edge of the airfield. Passengers scattered in all directions. Some ran toward the airplane and others raced back toward the terminal, where my family huddled close together at the door. I was about 50 feet from them. Without a second thought, I ran toward them as fast as I could.

When I reached the door, I pushed them inside the terminal and cried out, "I'm not going. I just can't leave you behind." My ten-year-old brother looked at me with tears in his eyes, for he understood it was our last moment together; after this, we would be separated forever. My other siblings were too young to understand why I was leaving the family.

My mother put her hands on my shoulders, leaned forward to kiss me, and then pushed me away as she cried out, tears running down her cheeks, "Go, before it's too late! You aren't safe here." I threw myself into her arms and hugged her for a moment. Then I turned to my siblings and hugged them, one at a time. "Go home," I told them, "It's very dangerous here. I'll be back in a few months." I stepped back, turned around, and left the building.

"Good luck and good-bye! I love you son." My mother's voice trailed behind me as I ran toward the plane, shouting at the top of my lungs for the pilot and crew to wait for me.

As I neared the staircase, two rockets flew over my head—one dropping in the airfield and the other just outside. I grabbed hold of the handrail and climbed the steps as fast as I could. From the top of the stairs, I looked back toward the terminal one last time. My family was nowhere in sight. I stepped inside the airplane and the door closed behind me.

Inside, it was very crowded. Passengers sat crammed into their seats, many with children on their laps or squirming on the floor at their feet. They all talked loudly and shouted across the aisle, for there were only two rows of seats against the walls. Babies whimpered and cried in their mothers' arms.

As I walked down the aisle, a rank, musty smell hit my nose. I stopped walking and looked around me. Then I realized that the carpet was wet and there were several crates filled with pigs, chickens, ducks, and pigeons piled up at the rear. I caught the eye of a boy on my left. Graciously, he and the girl on his right moved over to make a seat for me. I thanked them and sat down.

In my seat, I leaned against the wall and pulled a handkerchief from my pants pocket. I held it to my nose and mouth, trying to block the horrific stench. Aside from the animals, there were a hundred people in this small airplane; I wondered whether it would lift off.

As the explosions continued outside, the airplane's engines began to roar in preparation for takeoff. The plane moved slowly down the runway and stopped for about five minutes, idling. Then, it sped down the strip, going faster and faster, shaking, and lifting off just as a rocket soared past the left wing. The rocket crashed into the ground, sending plumes of black smoke rising through the air. As the airplane climbed high into the sky, the smoke below became dim and slowly disappeared.

The DC-3 turned 180 degrees and flew toward Koh Kong, a province bordering Thailand, west of Phnom Penh. Everyone cheered; for now at least, we were safe from the incoming enemy rockets of the Communist rebels. Nonetheless, we were flying above the enemy territory at least for another half hour.

A man sitting opposite me looked in my direction and gave me a smile. I politely returned it. Then I thrust my elbows on my lap and buried my face in my hands, thinking of the past five years of my life in Phnom Penh, the city where I had been born and raised.

I'm now on the flight to Koh Kong, preparing to leave Cambodia, for I believe that the Communists will take over and there will be many killings. I have to escape to Thailand for my life.

I ran away from home once when I was thirteen years old. My father brought me back home from the local police station, where I had been charged and held as a runaway boy. That was a long time ago. My leaving home this time is different. I have no idea when I'll be back or when I will see my family again.

The United States has been fighting this war against Communism in Southeast Asia for sixteen years, since 1959. The battles broke out in Cambodia in early 1970, when I was just a boy. There have been no American troops in Cambodia, but the United States has provided military intelligence and financial support for the war.

In 1973, the Communists took over most parts of my country and Phnom Penh, the capital of Cambodia, has been vulnerable. It has been battered by enemy explosions, whether rockets from the sky, bombs planted in public buildings, or hand grenades thrown in the crowds in public places. There have been so many deaths and injuries in the city. This horrific war has brought starvation, malaria, cholera, tuberculosis, and other diseases into the city.

Corruption in our government has torn the country apart. Money from the United States that was intended to recruit Cambodian soldiers has instead gone into the bank accounts of key government employees and military generals. Our government has been weak for the lack of money and soldiers. Phnom Penh has been much worse since the United States finally yielded to the Communist forces and was forced to pull troops out of Southeast Asia in late 1974. Communist reign is a sure thing now; it's only a matter of time. Most of the rich citizens are fleeing the country, but the poor are trapped.

Friends and relatives have advised me not to leave the country, saying that the new government will not harm its people. They believe that this inevitable Communist victory will be simply a transfer of power from the Capitalist system of government to the Communist. My mother knows better, though. She understands politics more than most of her friends, and she has encouraged me to leave, at least temporarily, just to be on the safe side.

"Son, the Communists will kill all the intellectuals and students if they ever catch them," she said.

"Are you afraid of flying?" the man sitting opposite me asked.

"No, but those rockets scared the hell out of me," I replied.

"I'm Samnang Lopez," the man said, extending his hand to me with a smile. "Let me introduce you to my family: my wife; my two daughters, Sophie and Mary; and my son, Vichenea."

"My name is Savy," I replied.

In her late thirties, Mrs. Lopez sat next to her husband, also smiling. Sophie, a young woman, sat next to her mother. Vichenea sat on my right, and Mary sat next to her brother.

"The plane's crowded and very uncomfortable," Mr. Lopez said.

"Yes, you are right, sir, the plane's crowded," I replied, turning to Vichenea and adding, "Thanks for the seat."

"That's all right," Vichenea replied.

"Are you going to take a vacation in Koh Kong?" Mr. Lopez inquired.

"It isn't a vacation. As we all know, the situation in Phnom Penh is unstable," I replied, looking him in the eyes.

"I assume you're still in school, if you don't mind my asking," Mr. Lopez said.

"I'm a sophomore in Phnom Penh University. The school is closing. I have no idea when it will reopen."

"The country is falling apart," Mr. Lopez said. "Things could turn out bad, very bad when the Communists come." He paused for a moment and continued, "The rest of your family is not leaving, is it?"

"No, my mother thought I should leave the city for a while," I replied sadly. "She said I will be more vulnerable than everyone in the family when the Communists come." I looked from Mr. Lopez to Sophie and back to Mr. Lopez again and said, "I have two brothers and one sister. My father passed away last year."

Our conversation was interrupted when the airplane shook and dropped altitude abruptly, making my stomach hollow.

"I can tell you're afraid of flying," Sophie said, looking at me and giggling.

"No, I'm not afraid, but the plane seems to be unstable," I said as our eyes met and we exchanged smiles.

Sophie was quite beautiful. At first glance she resembled a model, the kind you'd see on the pages of *Elle*. She had light skin and dark brown hair that fell a little below her shoulders, with a short fringe above her eyebrows in the front. Her face was a soft oval with a pointed nose and beautiful green eyes. Her lower lip was a little thicker than the upper. When she smiled, she showed perfect white teeth.

"My name is Sophia, but Mom and Dad call me Sophie," she spoke slowly, looking at her parents for a moment as though she needed permission to carry on our conversation. "You can call me Sophie if you like." She dropped her gaze to the floor. "We didn't know the plane would be this crowded."

"We need to get out of the city before the New Year," Mr. Lopez cut off our conversation. He was referring to Cambodian New Year's Day, which falls on April 13.

Just last week, news from unconfirmed sources had spread throughout the city that the Communists would take over Phnom Penh the week of April 13. "I don't think we will be safe either with the new government," Mr. Lopez added.

"We flew in a much nicer airplane when we went to Paris," Mary said. She drew her family's attention, and mine as well.

I turned to her and said, "Paris must be very beautiful."

"Yes, we've been many places in Paris, like the Eiffel Tower and this big church called Notre Dame. We took an elevator to the highest level of the Eiffel Tower. When we got up there we looked down below. There were so many cars and lights!" She looked at her sister and continued, "We went shopping on the Champs Elysees for hours and hours. You said you like that place, right Sis?"

"You're right, dear," Sophie replied and looked at me. "My sister, she likes to talk."

"That's all right. She's very cute," I replied, turned to Vichenea, and saying, "You had good times in Paris, I suppose."

"Yes, it's beautiful there. We went there a few times before the war and once two years ago. Mom loves it, right Mom?"

"Yes dear."

"We have a lot of friends there in Paris, and we've also been to San Francisco. My uncle lives there," Vichenea added.

"I've never been in Paris or the U.S.," I said and looked in Sophie's direction. I caught her smile and noticed my heart was beating fast.

"We wanted to go to Paris, but Dad said it was too late, so we are going to take a vacation in Koh Kong instead," Mary added. "This plane sucks. It smells."

"If you don't like it, why don't you jump out?" Vichenea said to his sister, smiling.

"You jump yourself," Mary retorted.

"That's enough kids. Stop talking. The plane's landing soon," Mr. Lopez said. I looked from Sophie to her father and then we stopped talking.

Not long afterwards, the airplane dropped in altitude and dived toward the Koh Kong airport. Through the window behind me, everything below was small: houses, cows, and buffalo on the rice fields, palm trees and others here and there. Everyone onboard seemed anxious until the airplane touched ground and landed safely. We landed right on time; it had been a short, forty-five-minute flight. The passengers got off one at a time. In the airport, before I bid farewell to the Lopez's family, I made sure to linger with Sophie for a little while. I hated to leave her.

Later, a taxi dropped me off in front of an inn that was a quarter of a mile outside of town. I went to the front desk inside to register and pick up my key. After finding my room, I lay my suitcase on the floor and walked to the window to let the fresh air in. The place was small and clean.

There was a queen bed set against the wall to the west, beside which was a night table with a small radio. A table and a chair sat in the right corner opposite my bed, and by the window, the only one in the room, a kerosene lamp had been placed in the middle of the table. The bathroom was in the corner to the left. On the wall above the table hung a large calendar for the year 1975, on which a picture of a beautiful woman was printed. With a big smile on her face, she held a bottle of Coke to her cheek. Above my bed, there was a picture of Angkor Watt, the magnificent temple in Cambodia. A print of traditional Cambodian Apsara dancers was mounted on the opposite wall, and there was a picture of the Palace Royal by the door.

It was about noon and I was hungry. I locked the door of my room and walked out to the street, heading downtown. Under the hot sun, I walked along the road that hugged the seafront. The vast sea stretched for miles to my left, and when I looked, I could see three islands on the horizon and half a dozen fishing boats far from shore.

As I walked, my eyes trailed to one of the islands, and I caught glints of the sun on the water. I took a deep breath as the breeze brushed my face; I inhaled the fresh air into my lungs, relishing it, as I had not seen the ocean for a long time. From the time I had gotten off the plane, I felt a sense of peacefulness. Koh Kong was like a foreign country to me; there were no sounds of gun fights or bombs.

I walked into a bar by the name of Thansour (meaning "the paradise"), one of the seafront restaurants in the city.

"A bottle of Tsingtao, please," I said.

"Yes."

The bartender looked at me, swept the counter with a wet towel, and brought me the beer and a mug. I sipped it straight from the bottle while the bartender handed me a menu.

"You aren't a local, are you?" he asked.

"You can tell?" I replied.

"Absolutely."

"My name is Savy. I just got into town this morning. I came from Phnom Penh," I said, extending my hand to him. We shook.

"I'm Tan," the bartender replied companionably.

"It's nice to meet you," I said.

"Likewise," he replied. "Are you ready to order?"

"Give me fried duck and a bowl of rice. It comes with rice, right?"

"Yes, you got it."

There were a lot of people at the bar, and a policeman sat at one end eating his lunch. I finished half the bottle of Tsingtao, but my food still hadn't arrived. I was hungry and kept drinking while I waited for my lunch.

"Tan, may I ask you a question?" I called to the bartender.

"Another beer?" the bartender asked.

"Ok, why not?" I said and motioned him to come closer. As he approached, I leaned toward him and asked, "I would like to cross the border to Thailand. I just wonder if you know someone who could help." I spoke in a whisper.

"Don't know and can't help you," he responded, looking at me as if the idea was madness. He walked into the kitchen. Five minutes later, he came back and placed my lunch unceremoniously before me on the counter. "Your lunch," he said and walked away.

I sipped my beer while mixing the fried duck with rice, brooding about the possibility of crossing the border.

"You want to cross the border, don't you?" A customer sitting on my right asked me as I began to eat my lunch. "I'm Khom. I've lived in this city all my life."

I looked at him and said, "It's nice to meet you, Khom."

"You want to cross the border to Thailand. I heard you ask the bartender."

"Yeah," I looked at him, "but I was whispering."

"But I heard you," he replied with a smile. "Where do you want to go?"

"Anywhere but here."

"You're crazy," Khom said, "but I can understand, because everyone who has come from Phnom Penh in recent months is planning to escape to Thailand."

"It isn't supposed to be this way," I said. "I'm a citizen of no country.

Sophie

Do you know how difficult it is to get a passport from our government?"

"Don't know and never thought about it. Besides, I've no need for it," Khom said.

"Applying for a passport is almost impossible."

"If you don't have a passport, you can't travel to other countries," Khom said.

"You're damned right," I replied.

"You don't have a passport?"

"No I don't. I applied for one four months ago but never heard from the bureau. And now here I am, planning to cross the border."

"You'll have to do it illegally. You're going to break the law."

"I know! Would you help me anyway?"

"No, besides, the border is closed," Khom said.

We looked at each other and I took a sip of my beer. Khom added, "I miss Prince Sihanouk. He was a good King who led this country in peace for nineteen years until the CIA came, kicked him out of his own country, and brought war to us all."

I must have been staring at him as he spoke, for he stopped, grinned and said, "What? Why are you looking at me like that?"

"Nothing," I replied.

"Spell it out. I don't like people looking at me like that."

"You know something, Khom?" I said.

"What?"

"Your King was a playboy and a coward."

Khom looked at me with anger and said, "Don't ever talk of my King like that. I could break your neck, you know that?"

I looked at him but said nothing. I just smiled.

"What do you want from me with your smile?" Khom asked.

"Friendship. Can we be friends? Leave aside our political views, would you?" I said.

As we were talking, the policeman stood up to walk out. He looked straight at me, and I dropped my gaze to avoid eye contact. Without paying his bill, he walked behind me and out of the restaurant.

"Khom, he did not pay for his lunch," I said to Khom.

"Who?"

"The policeman who just left," I said, gesturing to where the policeman had been sitting.

"You talk too much, my friend. First of all, this is none of your business. Second, keep your nose out of other people's business and you'll live longer."

"I thought the main job of policemen was to serve and protect."

"Yes it is, but first the restaurant owner pays them."

"I didn't know that was how things worked."

"I still think you talk too much. Please keep your nose out of other people's business, my friend."

"Are we friends now?" I asked.

Khom looked at me in the eye and said, "What do you want, smart boy?"

"Can you help me cross the border?"

"I already told you I couldn't help you there."

"I can pay."

"Look kid, the border is closed. Besides, it's illegal to smuggle people to other countries."

"I know. Would you help me anyway?"

"I have to go back to my boat. Someone has to make a living, you know," Khom said. "I've a wife and two kids. I won't go to jail for you."

"Thanks for the company," I said.

"Any time. See you around."

Khom left and I sat alone at the bar, staring at the empty bottle of Tsingtao.

"One more beer?" the bartender asked.

I looked from the bottle to the bartender and said "No, just give me the check." I paid the bill, tipped him, and left the restaurant.

I walked up along the shore, northward, away from town, under the hot afternoon sun. White clouds scattered and floated in the clear blue sky, pulled by a wind from the same direction as I was heading. On my right, an island extended to the west as far as my eyes could see, and to the north for what looked like a few miles.

There were two mountains on this island; the one in front of me looked taller than the one to the west, which stretched to the horizon. White clouds floated behind both of them, and the water lapped their shores with waves the color of the sky, but slightly darker. The island to the north, the larger one, appeared to be nothing but the steep slope of a mountain with a plateau on the northern end. It was covered with trees in some areas, but the top of the mountain and the plateau were largely barren, with rocks scattered over the plateau and hills. On the horizon, I could make out another small isle separated from the larger island by the dark, blue water like a strait leading to the open sea.

I walked a little further and sat down under a palm tree. Its trunk was straight, brown, and bare, with no branches within reach. The limbs stretched high overhead, and some interlocked to make a solid shadow on the sandy ground below. I lay on my back and looked up into the green leaves. The sand felt good against my back. I glanced up at the sky, through the branches, and then shut my eyes. I opened them and looked up again. There was a smooth wind high up in the palm leaves. I shut my eyes a second time and then fell into a deep sleep. When I woke up I felt very good.

I am not alone, I thought to myself, but hundreds of people in this city will leave the country when the Communists come. I leaned against the palm tree with my legs stretched out and pulled Victor Hugo's *Les Misérables* from my knapsack. Reading the story of a convict who turned out to be a good man blessed by Heaven, I found myself thinking about God, His love, and protection. I felt happy. I felt I had left everything behind, the need for thinking and the need to write. On the horizon as far as my eyes could see, the sun was large and bright red. It was descending slowly, and darkness had begun to cover the city, the lost paradise.

Chapter Two

I woke up the next morning in Koh Kong and again went downtown, for it was the only place where I would meet people and possibly find someone who could help me escape to Thailand. When I arrived downtown, I walked into the market, where I found all kinds of fresh seafood brought from the fishing boats in the early morning. There were red groupers; fat, shining pompanos; huge prawns; succulent lobsters and crabs; and many other items I didn't recognize spread over the tables.

Ripe vegetables curled in the baskets like beautiful snakes. There were fine cuts of pork and beef sold at the back of the market. There were live chickens and ducks with their legs and wings bound, lying across tables, constantly cackling. Sometimes, the birds tried to free themselves, but their attempts were futile.

Infants and children played on the ground near the stalls where their mothers busily worked, and people walked up and down the aisles to buy fresh food for the day's meals. Since there were no refrigerators to preserve food, grocery shopping was a daily routine for these market-goers. The place wasn't too crowded, for it was already late in the morning.

I walked out of the market to the seafront restaurant, where I sat at a table on the porch enjoying the beautiful morning. The sky was blue and clouds scattered and floated slowly northward. Flocks of seagulls flew up high, keeping themselves steady in the air. As I watched them, one seagull dived fast toward the sea, caught a fish in its beak, and flew away. It fascinated me.

"Here you are!" A voice came from behind me. It was a familiar voice. It was Sophie's voice.

"Oh! Hi Sophie," I replied as I turned around and saw the lovely young woman I'd met on the plane. I stood up and added, "What a pleasant surprise!" I pulled up a chair for her. "It's a beautiful day, isn't it? Do you care to join me?"

"Yes, indeed," Sophie replied.

"Sit down please," I said, motioning for her to sit. "Do you drink coffee or tea?"

"Coffee would be great. I like it strong."

"Where are your mom and dad?" I asked her politely.

"I don't need them to chaperone me everywhere I go," she replied with a smile, looking at me in the eyes and resting her left hand on my arm.

My heart was pounding and my blood seemed to freeze. I tried to keep my appearance normal and spoke in a calm voice.

"No, I didn't mean to say that."

"You seem nervous," she said and took her hand off my arm.

That's better, I thought. We chatted a bit, and then our breakfast arrived.

"Here is your omelet..." the waiter said and paused. He seemed to be searching for the right words to finish his sentence.

"Miss Lopez," I offered.

"Yes, Miss Lopez, your omelet," he said again, looking at Sophie. He turned to me and added, "Fried eggs over easy for you." The waiter put our breakfast on the table and stood there, staring at Sophie. He was not much older than us. When I looked at him, he said slowly, "You need something else?"

"No, thank you," I replied.

"Miss, is there anything else I could bring you?" he addressed Sophie.

"Thank you, I'm fine," Sophie replied politely.

"I cannot help it," I said slowly, "but I think you're staring at her!"

"Take it easy, man. Take it easy," the waiter replied.

I raised my head and looked him in the eye, ready to punch his teeth out.

"Oh, sorry, sir," he said and walked away.

"I didn't like it, but it's all right," Sophie said to me after the waiter had walked away. "I don't like people staring at me."

"You are very beautiful," I said.

"Do you really think so?"

"Absolutely!"

"You make me blush," she said, glancing at me. Smiling, she laid her hand on my arm once more. "You're so sweet," she added.

We were quiet for a while. I started talking to break the silence.

"This city's beautiful," I said as we began to eat.

My heart beat quickly as I looked at her. She was exquisite.

"Dad was impressed with you. He said you're a smart boy."

She was looking at the ocean as she spoke, the morning breeze blowing the rich, dark brown hair from her shoulders to reveal the soft, white skin of her neck and the large, round hoop earrings dangling from her left ear.

"Thanks!" I replied.

We paused a little and looked at each other in silence.

"Why do we have this terrible war?" Sophie asked.

"Who knows?"

"I'd like to hear your opinions, college boy," Sophie insisted.

"It's obvious: to stop Communist expansion in Asia," I responded. "It's a lost war for the United States."

"Why? The U.S. is so powerful and rich a country. How can it be?"

"The Vietnamese know their enemy well. Besides, this war is unpopular in the U.S."

"Did you hear this morning's news?"

"No! What happened? I missed the news because I woke up late and didn't have my radio on."

"The Americans dropped two big bombs on the middle of the

Defense Ministry and the Education Ministry this morning around eight o'clock, the two buildings that faced each other on highway Number One. They were blown into the sky, there's nothing left," she said, her voice trembling.

"Do you know how many are dead?" I said, finishing up my coffee and taking the last bite of my breakfast.

"No one got hit," replied Sophie. "Isn't it strange?"

"As I understand it, the two buildings contained crucial information about the military personnel, along with the credentials of the intellectuals and educated people in our country. To destroy the documents would save many lives from the Communists' persecution."

"They'll kill us all!" Sophie said, tears in her eyes.

"It's the end of a civilization, Sophie," I replied, looking at her sadly.

She leaned against her chair, looked into the sky, and said, "My uncle, given the fact that he had all means to leave the country, was still in Phnom Penh the day we left." She paused for a second and said again, "You want to take a walk?" I knew then she wanted to switch the topic of our conversation.

"Of course," I replied.

That morning, we walked side by side on the beach of rough sand and rocks. Sophie ran a few feet ahead of me, turned around, and yelled from a distance.

"I want to know more about you, college boy!"

"What do you want to know?" I shouted back.

"Everything about you!"

We walked for a while and found a big rock on the shore, which we dusted off and sat upon, looking out to the vast sea. We were silent as we listened to the sound of the waves beating the rocks along the shore and watched birds flying in the sky, singing.

"It's amazingly beautiful but frightening out there on the sea," Sophie started.

"You're right. It can be very violent sometimes."

"Tell me about your family."

I paused awhile and said, "I was the only child in my family for ten years, and then my mother gave birth to my two brothers and sister. They're two or three years apart."

"Do you look more like your father or your mother?"

"More like my mother, or so I'm told."

"You must have been lonely and spoiled, since you were the only child in the family for 10 years. Who did you play with when you were a kid?"

"My cousin Sarah is one year older than I. We've been friends since we were little. Now she is married and has three children," I replied. "My father passed away last year from multiple cancers."

"I'm sorry!" she replied. "Don't feel bad. There was nothing you could do to help him."

"I know."

"What do you think about the war?" Sophie asked.

"We'll lose the war for sure," I said. "Government corruption has made it impossible for the Americans to win this war."

"Corruption in our country is like a tradition. It has been worse these past five years," Sophie said and paused a moment. "We talked about it in our class discussions and most students thought poverty might be the root of corruption."

"No, it is the other way around. Corruption only brings disgrace and poverty," I replied sadly.

"What you just said implies that the U.S., France, England, and other countries such as Japan and Germany have no corruption since they are rich," Sophie said, leaning her shoulder against mine.

"I didn't say that. Corruption is a part of human evil and greed. My guess is that the countries you just mentioned have laws to deal with this problem." I felt her soft touch and got excited when she leaned against me.

"Do you think the President of the United States can be bought and corrupted?" she asked as she looked off to the horizon, her voice far away as though in a dream.

"Why do you ask that kind of question?"

"The President of the Untied States is generally rich and has too much power. No one dares to investigate him."

"You're right. I never thought about it."

We paused for a moment and then I said, "Lopez is not a Cambodian name."

"No, it isn't. To make a long story short," Sophie said, "I'm Spanish, Chinese, and Cambodian. My great-great-great-grandfather was Spanish with French nationality. He was a doctor who came to Cambodia with the French army during the French colonization back in 1870 and then married a Cambodian woman."

"That explains…"

"Explains what?" Sophie said and looked at me.

"That explains the shape of your nose and eyes," I said jokingly.

"Good or bad?"

"Beautiful."

"Are you sure? You're not flattering me, are you?"

"How could I?"

"Thanks. You're so sweet."

We enjoyed our morning at the beach until the sun was above our heads. It was very hot, so we decided to walk back. We walked side by side. She wore tight jeans and a white t-shirt. Her hair was let down to her shoulders. She was absolutely and astonishingly beautiful, her body, arms, and legs all proportionate to her height.

We strolled along the beach awhile. Suddenly, she stopped to untie her shoes. I turned around as she took off her shoes and handed them to me, saying, "Would you hold these for me? I'd like to get my feet wet for a while." She rolled her pants up to her knees and ran ahead down to the water. Slowing, she walked along the shore and let the calm waves of the sea brush her ankles and feet. She picked up seashells and rocks and turned around in my direction.

"Hurry up, the water's so warm," she yelled.

I held her shoes and walked faster to catch up with her. To please her brought joy into my heart. One of man's desires is to please the woman he loves, I thought. I caught up with her. Sophie was in shallow water near the shore and I on the shore, as far as I could go without getting my feet wet.

"I want to swim," Sophie said, looking at me.

"No one swims here. It's not clean."

"Look! It's clear. You know, I'm on the swimming team at school," Sophie replied. "Let's find a place to swim, ok?"

"I don't know where."

"You find out. There must be a place we can swim."

"Ok, I'll find out," I said, enchanted by her beauty.

We walked side by side, only a few feet apart.

Chapter Three

The sun set beyond the horizon just before seven o'clock. I was in my room, looking out the window. The sky was bright yellow and red in some spots and dark blue elsewhere as the night made ready to cover the city of Koh Kong. As I stood alone there, thinking of my family back home, the night sky claimed the city, swallowing it like a black hole.

The tree by my window began to seem larger than it actually was. Two branches jutted from the main trunk, forming two upward angles against each side. The thick leaves covering the tree seemed to transform it into a ghastly creature, as one might read of in a ghost story. I felt the breeze on my face as I looked outside. The night was perfectly quiet, except for the usual noises: the sound of the wind brushing the tree leaves and cries of crickets.

Sitting on the edge of my bed with my feet on the floor, I stared at the wall dreamily, thinking back to the beautiful afternoon I had spent with Sophie. Time moves very slowly since we parted, I thought to myself. I could not wait to see her again, and my heart beat rapidly as I thought of her. I missed her, everything about her: her beautiful face, her dark brown hair, and the way she conducted herself with me.

News on the radio earlier today announced that our troops had retreated from the towns and villages around Phnom Penh, and our government had mobilized student commandos to help the military protect the city. Hearing it was like a having a knife thrust through my heart. I felt terribly bad that, at a time like this, when I was needed most, I had abandoned my friends and country. We fought the war for five years, brother against brother. But there had been too many killings.

Mr. Lon Nol, President of Cambodia, his staff, and many of the high-ranking employees of our government had already left the country. Our troops fought with what was left, with no reinforcements from the Americans. In the end, it seemed as though we would lose the war as a result of governmental corruption. I pulled up a chair, sat at the table, and wrote a letter to my mother.

Koh Kong, April 5, 1975

Dear Mother,

I'm safe and sound now in Koh Kong. The city has its own charm, for it's by the gulf. A gulf and an ocean are no different to human eyes: both are vast water extending to the horizon as far as the eye can see. There are no explosions or gunfights here in Koh Kong. The city is at peace, in a kind of tranquility that makes me believe there is no war.

War! Why are people killing each other, and for what? Wealth and power: is that the answer? In the last month, many people have fled from Phnom Penh to this city with plans to escape to Thailand.

There will be a lot of killings when the Communists come. Like you said, it's a sure thing. I feel terribly bad that all of us are not together at a time like this. You've given up so much for me. You gave me life and an education, and you handed me the last penny of your savings for my escape to freedom. The country has been at war for a long time: five years. Mother, please leave the country if you have a chance. Life isn't worth living in a country where you can't express yourself freely.

Mother, the border is closed. If I could not cross it, we would be in the same situation, probably getting killed by the Communist dictator. You wanted me to cross the border for my safety. I'll do as you wish at all costs. Leaving the country, far and away from you and my siblings, I hope that I will find a home in a country where I can express myself freely.

Freedom is a gift from God, a free gift like air and water. The Communist government will take it away from us when they come. Lincoln, the 16th President of the United States, said, "Dictatorship in any form degrades the human race." Today it is the Communist dictator (where in the past it was groups of people who used their ideologies, philosophies, and theologies to control others) threatening to kill those who will not submit. These power struggles of the human race will not stop. Dictators do what they can to control others for their own interests. They must be stopped!

Mother, I love you. Please forgive me all my wrongdoings. You are always in my memory, and so are my two brothers and my sister.

Your son,

Savy

I folded the letter, put it in an envelope, sealed it, and put two stamps on the top right corner, readying to send it out the next morning. Then I laid the envelope on the table and walked outside to the hotel courtyard, where there were a few stoves affixed to the ground. I decided to make coffee and enjoy the evening alone.

I walked to the well, pulled a bucket of water from it, and filled the coffeepot half full. I put some more logs under the grill onto the fire and put the pot on. I went inside, brought out the kerosene lamp, and laid it on the wooden table a few feet from the stove. I sat on a bench next to the table, watching the coffee come to a boil. As I watched, the lid popped up, and coffee and grounds ran down the side of the pot. I took it off the grill, using an old newspaper to hold the handle. I put some sugar in the empty cup and poured some of the coffee out. I put the first cup of coffee on the table next to the kerosene lamp and read my book, sipping the coffee once in a while.

"Is it you, Savy?" I heard a voice from a distance. I followed the voice and saw my old friend Khemerin leaning against the hotel fence.

"You son of a bitch! What are you doing here?"

Khemerin jumped over the fence and ran toward me. We hugged and stood facing one another.

"It is you! It has been a long time," said Khemerin.

"I'm glad to see you," I said excitedly.

"Did you make coffee?" Khemerin asked, looking at the coffeepot on the stove.

"Do you care for a cup?"

"That's all you have?"

"Yep!"

"Of course, coffee would be great."

I poured the coffee in a cup while Khemerin paced back and forth between the table and the burning stove. I handed him the cup and said, "Sit down, here's your coffee. What are you doing here?"

"Leaving the country," replied Khemerin.

"Well, now that you put it so bluntly, how do you intend to cross the border?" I asked.

Khemerin stood up, his shoulders facing me squarely.

"The border is tight buddy, very tight. I've been here for two weeks. No one can cross the border," Khemerin stammered. "I have to get to him and give him what he wants. It's the only way."

"Get to who?"

"The Governor!"

"You want to bribe the Governor?" I asked.

"Absolutely. It's the only way out," said Khemerin, "He controls everything in this province. He's the King, Savy, he's the King."

We were quiet for a little while.

"You made good coffee, buddy," said Khemerin.

"Thanks," I said with a smile.

"We have to get out of this place soon, otherwise we're fucked!" Khemerin said. "The Communists are coming and will take over the country soon."

"I know!" I replied.

"We gotta stick together. We've got to get through to the Governor," Khemerin said. I was silent, thinking of Sophie.

"What? You're spacing out? Spell it out buddy."

"I don't think I can leave this city without Sophie," I said in a flat tone.

"Who the hell is Sophie? Is she some chick you met here in town?"

"Not some chick, Khem. We were in the same plane when we left Phnom Penh two days ago. She's extraordinarily beautiful."

"Oh! It's a romance in the middle of a crisis. I think you're bound to die like Romeo," Khemerin smirked and sat back down on the bench, looking at the fire flaring up in the dark night.

"Do you remember the night we camped in Takeo?" Khemerin asked again.

"How can I forget? It was the best time we had!" I replied and looked into the sky. There was nothing, no moon nor stars.

Chapter Four

In July of 1968, Khemerin and I took a trip by train to Takeo, a province located 62 miles southwest of Phnom Penh. It was a fine Friday morning. We embarked on the train from the central station in Phnom Penh at seven o'clock. It was crowded on the train, so we stood on the platform by the door with our backpacks on the floor. The train stopped at several stations and arrived at Takeo station, our stop, at ten o'clock. We got off the train and slung our backpacks on our shoulders. I held my fishing rod in my right hand. We stood in front of the station by the railroad as the train moved on, up the track, and out of sight. Then we walked to the other side of the track and proceeded on our journey into the vast land of grass under the hot sun.

We walked around a high hill, which was bare, with no trees. All around, there was nothing but sand and mud. The road climbed steadily. It was hard work walking up the hill with our heavy backpacks. We reached a bridge crossing the river; down below, the water was so clear. We could see many fish of all kinds—in the deep, fast-moving water, holding themselves in the current. We watched them awhile and then moved on, continuing the journey to our destination.

The road ran on, dipping occasionally, but always climbing. It was a hot day and we were exhausted after the long walk. Not far to our right, on a hill, was a large oak tree that offered plenty of shade from the afternoon sun. We walked under the canopy of leaves, laid our backpacks against the trunk, and stood there, taking deep breaths and looking at the horizon. Ahead as far as the eye could see was a forest of palm trees. Far off to the left was the curved line of a river.

We sat on the ground, our backs against the tree trunk. Khemerin took a nap as I stretched my legs out in front of me, reading quietly. I felt a breeze on my face and then my eyelids grew heavier and heavier and I, too, fell asleep in the middle of the afternoon.

After our nap, we continued our walk, following the direction of the sun. We kept on, going west toward the river, through a forest of palm trees that cast shade upon the ground in splotches. We were very tired when we reached the river, so we decided to camp on the edge of the forest, on a hill not far from the river, for the weekend.

At first, we made two small tents, one next to another, so that we could talk from our tents at night before going to sleep. We found level ground to set them up. Khemerin took the ax out of his backpack, chopped out two projecting roots, and pulled up all the sweet fern bushes by their roots. The place was ours for that weekend and was on high ground, from where we could see meadows and swamps far away along both sides of a small river.

I was tired from the long walk from the train station and from setting up the tents. I spread a blanket on the ground under a palm tree with enough shade. I sat on the blanket, my back against the palm trunk, stretching out my legs, and reading aloud to hear my own voice. Khemerin walked down the hill as I was reading. I read for a long while, until the sun went down behind the chain of mountains far off in the distance.

I stopped reading and stood atop the hill, looking down. What I saw was beautiful: so many trees, swamps, meadows, and the river glistening under the sunset. Khemerin was out there in the meadows shooting birds with a slingshot made from the forked branch of a sapling, large rubber bands, and a leather pouch made from an old bag.

That night, we made a fire and roasted the birds Khemerin had shot for dinner. What a feast that was! After dinner we did nothing. We sat by the fire, watching the flames lick the night sky. Then, after adding a few more logs to keep the fire ablaze all night, we crawled into our tents. It was a quiet night. We talked across our tents for a long time before we went to sleep. We talked about our parents, school, and about girls. We swore never to fall in love with the same girl at the same time.

In the morning, the sun was up early and our tents started heating up. I crawled out under the mosquito net stretched across the mouth of the tent to look at the morning and find Khemerin. He was sitting under the palm tree, reading. The sun was just over the hill. The river was clear, smooth, and moving swiftly in the early morning.

Later, I made a fire to boil coffee. I brewed two cups of coffee, one for Khemerin and one for myself, and put one sugar cube in my cup. Khemerin took two cubes for his. He tossed me a piece of French bread and a brand-new sealed box of "La Vache Qui Rit" cheese. Khemerin and I came from a similar educational background. We had been exposed to the French culture growing up, whereas most Cambodians did not have this opportunity, for they lived in poverty and lacked of education. We were accustomed to French food, such as cheese and bread for a snack; we preferred coffee to tea.

"Open it!" Khemerin demanded.

"Laughing Cow," I said, opening the box. I took three pieces of cheese from the box and tossed it back to Khemerin. I stuck the cheese between the French bread and took a big bite. I said to Khemerin with my mouth full, "It's not too bad! Good idea!"

"I picked it up from MeiLing last week," Khemerin said. MeiLing was an exclusive store in Phnom Penh; it sold only Western food.

"What else do you have in your backpack?" I asked.

"What do you mean?"

"Do you have French wine?"

"No! I was going to bring one bottle of Cheverny 1965, but Dad had found out just before we left for the train. He checked in my back-pack thoroughly," Khemerin said. "He said we are too young for that stuff."

"Right, we are too young," I said, rolling my eyes.

"You make good coffee," Khemerin said.

"Thanks."

Later, we went fishing at the river, where we sat on a big log at the riverbank under a big tree. I threaded the earthworm from head to tail with the fishhook and threw it into the river as Khemrin watched. The bobbers floated on the water for a while, and then moved fast, suddenly dipping below the surface of the water. Immediately, I rewound the fishing line with excitement. Then we saw it: a trout hooked to my fishing line, thrashing on the surface of the water. I reeled it in.

I unhooked the fish, hit it on the head with a piece of wood, and threw it in a basket. Then I started the same process all over again, putting bait to the fishhook and throwing it into the river. Khemerin rose and walked along the shore. He found a bamboo stick, two feet long, and sharpened one end, making a spear, with which he proceeded to catch smaller fish swimming close to the shore.

We fished all day and caught a lot of bluegill and trout. We camped another night, Saturday night, and then broke camp at dawn on Sunday morning, taking the trek we had taken two days earlier, all the way back to the train station.

Two years later, in 1970, the war in Cambodia broke out. It was the year that Khemerin and I were in high school, and so we were obligated to join the student commando to protect our school and city. We had basic training and went to a shooting range to practice. When we were on duty, we wore military uniforms and carried M16s like professional soldiers.

In October of 1970, we were sent on a one-week mission to guard a checkpoint near the Phnom Penh International Airport. Our mission was to provide security to the city and to ensure that people who were going in and out had proper identification and were not carrying illegal weapons. The great irony was that we did not even know whether the IDs we were examining were fake or not, and we did not have a metal detector to search for hidden weapons. The mission was actually a waste of time.

At night we rotated shifts to guard the city limits, hiding ourselves in our posts, which were dugouts surrounded by piles of sand bags. We crouched there, watching for any strange move.

One night, Khemerin and I were assigned to a post from midnight until four o'clock in the morning. We were very conscious of everything around us. We counted all the trees and bushes in sight. We were terrified when flares lit up the night sky; in actuality, they were far away, but they seemed so close.

The sounds of explosions burst out, "Boom! Boom!" far away. Then, black smoke flew up into the sky and fires lit up, seemingly in front of us. It was a horrifying spectacle. The explosions lasted for at least an hour. Then it was quiet for the rest of the night. Later, we found out B-52s had wiped out the whole village which was occupied by the Communists a few miles away.

At four o'clock in the morning, two boys came to replace us. When we returned to the campsite, it was absolutely quiet; nothing was to be seen or heard, except the occasional patrol. By eight o'clock, I was in the shower and Khemerin was in the one next to me. Suddenly, we heard the explosive sound of two rockets being dropped in our campsite, right there in the middle of the barracks. The sound was deafening. Then the shouts broke out: "We got hit! We got hit!"

I crawled hastily out of the shower and found Khemerin, already out of his shower, lying on the ground and hiding behind a tree trunk nearby. He signaled for me to keep my head down on the ground. One more rocket dropped and the shouting quieted down. It was deadly quiet for ten minutes, and then the yelling started up again: "We got hit! We got hit!"

Young soldiers ran all over the campsite to survey the situation. Half an hour later, the wailing swell of sirens filled the air. Four or five ambulances pulled into the campsite. Khemerin and I stood under the tree, leaning against the trunk, watching people running, screaming, and crying as medics scrambled to rush the wounded and the dead to hospitals nearby. There was blood everywhere. I rubbed my eyes with both hands, staring at the scene, unable to believe what I saw before my own eyes. We were too young to die. We were both terrified. It was a hell of a scene.

Chapter Five

The first time I met Khemerin, it was years before our army experiences. It was the first day of junior high, and I was a half hour late for class. When I got there, the door to my class was closed. I pushed it open, rushed inside, and then tripped and fell flat on my face. Everyone in the class laughed at me. I raised my head and caught the eye of a woman in her late twenties standing there in front of me.

"Comment vas tu?" she asked me in French. I realized then that she was my new French teacher.

"C'est bien Madame!" I replied, standing up and dusting myself off with both hands.

"Comment t'appelles tu?" she repeated.

"Savy!" I replied. She looked me up and down from head to toe.

"Prends ton chaise, s'il te plait!" I turned to my left. There was only one seat available in the second row from the front. Without a second thought, I walked toward the seat and took it. I was terribly angry at my carelessness.

"You just made a good scene. You're funny." I heard a whisper from my left.

"No, I'm hurt and embarrassed. It's not funny," I replied, frowning at the boy who just whispered in my ear.

"I'm Khemerin."

"You know my name," I whispered back, tossing him a hateful smile. Everyone in the class laughs at my expense, I thought. At the table to my right, two girls giggled, looking in my direction. They both were beautiful in their own way. Khemerin and I paid attention to the teacher for a little while and then started chatting.

"Elle est belle, non?" I wrote on a scrap of white plain paper and passed it to Khemerin.

"Oui," Khemerin wrote back.

"Comment elle s'appelle?" I wrote and passed the note back to Khemerin, my eyes looking straight at the teacher, who stood in front of the class.

"Bopha," he wrote back. It means "spring flower" in Khmer.

"Elle me plaît," I wrote: she delights me.

"Ferme la!" Shut up!

"Pourquoi?" Why?

"C'est ma voisine, mais son mari est un trou du cul." The note read: "She's my neighbor, but her husband is an asshole."

This written conversation was the beginning of our friendship.

The morning classes, from eight to eleven, were French and History. When the eleven o'clock bell rang, signaling that the morning classes were over, kids ran out of their classrooms, most heading to the bike racks in front of our building. Khemerin and I slowly walked out of our classroom to get my bicycle.

"Where do you live, Khem?"

"I live near Independence Monument." It was an area in Phnom Penh where houses were big, and only rich people could afford to live there.

"You live pretty far from here," I replied.

"Not really. It's only a fifteen-minute drive," Khemerin replied, adding, "How about you?"

"I live on the east side of town, across the river. It takes me at least 45 minutes to get here," I said.

"You spend at least 3 hours a day travelling from home to school," Khemerin said. "You waste three hours a day, 15 hours a week, and 60 hours a month. That's at least one and half working weeks in a month. Do you realize that?"

"You must be an economist if you think like that," I replied with a smile.

"You think I'm joking, aren't you?" replied Khemerin. "I am not joking. I can't tell a joke and I can't tell a lie. If you lost money, you could make up what you had lost, but when you lose time, it's gone forever."

"Khemerin, we're just passing through in this life. You know that right?"

"I never thought about that. You're probably right. We're just passing through."

"We'll start all over in our next life," I added.

"I think you're just as crazy as I am," Khemerin said. "Do you think school is important?"

"It was sure important to the Frenchmen," I replied.

"What are you talking about?" Khemerin asked, shooting me a quizzical look.

"Dad said that in his generation the French soldiers went door to door in our village, forcing boys and girls to go to school," I replied.

"I think you are absolutely nuts," Khemerin said. "If it is important to the French, it must be important then."

"What do you want to do when you grow up?" I asked.

"I don't know, how about you?"

"I have no clue," I replied.

"Now we prove our theory," Khemerin said

"What is that?" I asked.

"We are just passing through like you just said."

"You're damned right! Let's have a good time then," I said and smiled at him.

I unlocked my bike and walked out of the school compound, wheeling my bike along.

"Hey, you two!" it was a voice behind us. We turned around to see the two pretty girls from class walking toward us.

"You were funny this morning, the way you introduced yourself in class," Youvarine said, introducing herself.

"Thanks, but I was actually hurt!" I said. The other girl, Chantoo, did not say anything. She just smiled and listened to our conversation.

"How do you like our teacher?" Youvarine asked.

"I really like her," I replied, sneaking a smile at Khemrin.

"You two have something to hide?" Youvarine said.

"No, she is my neighbor," Khemerin answered. "We just discussed her husband a little. By the way, what's your schedule this weekend?"

"Why?"

"You two should come to my party," Khemerin said.

"What for?" Youvarine asked.

"For no reason. Just to have a good time and to get to know one another," Khemerin said. "You are coming," he said, turning to me. I did not answer.

"I have to ask my mom," Youvarine said, looking to her friend and then back at us. "Hey, I have to go. My mother maybe is outside waiting for me. We'll let you know tomorrow about the party."

"Ok. You two should come. I'll be counting on you," Khemerin said.

The two girls walked away as we looked at each other and smiled. Walking out of the school compound, Khemerin turned toward me and said, "My driver's here. I'll see you this afternoon."

"You have a chauffeur!" I said with surprise.

"Actually, it's Dad's chauffeur," Khemerin replied. He paused for a second and continued, "He's a government employee."

"That's even better," I replied. Khemerin put his hand on my shoulder and said, "You're all right and very funny. I'll see you this afternoon."

He ran to the car, as his chauffeur stood waiting for him by the door of the backseat. Khemerin climbed in, and the chauffeur closed the door and took his seat at the front. Through the window Khemerin waved at me. I waved back to him.

"Son of a bitch," I said to myself. The car turned around, drove away, and disappeared. I jumped on my bike and went home.

During recess, most days, Khemerin and I went to a refreshment stand near the school for snacks. Other times, we went to the railway station south of our school, a short walking distance. We walked along the tracks, back and forth for a little while, figuring the distance of the tracks from one station to the next. Sometimes we sat under a tree with Cokes in our hands, watching the trains go by.

One day, our afternoon class was cancelled and we decided to walk east, along the railroad track, all the way to the central station in downtown Phnom Penh. We walked and ran, chasing one another once in a while.

"Hey, I just figured out what I want to be when I grow up," Khemerin yelled at me over his shoulder.

"What is that?"

"The prime minister of this fucking country!"

"You don't like this good country?"

"I like it all right, but I want to make it better."

"Good thinking, but Prince Sihanouk won't let you do it."

"I know. That's what Dad said last night," Khemerin replied. "How about you? Have you figured out yet?"

"I want to be a writer," I shouted back to him.

"You're good with math and physics and all that stuff. You could be a damn good scientist," replied Khemerin.

"But I want to be a writer," I replied.

"You need to read a lot and write all the time if you want to become a good writer," Khemerin said.

"How much is a lot?"

"Don't know. Maybe you need to read all the books in our school library and all the books in the National Library downtown."

"That is a lot," I replied. I was silent then, walking slowly, kicking the dust on the ground, in deep thought. "First I'll write about you," I yelled out to Khemerin.

"Good, do that. It's a good start," he replied.

Our feet were stiff after the two-hour walk from our school to the downtown area, but it had been fun. We walked into the station and out to the street through the other door. This was the only train station in Phnom Penh, a big five-story building in the shape of a square, where all the railroad employees worked. The name of the station was engraved in French on the façade of the building: "Chemin du Fer Au Cambodge." Beneath it was a big round clock that always showed the most accurate time, day and night. This train station was one of the government buildings in Phnom Penh, and the railroad was also run by the government.

The train station was located in one of the more beautiful sections of the city. In front, there was a public park extending from the building to the riverfront of the Tonle Sap River. The green lawn was covered with row upon row of flowers of all kinds.

It was a good walking distance from the train station to the riverfront. Along both sides of the park, there were many beautiful public buildings; the two that remain clearest in my memory now are the city hall and central bank. Near the riverfront was a beautiful market called Phasa Chhas, or Old Market. In between the train station and Phasa Chhas there was an upscale refreshment stand. If you sat at this refreshment stand and looked to the south, you could see two big buildings facing one another. One was for the Ministry of Education and the other for the Ministry of Defense (the two buildings would later be blown up in 1975 just before the Communists took over the city).

We had a good time in the city and walked back to our school. Instead of going back the way we came, we took a shortcut, crossing the tracks, cutting through some houses in the area, and heading toward the music school, which was not too far from our school.

The music school was a yellow-brick building. We sat on the fence, listening to students playing instruments. It was beautiful: the sounds of violin, piano, and trumpet carried to where we were sitting. I loved music but never had an opportunity to learn any instruments. While enjoying the sounds, we heard the cracking of branches in the tree nearby. Suddenly, in front of us was a baby bird, just fallen from its nest.

We looked at each other. I jumped down from the fence, picked up the bird, held it in my palm, and gently caressed its down. Then I handed it to Khemerin and climbed back into the tree. Khemerin handed the baby bird back to me, and I climbed a few more branches up to the nest laying it in the nest next to its mother. I then climbed down the tree, and the two of us walked back to our school, where we waited until Khemerin's chauffeur showed up and we parted. I jumped on my bike and pedaled home.

Chapter Six

It was early morning in Koh Kong. Rays of sunlight glinted in the sky behind us as we crossed the market square from the center of town to a seafront restaurant. A mischievous raccoon darted from tree to tree in the quiet market square, for the market was not yet open. Another one rushed across the street into a tree hole. Inside the restaurant, Khemerin and I sat at a table with the three fishermen we'd arranged to meet.

Khemerin ordered two cups of coffee mixed with condensed milk—one for me and one for himself. Of the three fishermen, I'd met Khom on the first day of my arrival in Koh Kong at Thansour (the paradise where I ate lunch on the first day of my arrival in Koh Kong). The other two, I'd just met that morning. Sambat was in his forties and Ton in his late twenties.

"Life as a fisherman is tough," Khom said. "Look at my hands, they're very rough. Not smooth like yours." He extended his hands to us, showing his calloused palms.

"Our morning started at four. We made the first round for the early sales," Sambat said.

"We caught small fish and shrimp for our first early sales this morning," Khom added. "We'll catch bigger fish on the second round. We'll go a little farther from the shore."

"Have you ever seen a shark?" Khemerin asked.

"No, we haven't seen anything like that," Khom said. "I don't think there are any sharks in this part of the gulf."

"Not so sure," Sambat said, "We're lucky so far. A monster like that could easily flip over a boat our size."

Looking outside at the bright, clear sky, I listened to the conversation around the table without engaging, my chin in my hands with my elbows on the table. I was half asleep. Ton also seemed somewhat adrift in the conversation; he gazed sleepily outside, beyond the window.

"Would you fight if you encountered one?" I asked.

"I thought you were asleep," Khom replied, looking at me and sipping his coffee.

"No, I was not," I replied.

"You've watched too many American movies. We don't fight with sharks, we run away!" Khom said.

"Coward!"

"Look, kid, you're being rude and inconsiderate to the elderly. I'm going to teach you some manners," Khom said, rising from his chair. Sambat grasped him by the arm and forced him to sit back down.

"Guys, stop it," Khemerin interrupted. We fell silent for a moment. Khemerin continued, "Can you help?"

"We can't," Khom said, turning into my direction. "I told you the other day and you don't believe me? We're not allowed to go close to the border. The coast guard patrols every hour."

"A few months ago we might have been able to do something, but not now," Sambat said.

"Is the situation in Phnom Penh really that bad?" Khom asked.

"Yes," I replied.

Khemerin added, "We are losing this war for sure."

We looked at one another as if there was nothing more to say.

"Would you like to come with us and hang out on the fishing boat?" Khom said, trying to cheer us up.

"Savy, what do you think?" Khemerin nudged.

"Why not? It would be fun," I replied. We finished our coffee, paid the bill, and walked out of the restaurant.

"Wait," Khemerin said, "can I pick up a few packs of beer from here?"

Sophie

"That's not a bad idea. Of course, you can get as much as you want from the bar," Khom replied with a wink. Khemerin walked toward the counter as we waited by the entrance. A few minutes later he came back with two packs of Tsingtao in his arms.

In the blue sky, small clouds were travelling with the wind high above, making dark patches along the green water. A warm breeze blew out across the flat surface of the dusty sands. It was another beautiful morning in Koh Kong.

We got to the boat and climbed in. It was a fair-sized boat, not too large, with all kinds of fishing equipment. Khemerin put the beer aside and we toured the boat. In time, Ton untied the boat and pushed it away from the dock. The engine started and the boat moved slowly away from the shore.

Once the boat had travelled a few miles, Khemerin walked to the stern to take the wheel from Sambat. As he looked into the sky and surveyed the distance ahead through his Ray-Ban sunglasses, one hand on the wheel and the other holding his beer can, Khemerin seemed to be enjoying the beautiful morning. He was at ease navigating the boat on the vast ocean.

"You wanna take the wheel?" Khemerin yelled at me. I was at the bow, stretching my legs in front of me and leaning against the side of the boat.

"I'm ok," I shouted back. I was relaxed, enjoying myself as I inhaled the fresh air and looked to the horizon. Khemerin steered for a while and then came over to me, handed me a beer, and sat down.

"It's fun! But I really miss my family."

"I miss my family too."

"It's a long war, a terrible one, and we are losing it."

"Does your dad have a plan to get out?"

"I really don't know. He was worried the day I left."

"Did he try to stop you?"

"He only said the Americans may have plans to evacuate some people in high positions in the government, but he seemed unsure. He just said it would be wise if I got out of the country for a while."

Our conversation was interrupted when Khom came and joined in.

"Thanks for the beer. It tastes good in the hot sun, like we have today," Khom said.

"You're welcome, pal," replied Khemerin."

"It's amazingly beautiful out there. From this view, all I see is water extending far away under the blue sky." I said, looking to the horizon.

"It's beautiful all right," Khom said. "During a storm it is violent. Big waves could easily turn over a boat this size."

"Have you ever gotten caught in a storm?" Khemerin asked Khom.

"Not really, since I am always cautious and never go too far from shore," Khom replied. "In the past five years, I've lost two boats because they were hit by storms at night. The next morning, they were gone to the bottom of the sea."

I looked up to the vast sky, my mood sinking a little.

"What's on your mind?" Khemerin asked me.

"I am thinking of my cousin Sarah," I replied, looking from Khemerin to Khom and then back to Khemerin. "We were once caught by a big storm on a boat trip along the Mekong River when we were kids."

"Come on! Tell us about it," Khemerin interrupted me, eager to hear the story.

"Yeah, man! What happened?" Khom insisted.

Gazing out over the vast sky, I commenced the story of our horrific trip that night.

My grandparents, Sarah, my cousin and I embarked on a big steamboat with two levels at the port in Phnom Penh in the evening, walking up to the upper level. We laid our blankets on the floor for the night's sleep, as did everyone. There were no rooms, no cabins, except the empty hall. It was a dark night, but a fresh breeze hit us once in awhile as the boat rode along the Tonle Sap River for a short distance, making a U-turn at the reservoir in front of the Palace Royal.

The reservoir is huge. The Mekong River, flowing across China through Burma, Thailand, Laos, and Cambodia from the northeast, pours tons of water into this reservoir. From there, two rivers branch out—the Tonle Sap and the Tonle Bassac but from the sky, it looks like four rivers connect to the reservoir. The Mekong flows from the northeast and continues out to the right, eventually going south into Vietnam and spilling into the China Sea. The Tonle Bassac branches out to the left and also goes down south while the Tonle Sap River flows north during the raining season and reversed back when the season is over. The raining season lasts about six months, from May through October.

That night, in the steamboat, we headed north against the fierce current of the Mekong River. The view of Phnom Penh at night was beautiful, with twinkling lights and tall buildings scattered throughout the city. However, the village on the other side of the river seemed to be isolated from civilization. It was dark, and so were the villages along both sides of the Mekong River. There were no lights, nothing. It was completely dark, except for the silhouettes of tall trees against the night sky.

Soon the breeze seemed to die down. It was hot and humid, even at night. Sarah and I sat shoulder to shoulder at the stern on a bench inside the three-foot-tall iron railing. We talked nonstop, alone sometimes and other times not. Much later, we walked back to our place to sleep. I fell asleep as soon as I put my head on the blanket I had folded as a pillow.

Past midnight, I awoke to the sound of thunder and screams of fear coming from our fellow passengers. Standing up, I looked into the dark sky and saw purple lights flashing through the sky, followed by the sound of thunder again. Rain fell, making a rattling sound on the roof. Fierce winds jostled the boat and splashed the rain through the main hall.

I huddled close to my grandparents and Sarah. The boat was being hit by big waves and swayed from left to right, slowing down as we headed into the wind. Passengers were thrown all over the boat.

Suddenly, I fell backward and landed against the railing. I grasped it with my arms. I couldn't see my grandparents, but Sarah was struggling to hold herself five feet away from me. I extended my hand to her and yelled at the top of my lungs for her to come toward me. She jumped toward me, tears rolling down her cheeks, and grasped my legs as the boat swayed violently. I pulled Sarah toward me and the two of us grasped the iron bars tightly in our arms.

Lightning flashed in the sky, thunder roared, and the rain came down harder and harder. The boat kept inching farther from the bank to the *middle of the river, still against the wind, as it rocked back and forth. We held onto the guardrail with all our strength. In the sky to our right, we saw a bulging dark cloud. Inside it, red and white lights were flashing. It was the eye of the storm. The storm lasted nearly an hour and then died down slowly. We were sure we'd die that night.*

"You were lucky," Khom said.

"What a country we were living in. We couldn't travel 100 miles away from home without putting our life at risk. There was no warning system, nothing," I said.

"Are you kidding? We do not have any warning system here in the gulf today. Every morning we look at the sky and make our own best guess. Sometimes we are right and sometimes not," Khom said bitterly.

We were silent for a moment. "During raining season," I added, "the Tonle Sap flows northward, from the reservoir to the Tonle Sap Lake. You know, the Tonle Sap Lake is huge. It covers parts of five provinces in the northern region of the country. It was a major source of fish for the country's fishing industry before the war."

"The three rivers, Mekong, Bassac, and Tonle Sap, provide the supply of water for seventy-five percent of the people living in the country, and they were the main navigation system before the war," Khemerin added.

From the stern, Ton shouted, "There are three statues of Buddha submerged in the middle of the reservoir. These statutes protect our Kings and the Queen Mother from all harm, according to legend."

I looked at Khemerin and said, sarcastically, "He might be right!"

"You shut up, before they throw you out of their boat."

"What did I say?" I said, feigning innocence.

"Savy agreed with Ton. What is wrong with you two?" Khom said.

"Good, you two are friends now," Khemerin replied, and looked at me with a smile.

I looked from Khemerin to Khom and said "My grandfather and I used to go to places where they caught fish at the Tonle Sap River, to buy freshly caught fish and to watch them work. It was hard work and it fascinated me. They dropped a special kind of net deep in the water and pulled it out every hour.

Sophie

"There were so many fish trapped in that huge basket attached to the net. Fish swam with the current into the net and into the basket and then couldn't get out. They caught so many fish during the fishing season, from November through May. We never thought of a short supply of fish. Then the war started and two years later we had no food to eat: no rice, no fish.

"For years now, we've depended on rice from California, and we eat canned food if we have money, for the Communists occupy the agricultural regions of the country. On the way to school in the morning, I used to see an old man walking up and down the river bank in the docking area of the ferry. He was picking up dead fish that were floating on the river—they were his daily meal. My heart broke when I saw him. Life should not be this way."

"War is terrible, Savy," Khemerin said. "Remember in early 1970, our government commanded a massive deportation of all the Vietnamese living in Cambodia, transporting them to Saigon?"

"I did not understand it then and still don't understand now," I replied.

"The reason was that these Vietnamese weren't to be trusted. Some of them could have been Vietcong members," Khemerin explained.

"Most of them were born in Cambodia, though. It made no sense to send them to Saigon. They lost their homes, their jobs, and friends. It made no sense, whatsoever," I replied.

"There was no justification. It's a war," Khemerin said.

"They put these Vietnamese in camps spread throughout Phnom Penh, as well as on the outskirts of the city, before shipping them out. There were so many of them, a million if not two. I don't remember the statistics well. Their life in the camps was miserable. I've heard a lot of rumors, all kinds of rumors, about these camps. Things you don't want to hear," I said.

"Generally, rumors aren't true," Khemerin said, "These people may have joined the Vietcong when they got to Vietnam. Now they might come back and fight our troops. Our government made a big mistake with this deportation business," Khemerin said.

"It was stupid, actually," I commented.

"I like Vietnamese women, you know, they are sexier than Cambodians!" Ton yelled out.

I looked at Khemerin with a smile and said "Do you agree, Khem?"

"In general, Cambodian women are nice, good women, you know, but Vietnamese women are not so good. They're bad girls. Do you like bad girls or good girls?"

"I know you like bad girls," I said.

"And you do not?" Khemerin asked.

"Tell me some good stories," Khom said, looking at me.

"One day," I said, "our town was hit hard by a big storm. As always, school closed when we had a storm. That was when I was in elementary school. I slept late that day and was happy, for I did not have to go to school. In the afternoon, Sarah and I went fishing in the lake behind our houses. It was a big lake, which extended miles and miles to the east and the north, as far as my eyes could see. We had a lot of fun at the lake. We sat on the bank watching canoes rowing slowly on the surface of water, we ran along the bank to catch butterflies, and we fished the lake with our fishing net, which was simply an old mosquito net cut into a rectangular shape."

"You call that a good story, city boy?" Sambat shouted and laughed from a distance as he held the fishing line.

"What do you mean by a good story?" Khemerin rebutted in my defense.

"When was the first time you got laid?" Khom prodded, grinning.

"I had no patience for romance and marriage and all that stuff. I relieved my anxiety at the Harem House," Khemerin said.

"You lost your virginity to a prostitute?" Khom replied with loud laughter.

"You could say that," Khemerin said. I sat quietly, just listening to the conversation, sipping my cold beer.

"These women were hot," Khemerin said. "I went back a couple of times a week. Later I became a regular. True, prostitution is illegal, but it's all over in Phnom Penh. Business has been booming since the war broke out. These whore houses are guarded by armed soldiers." He paused for a moment and continued, "It makes no sense. On one hand we talk about traditions, what we can and cannot do, but at the same time sex is sold on the streets."

"Sex has been sold on the streets since the beginning of time, Khem," I said.

"Thanks! That makes me feel less guilty," Khemerin replied with a smile.

"Did you lose your virginity to a prostitute too?" Khom looked at me.

"I'd rather not talk about it," I replied softly.

"Why?"

"Because I didn't have sex with prostitutes," I said.

"You can try," replied Khom.

"No."

"So you're a virgin," Khom said. Khemerin was silent, smiling.

"Neither."

"And?"

"And, I won't talk about it. Can we move on to another subject?"

We sat silently for a while and sipped our beer. Then we heard Sambat singing a song loud enough for us all to hear.

"I've never been drunk, I've never slept with a woman, and I've never told a lie."

I looked at Khemrin after Sambat finished his stupid poem.

"He gets on your nerves, doesn't he?" Khemerin asked me with a smile.

I nodded my consent and looked far off into the horizon.

"Any place around here where we can swim?" I asked Khom.

"From the restaurant where we had breakfast this morning, you go south a mile and you'll find a decent beach. You can swim there. I always take my kids there."

"Is it safe then?"

"Absolutely."

"Ah! What is your secret? Spit it out buddy!" Khemerin said and slapped me on the back.

"I have no secret, Khem. Sophie mentioned that she would like to go swimming. I'll check it out, just in case."

"You're trying to create a love scene here in this little paradise?"

"There is no romance, buddy. We're just friends."

"You said you like her."

"That's true, but I don't know how she feels about me."

"You need to take good care of yourself," Khemerin said. He paused for a moment and added, "Take it easy man. Don't go too fast."

"I know," I said.

"Hey Khem! Will he tell you everything when he gets to the battlefield of Normandy?" Sambat yelled out to us.

"Not sure!" Khemerin yelled back.

"What are you talking about?" I asked.

"I think he's referring to the final step of the big battleground of all men's dreams," Khemerin replied. He paused for a second and then said with a smile, "You know: S. E. X."

"You guys are crazy. You know that, don't you?" I asked.

I sipped my beer, looked at Khemerin uncomfortably, and then changed the topic. "Is there anyone living on those islands?" I pointed to the isles in plain view on my right.

"Nobody lives there. They're jungle islands, overrun by thick trees, plagued by mosquitoes, poisonous snakes, and all sorts of other insects and reptiles," Khom said and paused for a second to look more closely at the island coast. "We put a shack on that isle," he pointed to the one farthest. "We used it to smuggle people to Thailand. We put them on the isle for a week or two until our partners on the other side of the border came to pick them up. But that business is tough now; we can't do it anymore."

Upon hearing Khom's comment, I got up and paced back and forth, a million things on my mind. I turned in Khemerin's direction and said, "Khem, you don't know what poverty is all about. After my father passed away, we were unbelievably poor. My mother worked her fingers to the bone to keep us in school. She went through a hell of a lot. I miss her, Khem! I miss her!"

Khemerin looked at me with compassion. I knew he felt my pain.

"I miss Prince Sihanouk. He led our country in peace for a long time," Sambat interrupted.

"He was all right. I think he made a lot of mistakes during his leadership. He shut the door to the western world by adopting an anti-American Socio-Economic Policy. It was a stupid policy. He killed many Cambodians whom he believed to be the secret agents of the CIA. He made alliances with Communist countries. He was very popular in Cambodia, no doubt, but I don't think he was honest with the people who put their trust in him." Khemerin commented.

"He's a politician, what do you expect?" I said.

"He is definitely a Communist," Khemerin said.

"If he shut up and retired in France, this war would not have lasted so long, and many lives would have been saved. Instead, he went to China and mobilized people to support the Vietcong."

"Absolutely! The Americans miscalculated Prince Sihanouk's popularity. Stupid, stupid Kissinger!"

"You're right, Khem, he's a dumbass! He thinks just because he has B-52s, he can drop them wherever he wants. The Americans have dropped bombs in Vietnam since 1965, and the entire operation has been useless. The Vietcong and North Vietnam grow stronger and stronger!"

"Unless the American policy is to prolong the war, which is something you and I would never know. The U.S. has too much power. She can do whatever she wants in this damn world!" Khemerin said.

"I'm not so sure, Khem. I still think Kissinger is stupid," I said. "Remember in 1972, the U.S. was short of oil because these Arab countries reduced the oil supply? It affected the United States, our country, and many other countries in the world. Remember you had a damn hard time filling the tanks of your mini-bike and Mini-Austin? It was a very difficult time for all of us for a while. These Arab countries might strike again, and then they would make the United States vulnerable. I still don't believe that the U.S. is losing this war and cannot control these Arab countries."

"If you have a problem with Doctor Kissinger, go to America and tell him."

"I would if I could. He just miscalculated Prince Sihanouk's popularity. A true genius is not allowed to make a mistake like that!"

"Oh, like you don't make any mistakes!" Khemerin said with a smile.

"I always wanted to go to Phnom Penh before the war but never had a chance, like I said. I would have liked to play games at the casino when it opened back then, during Prince Sihanouk's regime," Khom said, changing the topic.

"Prince Sihanouk opened the casino in Phnom Penh in 1965. It was a smart move, I think, to raise funds for the city," I said.

"I'm not sure the money from the casino went to the city. Corruption has been a major problem in our society," Sambat shouted from the stern.

"If you crossed the border, where would you go from there?" Khom asked.

"I'll cross the borders and watch the situation from Thailand," Khemerin replied. "If the situation's all right, I'll return; otherwise I'll have to think of something. I have a few friends living in Paris. I hope the Americans have a plan to evacuate key employees of our government. In that case, I'll join my family in the U.S. The Communists are definitely gonna take over the whole region: Vietnam, Laos, and Cambodia. We're all fucked."

"I agree with your assessment, Khem," I replied. "Even though I don't have a long-term plan lined up like you. I need to get out of this country alive, and then I will figure out my options."

"You have any plans, my friend?" Khemerin asked Khom.

"I'll stay put. I'm just a fisherman; no one wants to kill me. I'm ok," Khom replied. "I need to go back to work. Enjoy your beer and the sunshine." He tossed his empty beer can into the sea.

Sophie

Chapter Seven

That afternoon, Sophie, her two siblings and I stood in line under the shade of a tall tree on the seafront to buy ice cream cones from the small, bicycle ice cream cart: vanillas for Sophie and me, chocolate for Mary, and coconut for Vichenea. After paying, we walked out from the crowd, crossed the street, and stood in the shade of a palm tree.

Pedestrians on both sides of the street walked by, passing us in both directions as we enjoyed our conversation and the cool sweetness of the ice cream. As we talked, I noticed that some passersby glanced in our direction, just to catch Sophie's eye.

The traffic was slow. There were no cars, except military trucks and jeeps passing us once in awhile. Bicycles and motorbikes were common in the street. The wind blew softly, brushing our faces with fresh air, scattering the dried leaves on the ground, and rustling the palm leaves above us. Sophie cried with laughter when the wind blew her hair in all directions. She, as trying to keep it decent, at the same time held her skirts firmly with her other hand.

"You'll come to dinner with us tonight, right?" Sophie asked me.

"Yes," I replied.

"Mom and Dad would be pleased to have you join us."

"Oh, Mom and Dad would be pleased to have you join us," Mary mimicked her sister.

"What's all this, dear?" Sophie asked her sister, taking a handkerchief from her purse and pressing it gently on her sister's cheek to remove a small fleck of ice cream.

"Do you like her, Savy?" Mary asked me.

"I like you. You are the most beautiful girl in the world," I replied.

"Liar! Liar!"

"No, you don't say that!" Sophie chastised her sister. "It's rude. You have to apologize to him. Go ahead and say sorry to him. I don't want you to talk like that to him or anyone, understand?"

"I'm sorry," Mary said to me.

"That's ok, cutie," I replied and turned to Vichenea. "How're your mom and dad?"

"They're ok. Dad's sort of worried about the current situation. He said getting out of here would be very difficult, especially for us because we have a big family."

"It's difficult for everyone who wants to cross the border at this time," I responded.

That afternoon, Sophie wore a light blue, elbow-length blouse that tightly hugged her body. She wore foam sandals and a dark blue skirt that fell to her ankles and sandals. Her hair was loose and spread below her shoulders. Her beauty attracted almost everyone who walked by. As we just finished our ice cream, Khemerin waved at me from a distance.

"I couldn't find you at the hotel," Khemerin said as he arrived. "I knew I could find you here."

"I would like you to meet Sophie, Vichanea, and Mary." I paused for a second and continued, "Everyone, here is Khemerin, my best friend. We went to school together."

"It's nice to meet you," Khemerin said.

"It's nice to meet you too. We've been here almost a week," Sophie replied.

"I know," Khemerin replied, "I arrived in this city two weeks before all of you. You are very lucky, because your flight was the last flight out of Phnom Penh. The airport closed just after your flight took off."

"Let us know if you found a way to cross the border to Thailand. Dad is worried," Sophie said.

"Nothing's impossible; it's just difficult, right Savy?" Khemerin said and slapped me lightly on the back.

"I'm in my last year at Lycee Descartes," Sophie said.

"I'm not surprised. I knew you were one of the Descartes girls the minute we said hello," Khemerin replied with a smile.

"How did you know?"

"It's obvious," Khemerin replied, obviously trying to impress her with his charm. "It's also my last year at Lycee Toul Kork."

"Really! It's a very good public school, actually," Sophie replied.

Sophie looked from me to Khemerin, puzzled.

"He did not complete formal education like most of us," Khemerin said, looking at me. "He went to college as the rest of us were struggling to pass the national exams in high school. He skipped two years ahead of me, and I was struggling to pass each exam and this year is my last year in high school."

Sophie looked at me with a smile and said, "That explains it. We are the same age."

"Thanks for the compliment, Khem," I said. "You have just embarrassed me."

"Savy talked a lot about you," Khemerin said to Sophie.

"Oh! What did he said about me?" Sophie asked Khemrin with a smile.

"He said he met you on the plane."

"It's true," Sophie said. "That's all you two talked about?"

"I told Khemerin that if we ever found a way to leave the city, we would share the information with your father," I said.

"That's nice of you two," Sophie replied. She paused for a moment and asked, "Do you two have any plans for the rest of the afternoon?"

"No, just hanging out around here," Khemerin replied.

"Me neither," I said.

"I want to go home," Mary nagged. Sophie looked from me to Khemerin and back to me and then said to her brother, "Vich, take her home." Sophie went over to her sister and put her hands on her shoulders, coaxing. "You go ahead and tell Mom and Dad I'll be home soon, ok?"

"Yeah, let's go Vich," Mary cried out.

"She's spoiled," Sophie said apologetically.

"She's very cute," replied Khemerin.

Mary glanced back at her sister as she and her brother walked away from us.

"I love the sea and the fresh air," commented Sophie, waiting for a response from Khemerin.

"I love it too!" Khemerin answered. "Would you like something cold to drink?"

"We just had ice cream," I said.

"Come on. I'll buy you a drink and we can chat," Khemerin said.

We walked into a restaurant on the hilltop and sat by the window, facing the sea. White clouds scattered in the bright blue sky and the deep, blue water extending as far as my eyes could see. On the horizon, I could just barely make out a slow-moving barge. I wondered where it had come from and where it was going. The area below us was covered with all types of trees and green plants. Only the palm trees stood out. There were many rocks—large and small—on the shore. Once in a while the waves splashed against them.

"Once we leave this country, I don't think we can come back," Sophie said sadly.

"You never know. Things may not be as bad as we think," Khemerin said, comforting her.

"We'd been so many places until the war broke out. We are trapped now," she sighed.

"We were in Paris just before the war, in February 1970," Khemerin said. "We came back sometime in March, and then the country was in trouble. Since then, we've never had a chance to get out of the country."

"Have you been to Siem Reap?" Sophie asked me.

"Yes."

"We were there once when I was twelve years old. I don't remember it much. The place was filled with temples all over, and some of them had fallen apart," Sophie replied.

"What part of Angkor did you go to?" I asked.

"Don't know. It was all the same to me. Like I said, it was a long time ago," Sophie replied.

"The entire area is the Angkor, and Angkor Watt is one temple of the Angkor," I said.

"When did you go there?" Khemerin asked.

"Just before the war," I replied.

"Did you like it?" Sophie asked.

"Yes, actually, I liked it a lot," I said.

"What is your opinion of the place?" Sophie asked, turning to Khemerin.

"It's an interesting place. There is a lot of history there," Khemerin replied.

"Tell me!" Sophie demanded.

"Savy, you tell her," Khemerin said to me.

"No Khem, she's asking you. You tell her," I said, annoyed.

"You tell us what you know about the place," Khemerin nudged.

I said nothing. I just leaned back in my chair and sipped my beer, looking away from the two of them.

"You two! Is there something wrong that I should know about? Would you like me to flip a coin and decide who is going to talk?" Sophie joked, seemingly peeved.

"Ok, I don't mind. Let me describe what I remember," I said, hoping to avoid irritating her further. Khemerin slapped me on the back. I began telling the story of the Angkor as precisely as possible.

"Angkor Watt was built around the 12th century. It's probably the most beautiful temple in the world." I paused and looked at Khemerin as Sophie sat smiling up at me. She was so beautiful. She filled the room with joy and happiness. I continued, "Angkor Watt was surrounded by a moat approximately 1,000 feet wide and an outer wall five miles long. On the west side of Angkor Watt, a man-made reservoir extended as far as five miles long and one and a half miles wide; that's enough water to fill 17,000 Olympic swimming pools."

"I remember the reservoir. It was huge and the water was so clear," Sophie said, giving Khemerin a quick sideways glance. I smiled at both of them and continued my description of the Angkor Watt.

"Angkor Watt has five beautiful towers built on each of the corners of the temple and one in the middle. The towers were built to replicate the closed-up bud of a lotus flower. They said the central tower of Angkor Watt is as high as some domes of cathedrals in Europe. The overwhelming impression of Angkor Watt is one of grace and beauty.

"A huge walkway was built across the moat to the west entrance and to the inside of Angkor Watt. There is a hall leading to the central shrine inside the central tower at the heart of Angkor Watt, the Holy place of worship for thousands of devoted Buddhists each day. The shrine is small—smaller than most people's living rooms."

I paused, sipped my beer and looked at both of them. They seemed intrigued, so I continued: "Each of its walls is decorated with the mythologies of Hindu and Buddhist inscriptions in Sanskrit. There's a chronological list of all the Cambodian kings and their temples and beautiful women dancers, called Absaras. There are so many of them, and each one of them is different.

"They have different expressions, different clothes, and different hairstyles. Each step and each move of the dance carved on the walls is a source of the Absara dance today. This dance has become the classical Cambodian dance and has spread into Thailand and Laos, our two neighboring countries."

The waiter, who had stood by for some time, chose this moment to interject.

"Do you care for one more round of beer?" he asked. "How about you Miss?"

"Yeah, give us one more round," Khemerin said. "Sophie, do you want something from the bar?"

"No, thank you," Sophie replied.

"The Angkor site," I continued, "is as big as Manhattan in New York, that's what they said, with hundreds of temples scattering the site—some of them in good condition and others not. In the Angkor site, King Suryavarman VII built a city of nine square kilometers, where he put 54 huge towers of quadruple human faces." I glanced briefly at Sophie and caught her eye. "There are 54 huge towers and four faces on each tower, with 216 faces carved in stone looking down from above as you walk through the city. It's amazing."

"Whose faces do you think they are?" Sophie asked.

"Historians believe that these were the faces of King Suryavarman VII himself, bearing Buddha's expression of compassion. King Suryavarman VII built the city with five gates, soaring towers with great entrances and temples with gods and demons in a tug of war, using a giant serpent as a rope. Also carved in the walls of each of these temples are images of fish and crocodiles being cut to pieces underneath the tug-of-war. The great king also built the Bayon, the most mysterious temple of all in Angkor Thom in its designs and architecture. At night under a full moon, the Bayon seems a very strange place to the modern world."

"You mean creepy," Khemerin added.

"Yes, creepy," I said.

"Why didn't you say that?" Khemerin asked, goading me.

I looked at him, but stayed silent.

"Creepy describes Bayon at night as I remember it," Sophie added.

"I know," I said, irritably. I was not too thrilled when Sophie agreed on any issue with Khemerin. I should kill Khemerin or kill them both, I thought.

"There were many stories related to these mysterious palaces in Angkor Thom," Khemerin added.

"You mind sharing with us?" I demanded.

Khemerin looked from me to Sophie and said, "One of the towers in Angkor Thom was a sacred place, the palace of a god. This god took the form of a snake with eight heads. Every night, the snake transformed itself into a beautiful woman and came to the king every night to have the king make love to her. If there was a night the king failed to make love to her, it was a sign that death would soon come to the king."

"Thanks, Khem. It's a good fairytale," I said, snorting.

"It is a good tale, actually. I like it, Khem," Sophie said. She quietly drank her ginger ale. We both looked at her, admiring her beauty. It's time to kill her, so that no one else will have her if I can't have her, I thought again.

I looked at the two of them and continued, "The Angkor site was abandoned for 500 years. A civilization was once raising and building the most beautiful temples the world has ever seen. It was more than a thousand years ago. The mystery remains: why did they abandon the jewels and city they created? Until 1860, Henry Mahout, the French explorer, hadn't discovered the place. It took French archeologists many years to clean up the jungle and bring the Angkor back to life. The glory of the Angkor was built in the period from the 9th to 14th centuries."

"You told it beautifully," Sophie said. "From the 9th to 14th century, 600 hundred years of glory, building hundreds of huge temples and then abandoning them. Isn't that weird? The GDP of the empire for all these years poured into these temples."

I looked at both of them and said, "You're right, Sophie. I couldn't find any better words to describe what these kings had done to their people."

"What was his name again?" Khemerin asked.

"King Suryavarman VII," I replied, looking at Khemerin. "Why?"

"Son of a bitch," Khemerin blurted.

We were silent for a while, sipping our beer and leaning back, looking out at the horizon. It was a beautiful day and the sky was clear.

"Hinduism is a religion older than Buddhism and the two are not the same," Khemerin said. "Is it fair to say that Buddhism is a branch of Hinduism? Is Buddhism is a philosophy or a religion?"

"Buddhism is the teaching of Buddha. It's a philosophy, not a religion," I said.

"The concept of heaven and life after death according to Buddha's teachings are completely different than Christian, Jewish, and Muslim faiths," Khemerin replied.

"You are right," I agreed. We both looked at Sophie.

"I don't want to discuss about religion. I am glad that Jesus died for me and I don't have to do anything in order to go to Heaven," Sophie said, tossing us a smile.

After a period of silence, Khemerin said, "I can't wait to cross the border, can't wait to see the Thai Boxing. They don't just fight with their hands in gloves, they kick and hit with elbows. It's fun to watch. If you know Taekwondo it helps you win the fight. Once, when I was twelve or thirteen, I went to see a boxing match at the sports center. It was exciting. I really liked boxing and practiced it whenever I had time. I asked Dad if he'd let me join a boxing club, where I could have proper training. He didn't like the idea. Instead he sent me to a Judo club. He thought Judo was more fun and not too dangerous. He's right and I like Judo very much now."

"And you have a black belt," I added.

"That's very impressive!" Sophie said and patted Khemrin on the shoulder.

"Yes, actually I have never fought outside of tournaments. You don't participate much in sports, do you?" Khemerin asked me.

"Not really. I played soccer with friends in the neighborhood when I was a kid, and later I lost interest in sports. I know it isn't good. I need some exercise to stay healthy. Look at you, Khem! You spend a lot of time in the gym to stay built up like you are now. It's hard work and requires a lot of time!"

"You need to exercise regularly, Savy. You need to set time aside daily, at least 10 to 15 minutes. It's good for you to exercise."

"Thanks, Champ. I wish I had everything," I said and looked off into the distance, a thousand thoughts in my mind.

"Have you been in Kirirom, Savy?" Sophie asked.

"Yeah."

"I like it there more than other places I have been in Cambodia," she said. "Kirirom is so beautiful—it's a plateau 2,300 feet above ground and is the only place in Cambodia where a pine tree can survive. I love pine trees. The temperature there is also nice. It reminds me of Paris in spring. I love Paris.

"The roads in our country are terrible. It took us three hours from Phnom Penh to Kirirom for a distance of 55 miles, with potholes everywhere once you were five minutes out of Phnom Penh. In some places, we had to get out of the car and push it. It was not fun." She made a face.

"I like Kirirom too," said Khemerin. "I used to walk through the pine forests for hours. There were a lot of birds, all kinds."

"I love a waterfall," Sophie exclaimed. "There was one in Kirirom, but I liked the one in Kampot much better. We used to go to the one in Kampot every month."

"Dad and I once spent one weekend in Kirirom and caught some big fish in the lake at the foot of the hill. The water there was quite clear. We loved it!" I said.

"We had a lot of fun before the war, and now the war is destroying everything," Sophie added.

"I know," I said.

"Savy will come to dinner with us this evening. Khem, join us too! Mom and Dad won't mind if we have one more guest."

"Am I invited for dinner with your family? It's an honor," Khemerin said and looked at Sophie with a smile.

"Khem, cut it out. Will you come or not?" Sophie replied.

"Sure. It will be fun," Khemerin answered.

"Good." Sophie said.

Chapter Eight

Back in the hotel that night, my thoughts drifted back to the first day of my last year of high school. It was a great achievement for a student to complete thirteen years of formal school. The curriculum was rigorous and each student was required to pass four national exams.

The school bell rang at seven o'clock in the morning, and students walked in both directions down the hall to their classrooms. As I dodged through the crowd, I crashed into a girl, knocking her school-bag to the ground and spilling her books, pens, and pencils on the floor. It caused a commotion, and some students walked around us while others cut between as we gathered her things, which were scattered all over the floor.

"I'm sorry, Miss," I said.

"It's okay. It was an accident. Not like you did it on purpose!" she replied. Her voice was soft. I looked at her, catching her smile. She was older than me. "You're probably in the wrong building," she said. I did not reply to her comment but continued helping her gather her stuff.

"I'm very sorry," I said again.

"It's ok!" she replied, still smiling.

I stood up, facing her, and handed her the last piece of paper that had dropped on the floor. Again, I said, "I'm sorry," and then, "Goodbye."

I walked into my class, the room on the right. While listening to Dr. Phounan's lecture on human anatomy during my first morning class, the image of the girl whom I had bumped into kept flashing in my mind.

She wasn't beautiful, per se, but certainly attractive in her own way.

For the next few weeks, we exchanged smiles when we saw each other in the hall running to our classes, even though we did not say a word. She seemed to become more beautiful each time I saw her, and I started to think of her throughout the day.

Oh well, I'm seventeen years old and a virgin; maybe I am attracted to all women I bump into, I thought to myself. It's impossible to fall in love with any woman at first sight. Women have beautiful bodies, in general—even unattractive women are still sexy when you see them from behind. It is how God makes them. Oh well! Not all men are created equal and not all women are beautiful.

I used to read work by Sok Pauline, a well known Cambodian contemporary writer during the '60s and '70s. Most people did not like his books, since he wrote about sex sometimes, and it was a topic that was considered offensive in our culture. However, I enjoyed his writing, not so much the sexual aspect of it. Rather, I believe he tried to express his right to free speech in an oppressed society. He wrote many books—at least ten—and I read them all.

One morning, two weeks later, I stood against the wall in the hallway in front of my class, staring at the ceiling and letting my mind go free.

"You're really in deep thought!"

"Oh! Chantal, hi," I said and looked at her with a smile. It was the girl I'd bumped into weeks earlier.

"How do you know my name? I don't remember us being properly introduced."

"Did I say your name?" I asked. "I'm sorry, a friend of mine told me."

"Why?"

"I thought I should find out your name, just in case we have a chance to talk, like now," I replied.

"Hear any other gossip about me?"

"I know you're rich."

"And anything else?"

"I know you're a literature student."

"It's obvious since my classroom's just across the hall from yours, you're a mathematics major."

"Yes, adding numbers seems to be easy for me," I said. She had a thick book in her hand, so I asked, "What are you reading?"

"Socrates: the father of Western philosophy."

"You know, he was married to a woman a lot younger than he was. Her name was Xanthippe. They had three children. Can you pronounce her name with a strong P?"

"I am trying to learn about his work, his ideas, and philosophy."

"You know what his wife said before he was executed?"

"What did she say?"

She said, 'He was good for nothing.' Do you believe that?"

"It's funny. You made it up."

"No, really! I've never made anything up!"

"It's charming. Come on, I'll buy you a cold drink at the refreshment stand. I don't feel comfortable chatting in the hall."

We walked side by side from the building, across our school yard, and toward the refreshment stand.

"Socrates was married to a woman younger than him," I said again as I looked at her.

"Why do you keep bringing up his marriage?"

"My future wife might be a few years older than I am, as opposed to Socrates, who was married to a woman who was younger than he."

"How much older will she be?"

We arrived at the refreshment stand as she finished her question. We pulled up two chairs and sat down.

"What was the question?" I asked her after we had settled and were waiting for a waiter or waitress to serve us.

She looked at me and said, "How much older would she be?"

"Oh that," I said and looked at her, searching her face for the answer: "Four years?"

"Oh my God! How much do you know about me?" she said. "And how? You've been spying on me." She paused as a waiter arrived and took our orders. We both ordered Pepsi. When the waiter walked away, she continued, "People told me that some of your friends are still in 10th grade and you are here ready to go to college. I'm not smart like you. I failed the exam and this year is my second attempt. If I fail again, you know, they will kick me out. My life will be over then."

"You know, the exam for the last year of high school is very difficult. Don't feel bad if you don't pass the first time," I said. "So, it sounds like you checked up on me as well. Why?"

She smiled and said, "I thought you looked too young to hang around in our building when you crashed into me that morning, two weeks ago. Besides, you're sort of cute."

"What does all that mean?"

"It means I won't date you, but I like you as a friend. Maybe you can help me with those stupid differential equations."

"Oh, you call that stupid! That really takes smarts!"

"I'm a literature student. I don't need to know these mathematical formulas."

"I can help you. Maybe you can teach me how to write."

"You are something, aren't you?" she said, and added, "Let's get this straight, ok? Forget about your 'future wife' being four years older. I am not dating you; we are just friends. You are too young for me. In fact, I am engaged to be married." She paused for effect and then added, "I want you to help me with calculus. I do not have a strong mathematical background. I know you can help, and that's why I want to talk to you. I can pay you."

"No, you don't have to pay me. I'm glad we're friends." I said, sipping my drink. "You know, some people are very photogenic, but you are different."

"How? What do you mean?" Chantal asked.

"You've a special charm and beauty. The longer I look at you, the more beautiful you are."

"Forgot about the way I look, ok? We're friends. Can you handle that?"

"Yes."

"Good."

"Tell me about your fiancé?"

"He's a friend of the family. Mom and Dad like him very much. He's a lieutenant in the army, working in the Finance Department."

"That's wonderful."

"He's 27 and I'm 21."

"Do you like him?"

"Sort of... He's all right. I told Mom and Dad I want to go to college, at least for two years, before getting married."

"Why?"

"Because I feel I'm not ready; besides, I would like to go to law school," Chantal said, "How about you?"

"No, I have no plan," I replied.

"You'll do fine whatever you do," Chantal said and looked me in the eye.

"Thanks for the compliment," I replied. "I don't want to teach."

"I can understand that."

"Look, it's time to go back in," Chantal said. "I'm helping children at the orphanage in the city. Do you want to come this afternoon?"

"What do you do there?" I asked.

"I help in the kitchen and read to the children sometimes," Chantal said, putting her hand on my left arm, "Come with me this afternoon. You can teach the boys how to play soccer."

"What time?"

"From two to four, and after that we can study until six, if you want. I have a ton of questions to ask you. You'll help me to pass the exam. ok?" she said with a smile.

"Yes, I'll help you."

We stood up and she motioned that she would take care of the tab. After she paid the bill, we walked back to our classes.

That afternoon, we went to the orphanage as planned. Everyone there greeted and accepted Chantal warmly. We spent the first hour reading to a group of children ages eight to nine, and then I took the boys outside to kick the ball while Chantal cleaned the kitchen. It was a wonderful afternoon.

We came back to the school, wandering from one classroom to the next, looking for a vacant classroom to study in. We found one and walked in. I helped Chantal solve a few mathematical equations by showing her the method I used, with the theorems applicable to the method. There was more than one way to resolve one problem, I explained, as long as the theorems applicable supported the methods.

"The war's terrible," Chantal said.

"Whether we like it or not, it's war, Chant. The Americans' policy selected South Vietnam as a battleground to stop the expansion of Communism, and the war spread to our country."

"I know. There are so many people who died because of this war. I read in *Paris Match* a few months ago, three to four million Vietnamese have died since the war started and more than 50,000 Americans have lost their lives."

"The war drags on too long. It started in 1959 and now spread to our country," I said. "To understand this war I need to understand its history, but there are no books written about it."

"As you know," Chantal said, "we are living in a society that views knowledge and inquiry as unimportant. People do not read enough and as a result, there are not many good writers to inspire reading. All of us go to school to get a diploma and then go to work for the government. Socrates said that men should not seek material gain or powers, but wisdom."

"Socrates said a lot of things that the world neither agrees with nor understands," I replied. "Tell me the history of the Vietnam War if you know about it."

"We have *Paris Match* and *Time* at home. They print insightful information about it sometimes. The war is all about politics and power."

I looked at her, inquiring.

"Ok. I'll bring the articles tomorrow and you can read them yourself."

"Tell me what you know," I asked, just to prolong the visit. I enjoyed being around her and listening to her.

She glanced at her wrist watch and said, "Ok, we have half an hour. I need to be home before six. I just don't want to explain to Mom and Dad when I'm late. They don't keep track of where I'm going, but they expect me to be home at a certain hour."

"I understand. You can bring me the article whenever. I'd love to read about it," I said.

She smiled and said, "I know you want me to tell you. I really enjoy your company too."

"You do?"

"Yes," she said. Then she paused and started pacing back and forth, looking at the ground. "The bloody battle of Dien Bien Phu in 1954 was the final French defeat in Vietnam. Communist Vietnam won the battle in Diem Bien Phu because of support from China and possibly the Soviet Union. At the Geneva conference that year, the French granted independence to Vietnam, Cambodia, and Laos."

"Wait a second," I interjected. "We were told that Prince Sihanouk alone got independence from France in 1953, while Vietnam and Laos fought for their independence."

"I know. It's not true," Chantal said. "We got our independence after the Vietnamese kicked the French out of Dien Bien Phu. Vietnam was divided along the 17th parallel. In the north, Ho Chi Minh created a socialist state. In the south, a non-Communist state was established under the Emperor Bao Dai. Millions of people fled from north to south because they feared the Communist persecutions. The French left South Vietnam and the Chinese, North Vietnam at the same time, in 1956. China was deeply involved in the conflict in Vietnam from the very beginning."

"Of course, without support from China and the Soviet Union, Ho Chi Minh couldn't chase the French out," I added, understanding now.

"Right. There were some articles written claiming that the U.S. provided support to the French in the Vietnam conflict after World War II," Chantal said. "The demarcation line along the 17th parallel was supposed to be temporary and there would be an election in 1956, as established in the Geneva conference in 1954, but the election never took place."

"What election?" I asked.

"Well, exactly. It was supposed to reunite the country under one government, but the election never occurred," Chantal replied. "The conflict between North Vietnam and South Vietnam started in 1955, when President Diem acted against the Americans' advice. He wiped out a religious sect, claiming that this group harbored Communist agents and were arresting and torturing others whom the government believed to be Communists."

"So the Americans were behind the South Vietnamese government," I said.

"I guess so. I believe the Americans were in South Vietnam to prevent the spread of Communism in Southeast Asia," Chantal said. She paused for a second and continued, "The Americans' pledge to support President Diem was in the summer of 1955. Since then, the war escalated. The war in Vietnam became the American war that had started in 1959. Then it spread to Cambodia because Prince Norodom Sihanouk allowed the North Vietnamese troops to have sentries in Cambodian borders."

I said nothing. Chantal paused for a second before continuing. "Sihanouk was very smart. He knew the Vietnamese would be the main military force in Southeast Asia, so he had to play along to survive, hoping that Ho Chi Minh would give him a break."

"It's your theory."

"Yes." She looked at me sadly and said, "Look, I need to go."

"Thanks, Chant."

"See you tomorrow. You seem taller than this morning," said Chantal with a smile.

"You think so?"

"Keep your chin up and study hard, ok?"

"Ok, see you tomorrow, Chant."

Chantal and I became close friends during our last year of high school. It was wonderful just to be around her and see her smile. We spent a fair amount of time during recess at the refreshment stand outside school. Sometimes we just sat there sipping our Cokes or Pepsis without any words for a long time. Sometimes I could see sadness in her eyes, but I was not willing to pry in her personal life.

I listened and tried to support her as much I could when she told me of her problems at home. She told me about some nonsensical rules she had to follow as a daughter. There wasn't much I could do to help, because our culture has rules and traditions to follow. She did not tell me much about her fiancé, except that he was a nice fellow and her parents loved him.

Sometimes after school in the evening, we would drive downtown for ice cream before we parted for the day and saw one another again the next day in school. Some weekends we met at the National Library, which was located behind Watt Phnom, one of the well-known Buddhist temples in the city. The library was opposite Lycee Descartes, the elite French private high school in Phnom Penh.

We spent many hours at Watt Phnom; it was a place of solitude for the two of us. There, we talked and shared our views on the literature we had read, also discussing politics, religion, and the philosophies of Socrates, Plato, and Aristotle. I was not a philosophy student and found philosophy dull and nonsensical sometimes, but Chantal seemed to enjoy abstract concepts more than I. I liked her so much and found her very beautiful, but there was not one occasion where I behaved inappropriately towards her. Her smiles always cheered me up when I was down; she was terrific.

Our work at the orphanage strengthened our friendship. Working there also helped me to grow as a person and to love and to have compassion for other human beings. At the orphanage, we worked together —but sometimes I played with children outside while she worked inside, helping the girls. On such occasions, we smiled at one another through the window when our eyes met. I was lost in her smiles.

I felt uneasy when she was in the office of the orphanage director, a man in his mid-thirties, for a business meeting behind a closed door. I had to control my feelings, not to let her know how much I cared for her. Actually, I was in love with her. It's a terrible thing, I thought. One evening I bumped into her and her fiancé at a restaurant in the central market while they were having dinner. I decided to stop by and said hello.

That evening, I couldn't stop thinking of them, trying to guess where they would go and where they would be after dinner. The next day and the following days I avoided her; I just did not want to see her or talk to her. However, she caught me by surprise one morning as I walked to my classroom.

"You've been avoiding me these past few days."

"No I'm not. I have too much work to do."

"You're avoiding me since the day you bumped into me at the restaurant. You're jealous! He's my fiancé and you and I are just friends!"

"I know, Chant; I'm telling you, I'm busy. Besides, I'm worried. My dad is not well."

"What's wrong?"

"Lately he's had stomach pains and unusual hair loss."

"You're not jealous when you saw me and Sarey together?"

"No, why should I be? He's your fiancé."

"He said we should get married at the end of the school year."

"Good! Congratulations," I said, walking faster.

"You want me to tell you what I said to him?"

"You said yes, and you're happy," I said, looking at her and walking even faster.

"You! Slow down. I told him no."

"Why not?"

"I told him I'm not ready."

"When will you be ready Chant? Get married, ok?"

"I want to go to law school."

"Yes, you told me about law school about a hundred times."

We stopped in front of our classes. I turned to her and said, "I have school to take care of." I walked two steps to my class, heard Chantal call my name, and turned around to look at her. She said with a smile, "You asshole, I miss you. Wait for me after school, ok?" I smiled and said, "Ok. I miss you too, Chant."

I was very happy when I was with her, and I missed her terribly when I was not. Several times she dropped me off at home and picked me up in the morning before school. I introduced her to my mother and father. My mother did not like the idea that I hung out with Chantal. She thought we might be involved in a romantic relationship. She said that it was impossible for a man and a woman to be in a relationship just as friends. She said a man was bound to be vulnerable if there is a romantic relationship between two sexes. My father did not talk much, but I knew he shared my mother's views.

At the end of the school year, we sat for the national exam. Chantal passed with a good score and I barely passed; it was good enough. Now I could move on with my life. I did not want to go to the engineering school and didn't want to teach mathematics. I decided to go to law school, a four-year program. I could practice law, or I could join the army as an officer when I graduated. If the war continued for the next fifteen years, I would become a commander, or possibly a general by the age of thirty-five. It was a good deal. Chantal also enrolled in law school, as planned. It was 1973.

One morning, Chantal and I stood in front of the law school in Phnom Penh. It was seven o'clock, and we had been assigned as sentinels, guarding the front entrance of the university.

"Are you daydreaming? It's seven o'clock in the morning," Chantal yelled at me from a distance.

"Yes, I was thinking about us, last year, in high school. It was a wonderful year," I replied and walked toward her.

"Yes, we had a good time. You almost flunked the exam, you goofball!" Chantal said.

"Tell me about your fiancé; do you like him now?"

"Are you talking about him again?" Chantal asked.

I raised my courage and asked her, "When are you two getting married?"

"I told Dad I need two more years. I want to finish the first two years of law school at least."

"Two years is a long time for the postponement of a marriage. What are you two doing for the next two years?"

"You shut up! We do nothing, ok? It's time to work, people are starting to come. We need to behave like real soldiers. After class we'll go to lunch and then you can tell me what you are going to do when you finish law school," Chantal said. We stood by the gate, watching students enter the school compound. Most students still rode bicycles, but some were on scooters or motorcycles. The rich students drove cars.

At nine o'clock we closed the gate, and no students were permitted to enter the premises without proper identification. We entered our bunker, which was protected by sandbags, piled three feet high. We sat on the edge of the bunker and continued our conversation, our eyes fixed on the front gate.

"This is a lost war," Chantal said. "In the United States this war is very unpopular, and here at home our troops are on the defensive more than the offensive. The war will end before we'll become lawyers."

"It may or may not, depending on the U.S. If she continues to fund the war, the fighting will last for a long time," I replied.

"I don't want to live under the Communist government," Chantal said.

"Me neither. What do you think about the future of this country?"

"When the Americans pull out, the Vietnamese will take over the region."

"You're probably right," I said.

Suddenly, the sound of a bomb blast burst out nearby. I instinctively jumped over Chantal, threw her to the ground, and covered her with my body. One after another, we heard three bombs dropping within five minutes, and then one more dropped a few minutes later. The explosions were so loud, they seemed as though they might destroy my eardrums.

It was quiet for a while—very quiet. Then yells and screams burst out all over the place.

"Savy, are you ok?" Chantal asked.

"Yes, are you ok?" I said softly.

"Ok, then wake up. You're heavy," she gasped.

"Chant, I can't, my legs are numb," I said to her. We were covered in debris. I dusted it off, looked at my hands, and said softly, "Chant, I got hit, look." I showed her my hand.

"Oh my God!" she screamed and pushed me off slowly, freeing herself. Then she screamed louder, "Oh my God, please over here, we're hit over here!"

She ran to look for help; in the meantime, I lay on the ground in a pool of blood. Then I heard a siren and saw lights flashing all over. "Where is Chant?" I thought. Not long after, she came back with two men carrying a stretcher. They lifted me up, laid me on the stretcher, and carried me to the ambulance. The sounds of yells, screams, and moans nearby made me wonder how many deaths had occurred and how many were wounded. I thought of my mom and dad; death was near for all of us, it seemed. I was pushed in the ambulance, where two injured lay on their stretchers. I heard voices arguing, back and forth.

"Miss, we cannot allow you in there." It was a man's voice.

"No, you get out of my way. I'm with him. I have to be with him." It was Chantal's voice. There was a commotion between Chantal and the medics before the door closed. Finally they let her in. She rushed over and sat next to me. She took my hands in hers.

"You'll be ok," she said. The ambulance was moving and the sirens starting up their piercing wail. I was being transported to the hospital. I looked up at Chantal, trying to show her my appreciation and joy for her being with me at that moment.

"Why did you do it?" Chantal asked. I barely heard her. I felt weak and sleepy.

"No, talk to me! Open your eyes. Talk to me!" Chantal screamed, but I closed my eyes and started to fall asleep. Chantal shook me to keep me awake. I opened my eyes and saw tears on her cheeks. "Talk to me, you understand? You cannot die. Why did you do it?" she asked, just to keep me awake, just to keep me talking to her.

"I couldn't let you get hurt." My voice was barely audible. "Chant," I grabbed her hand with what remaining strength I had, "I love you. Each day I grow to love you more and more. I just want you to know, in case."

"You think I don't know that? Keep talking. I love you too," Chantal replied and smiled at me through her tears. I was sleepy and closed my eyes, drifting off into a deep sleep and a hazy new world. The sounds around me in the ambulance now seemed so far away. My body was being shaken but I could barely feel it.

I heard a voice from far away saying, "Wake up you, you son of bitch! You don't die on me!" The voice grew quieter and quieter, and then it was gone.

Sophie

Chapter Nine

I was in the hospital for three weeks and stayed home for another two weeks before I could go back to school. Metal shards from the bombs had cut through my right leg and the lower part of my body; fortunately, none of my organs and bones had been hit. I had, however, lost a lot of blood by the time I arrived at the hospital.

A year later, my father became very sick and had to be hospitalized. At first, the doctors couldn't diagnose his illness. I stayed with him every day after school and on the weekends, watching as his condition deteriorated. I hid my tears, for I could not bear to see him suffer. Day after day, he lay hopelessly on a bunk bed in the hospital hall, wounded soldiers around him screaming in pain. The hospital was too crowded for the government to offer my father the private room he was entitled to as a government employee.

It was a difficult year for me, not only because my father was sick, but also because school required a lot of my time. Besides, the situation in Phnom Penh was getting worse. People were killed at random by rockets launched through the sky, hand grenades thrown into crowds, or bombs planted secretly in public buildings. Regardless, Chantal and I managed to spend as much time together as we could, enjoying what time we had together.

We talked, told each other jokes, and planned our future. Chantal was wonderful to me; she visited my father at the hospital two or three times a week and brought him flowers and fruit baskets. I sat on one side of my father's bed and she on the other side, as he looked at us and struggled to speak a few words. We just couldn't hide our sadness at seeing him like this, and tears rolled down our cheeks.

Some evenings, we parked at the lakefront before the Palace Royal, Chantal driving her red Mini Austin (a small, English-made car), and strolled along the riverbank and in the public park in front of the Palace Royal. The building was enclosed with thick, high walls with four gates, one on each wall, guarded by uniformed soldiers at all times.

Inside the Palace Royal, there were several buildings, but the biggest was the one behind the east wall. It was a magnificent yellow monument standing tall with its dome pointing into the sky. The public park outside the Palace Royal was covered with green grass, 500 feet from north to south, and 200 feet to the east. In the middle of this big, beautiful lawn was a circle boasting all kinds of flowers: lilies, monkhood, tulips, daisies, and others I couldn't recognize at all.

There was a pathway around the green lawn where we walked, crossing the cool grass. We liked to sit on the bench across the street from the park, facing the river, where a garden of flowers stretched along the riverfront approximately a half mile from north to south. They were lush and fragrant, which made us temporarily forget our worries and sorrows.

At sunset, the lights in the park came on, and we sat there on the bench in the lamplight, hand in hand, talking about our future and the future of our country. I loved the way she talked and her smile. One time, I put my hand on her soft, beautiful face and kissed her gently on the cheek.

There was another park in front of the Independence Monument where we also loved to spend time together in the evening. The park was clean, modern, and illuminated by electric lights that fell from two rows of lamp posts. It was even more beautiful at night, lit up by the stars and the full moon on some evenings. We liked to sit by the edge of the fountain, talking, holding hands, and kissing. The fountain shot streams of water 5 to 10 feet into the sky. The evening always seemed beautiful when we were together; it was a wonderful life in the middle of the hell of our country's war.

Another place we enjoyed spending time together was Watt Phnom, a Buddhist temple in the middle of the city, about four miles north of the Palace Royal. The temple was built on a hill and was the sacred

Sophie

ground and place of devotion for Buddhists. The temple was surrounded with Bodhi trees, which provided shade that cooled the ground from the hot afternoon sun.

In the shade, on the sacred ground of Watt Phnom, Chantal and I walked around and watched young couples like us kneeling in front of Buddha statues, folding their hands together at chest level, and praying to the statues and the spirit of Buddha. They prayed for their eternal love, promising to be true to one another as the statues stood witness. One time, watching the couples, Chantal looked at me and said, "We don't need that."

I looked at her and pulled her toward me, my hands on her shoulder. She said, "I know that in your heart you love me. We don't need to express our emotion in front of the statues." I said nothing, pulling her in my arms and kissing her soft, black hair. She smelled perfect. There were no monks living in this temple. It was more like a museum, or a public place of worship. We walked down the hill and sat on a bench under a Bohdi tree.

"It's interesting up here. It's peaceful," Chantal said, and leaned her head on my shoulder. I extended my arms and drew her closer to me.

"I love it here," she said, looking into my eyes.

"Do you know why every temple has Bohdi trees?" I asked. "The tree must be connected to Buddhism in one way or another."

"You don't know that?"

"No."

"Under a Bohdi tree, Prince Gautama Siddhartha became Buddha, meaning the 'Enlightened One'," Chantal replied, her head resting comfortably on my shoulder.

"It happened in India, right?" I asked with a smile, feigning ignorance.

"Look! It's not funny," she replied, her spine stiffening as she turned to face me.

"Sorry!"

"I know you're not Buddhist, but you should not make fun of what other people believe," she said and patted my head.

"Was it in Nepal?" I asked her again, trying to assure her I really didn't know.

"Was what in Nepal?"

"The place Buddha found his Enlightenment."

"Nepal was the birth place of Buddha. It was Gaya in Bihar, North India, under a Bodhi tree, where Gautama Siddhartha became Buddha."

"Was Gautama his last name or Siddhartha?"

"I don't know. You always find humor in everything."

"It must have been hard on his wife, his son and parents, when he left them to find the true meaning of life. When he found it, he did not return to his family," I said and looked at her, searching for her answer.

"You knew the story! Why did you ask?"

"I know just bits and pieces."

"Yes. He left his family when he was 29 years old. It took him seven years to become Buddha. His teaching was focused on self-denial and reincarnation."

"Like going to college to get a Ph.D.," I said and continued before Chantal had a chance to reply, "You know Socrates also believed in reincarnation. It's very complex. I never understood it. Buddha remembered his past life, but Socrates did not."

"Charming. If you talk like that I think we should go home," Chantal said after hearing my comment.

"Sorry! Tell me what you know about Buddha," I replied.

"Three months after Buddha's death, his 500 disciples came to agree about the teachings of Buddha, which became the foundation of Buddhism. Based on the 500 opinions of his disciples, only 18 groups of Buddha were formed in 100 BC. Our practice of Buddhism is not the same as the Vietnamese's. You know that, right?"

"Yes," I responded.

"It's also different than the practices in Japan and China," Chantal added.

Chantal was beautiful and had a good heart. She was committed to the teaching of the Buddha. She regularly attended services at the temple near her home with her parents and brought along, as a symbol of her faith, a small silver pan filled with rice for the monks who lived in the temple.

She broke up the engagement with her fiancé a few months after my recuperation from my bomb blast injuries, and we had been together since then. I loved and respected her and never asked her to sleep with me, though I really wanted to.

She spent a fair amount of time in orphanages each week, helping the staff and reading to children. She raised funds from government agencies and wealthy people, helping to put more rooms in the orphanages and build shelters for refugees. Because of her volunteer work, she became well-known among faculty members in our university, the leaders of some non-profit organizations, and some important people in our government. Her father's status in the government helped as well.

Even though we did not see each other as much as we would have liked to while my father was sick, our love was still strong. Sadly though, my father's condition grew worse each day. He lost a lot of weight and soon, there was nothing left but skin stuck to his bones; he hardly moved his arms. The family decided to bring him home so we could give him our full attention. The day we brought him home, my five-year-old sister knew very little about our father's condition. I carried her and we sat next to our father. My dad held her hands tight, tears rolling down his pale, skinny cheeks.

When I was ten years old, my mother had given birth to a cute little boy: my brother. We all loved him, but dad wanted to have a girl; so, three years later, my sister was born, followed by my youngest brother two years after that. Since the day my sister was born, my father was ecstatic. She was the apple of his eye. Everywhere he went, he took her along with him, of course except when he went to work. We all loved her, for she was exceptionally smart and beautiful.

Near death, in the hospital, my father held his daughter's hands and cried; he knew his life was near its end, and he would not be able to love his daughter and provide her with the future he dreamed of. Life was unfair to him.

My mother and I were at my father's bedside all the time, especially at night. We took turns watching him. We couldn't tell when he was asleep or awake. He just lay in bed, sometimes with his eyes closed, and other times blinking up at the ceiling, drifting off into another world, a world where there was a God and Heaven. For almost three months, my father lay in bed this way.

His condition ate away at both of us, my mom and me. We loved him so much, but we knew that there was no way we could help him. My father was forty years old: too young to die! Even when he was this sick, he still had a sharp mind. He never forgot the date and time at any moment.

When he gained some strength, he asked me about school. He said that it was very important to have an education. He was a very smart man and very handsome as well. He had lived a good life until the day he first lay in bed in that hospital.

Chantal visited my father very often during those weeks, knowing that he would not live long. I did not know how I could live without her at a time like this, since she always comforted me. One Thursday, early in the morning, I was sitting next to my father when someone knocked on the front door. It was Chantal, standing there with a smile on her face.

"Hi everyone," said Chantal as she walked in. She had become a part of our family.

My dad smiled and waved at her. She brought with her a basket of fruit, which she laid on the table near my father's bed. She sat beside him, reached for his hands, and kissed them.

"Thanks for the basket," said my father, and smiled at her.

She looked at me and said, "We're going to school together." She paused and turned to my father, "Mom and Dad left this morning to Kompong Some on business. They won't be back until tomorrow night."

"Chant! Do you need company?" I asked.

"It's not a bad idea. I'm afraid of being alone at night in a big house," Chantal replied.

"It's not a good idea. You two are too young to be alone," my father said.

"Dad! We are old enough to understand sex and stuff. We've not done anything against our culture or tradition," I said politely. "Besides, we could have broken the rules and traditions by now if we chose to."

Chantal leaned to kiss my dad on his forehead.

"Ok. Take good care of one another," my father said and closed his eyes.

We sat next to him for a while, kissed him goodbye, and then went to the kitchen to say goodbye to my mother. We walked outside and toward the car parked in front of our house. Chantal opened the door and sat behind the wheel as I got in the front seat. She put on her shades and drove north for a quarter of a mile, then turned right, made a U-turn, and came to a complete stop at a check point before crossing the bridge.

It was the only bridge in Phnom Penh that crossed the Tonle Sap River. The sentinel at the checkpoint checked us thoroughly before we were allowed to cross the bridge. When we were clear to go, Chantal sped ahead, crossing the bridge as the breeze brushed our faces. The current of the Tonle Sap River below flew fiercely under the bridge, heading south.

We drove on the bridge for less than five minutes, but it seemed like a long time. We crossed the bridge and headed into the city. We went from one street to the next, turning right, then left, and again straight, dodging the morning traffic. In less than a half-hour, she pulled the car over to a corner in front of the Central Post Office and looked at me with a smile.

"Do we really need to go to class today? I don't have any assignments, except one in civil law class," Chantal said.

"Why do you want to skip class?"

"We can spend time together if you want. We have not seen one another for ages; however, if you think that the classes are important we'll just go to school then."

"I'd rather spend time with you. I have two classes this morning, but I'll catch up later and just read the textbooks," I said.

"Are you hungry?" she asked. Without waiting for my answer, she pushed the gas pedal gently, inching the car forward and stopping across the street in front of La Lantern, an upscale French restaurant. We walked through the restaurant and sat at a table outside on the sidewalk. On the other side of the sidewalk, pedestrians walked back and forth. The traffic was very light, since the restaurant was located in a secluded area of the city.

"Why did we come here Chant?" I asked.

"You're hungry, right?"

"Yes, but ..."

"But what?"

"Too expensive here."

"They have good food here. Everything is good," Chantal replied.

"Ok, if you say so."

We ordered coffee, orange juice and scrambled eggs. The service at La Lantern was exceptional and the place was meticulously clean.

"I'm sorry for your dad," Chantal said. I could see sadness in her eyes.

"Thanks. It's very hard on Mom."

"You are going through a lot. You're not alone. Remember I'm with you all the time."

"I know," I said and reached for her hands, holding them in mine, "You are very beautiful. Everything about you is so beautiful, so perfect. You were my dream girl even before I met you."

"That's very sweet; I must have done something good in my previous life, which led me to meet you in this life," she said and continued, "You seem uncomfortable. What's bothering you?"

"Why do you say that?"

"Body language. It's your eyes, you're so predictable. You're incapable of hiding the truth. That's the quality in you that I adore most."

"Simply because you're a psychic," I said, leaning toward her and kissing her on her lips. It was a sweet and passionate kiss." She returned it for a very brief moment, then drew back a little and said, "We're in a public place, my darling." She paused for a while and said, "What's bothering you?"

"You should give me two weeks warning at least, so that I can save enough money to buy you breakfast in a place like this."

"Oh, that! Is it the only reason?"

"Yes," I answered with a smile.

"You're silly. How long have we been dating?"

"It has been a year and a half, officially," I replied.

"How do you feel?"

"About what?"

"Our relationship," she replied.

"I cannot live without you. You know that."

She paused, leaned against her chair, looked at the slow traffic in the street, and said without looking at me, "We are not going to win this war."

"I know," I replied, looking at her and searching for an answer behind her statement.

We were silent for a moment, and I caught her eye. I felt that she wanted to say something; there were tears in her eyes.

"What's wrong? You're crying," I said.

"Dad wanted me to finish school in Paris," she replied. I was dumbfounded by the news. I did not know how to react.

"It's good, good for you," I said softly and continued, "We will not see each other anymore, I guess."

"No, you misunderstood completely. Mom and Dad don't want to separate us," she replied.

"Why do you have to go to Paris, then? What's wrong with school here?"

"Dad said we are not safe here. No one knows what'll happen if this place goes down."

"He's right; this place is not safe," I said, and asked, "When are you leaving?"

She leaned toward me, grasped my hands and said, "I told Mom and Dad that I am not leaving without you."

"You should go. It's a big opportunity for you, and you'll come back when you finish school," I said with a smile. "I'm happy for you."

"No, I'm not going without you. I don't want to live without you," she said, tears rolling down her cheeks.

"Don't cry," I comforted her, "You're in my mind, every breath of my life, and it does not matter if you're here or in Paris." I paused and added, "Think it over, ok? It is safe in Paris." I stopped speaking for a few moments, leaned against my chair, and said, "We'll get married when you come back."

I took my handkerchief from my pants packet, pressed it gently against her cheeks to dry her tears off, and said, "We'll be fine. Your father is right; it's dangerous here."

She leaned toward me, put her arms around my neck, and whispered in my ear, "I am not going anywhere without you." Then she sat up straight and gave me her beautiful smile.

"You need to listen to your parents. We'll get married when you come back," I said and returned her smile.

"Just drop it, ok? I'm not going anywhere." She paused, looked me in the eye, and said, "I'm sorry I'm telling you all this."

"Why sorry?"

"I brought it up because I couldn't help it. I need to confirm my decision. You're happy for my safety, but I can see it in your eyes; you're falling apart, knowing that I might leave you."

"What would happen if this place fell apart?" I asked.

"We'd die together," she said. I was silent, kissing her gently on her lips. She continued, "You'll make a good husband."

We ate as we talked, and we finished our breakfast an hour later.

"Let's go. I want to stop by the bookstore to pick up some magazines," she said.

Then she asked the waiter for the bill. She paid for breakfast and we left. It's nice to be rich, I thought.

That morning we drove into the city, stopped by the Central Market to pick up fresh fruit, and then headed to the bookstore that sold books, magazines and newspapers. We spent a few hours there and then drove to the waterfront near the Palace Royal. We parked the car on the riverfront, walked in the park, and sat on a bench facing the sun, looking at the Tonle Sap River flowing southwards. There were a few canoes floating on the river; some were rowing slowly upstream, and others were just floating along with the current.

"Remember the canoe races on the river at this time of year, before the war?" I asked her.

"How could I forget? It was the biggest national festival during the year. People from everywhere in the country came to participate; there were millions of spectators! It was fun. At night when it was dark, fireworks went on for hours and reflected along the river for miles and miles. They were beautiful. The whole city was animated with crowds, lights shined from the lampposts along the streets, and jugglers and magicians showed their talents to the public in the streets. The war destroyed it all."

I leaned to kiss her on her cheek and said, "Let's go back. It's beautiful, but I don't feel safe at all."

"We're not safe anywhere in this city," Chantal replied.

We drove down the street, passing the Independence Monument, toward Watt Phnom, the place we liked most. It was a place of solitude, so peaceful, the shadows of Bodhi trees serving as a cool canopy as we walked or sat together. That day, we spent a few hours in the back of the National Library, in the shade of a tall tree, shoulder to shoulder, talking about our future, politics, and other things that came to our minds.

At sunset, we drove back to her house in Toul Kork. The car stopped in front of the main gate. I got out of the car, unlocked and opened the gate, and watched her drive slowly through the gate into the compound of her mansion. I locked the gate as she parked the car in front of the mansion. I had been in the house numerous times, but at least one of her parents was always at home.

"I'm hungry," Chantal said.

"I can cook. Do you want me to make something?"

"That's a good idea," she replied. I put my arms around her and whispered in her ear, "You are very beautiful," and kissed her on the forehead. She raised her eyes, looking at me, and then I pressed my lips against hers. We kissed for a while, and then she pushed me away and said, "Go and refresh yourself, make yourself at home. Then we'll prepare food together."

I went to the kitchen, put on an apron, and started cooking. I am not a good cook, but I can't go wrong with meat, I thought. I took ingredients out from the refrigerator: meat, green beans, potatoes, tomatoes, mushrooms, and cauliflower. I placed the meat under the faucet and let the hot water flow over it to thaw it. I cut the vegetables into small pieces and rinsed them in the basin.

"What are you doing?" Chantal asked as she walked toward me.

She wore a sarong and a loose, bright yellow blouse, open-necked, showing the smooth skin of her neck and her broad chest. Her hair was loose, spread over her back and falling below her shoulders. She was barefoot. I noticed she did not wear the necklace she had on earlier. I walked slowly toward her, held her in my arms, and kissed her beautiful neck; no words could describe my happiness at that moment.

"You are very beautiful. I love your outfit," I said. "It's different. Where did you get it?" slowly I released her.

"What are you doing?" she asked me again.

"Cutting some vegetables and thawing the meat."

"Go take a shower. When you're done showering, the meat will be ready to be cooked," she told me.

I went to the shower and came back in less than half an hour. I put on the new pants and shirt I brought with me that day. When I came back, Chantal was stirring the meat and vegetables in the frying pan. She sprinkled a little salt in the pan to spice up the food and then adjusted the stove to 120 degrees, covering the pan to keep the heat circulating within. While she cooked the meat and vegetables, she set the rice going as well; it was all ready in less than an hour. As she finished up, I stood behind her, put my arms around her waist, and kissed her neck and cheeks.

"Chant, I love you. Can I sleep next to you tonight?" I whispered in her ear.

"No, you sleep downstairs," she said with a smile, and she turned toward me with a look that suggested my request was a joke.

I pressed my lips against her gently. She pushed me away a little and walked toward the fridge, taking out four oranges. As she peeled and sliced an orange for dessert, I stood next to her, watching how her delicate hands moved.

"What music do you like?" I asked.

"I like the Beatles."

"They are good, aren't they?"

"I want to hold your hand," I said. "You know, the song."

"I know," she replied with a smile, putting her hand on mine.

" 'I'm Just a Jealous Guy' is the other song I like."

"That was John Lennon, baby."

"They are great, aren't they?"

"Yes, they're more than great."

I turned her to face me and said, "Just dance with me, baby, just follow my lead."

I pulled her toward me, held her left hand and rested my free hand on her waist. I led the dance and sang:

"When the night has come and the land is dark... and the moon is the only light we'll see. No I won't be afraid, no I won't be afraid... just as long as you stand, stand by me..."

I released her when I stopped singing.

"It's beautiful," she said. "You just sang in English. Do you know what it means?"

"No clue. The song was beautiful and I just sang along when I listened to the tape at home," I said.

"Yes, it's a beautiful song," she said and leaned to kiss me.

"The Americans are so free, like birds in the sky. They do whatever they feel. Isn't it great?" Chantal said, and pulled me to the living room, pushing me onto the sofa and throwing herself in my arms. I embraced and kissed her. Our lips met, our bodies melted, and I felt her breasts pressing against my chest. I was lost in a dream, the best feeling I had ever had. Then, suddenly, she pushed me away and stood up, saying,

"It's wrong. We should not do this; it's very wrong." Then she walked to the kitchen as I sat on the sofa wondering what she was doing and what she would do next.

"Come on baby, we eat in here," she yelled out from the kitchen.

"Let me help you," I said, walking toward her.

"Ok. You can help if you want to."

In the kitchen, she put the food on the table and I pulled out the chair for her.

"Thank you. It's very sweet of you. I think you watch too many American movies. That's why you know how to kiss and please a woman."

"Is it bad to please the woman you love?"

"No, let's face it. Most men in this country treat women with less respect, out of their conscience. I hope you are not just flattering me when you adore me."

"No, I am not flattering you," I said, leaning to kiss her lips.

I sat down and poured the water from the pitcher into two glasses. Suddenly, she stood up.

"Where are you going?" I asked.

"I have something that will go well with our dinner," she said, walking toward the cabinet and pulling out two wine glasses and a bottle of wine.

"Can you open it?" She handed me the wine and the opener.

"Dumain de Mavette Cotes du Rhone, 1965, Rhone, France," I read the label on the bottle as she walked to the next room to turn some soft music on.

"Just open it," she said when she returned.

"Is it too much?" I had never had alcohol in my life. It was my first time, but I hesitated to admit it.

"It won't kill you. We are going to break our tradition."

"Break the tradition," I repeated.

I opened the wine and poured it into the two wine glasses and sat down. We looked at each other with a smile, then touched our glasses together and said, "Cheers!"

It was the first sip of wine I ever had. It was surprisingly good.

"Where were we?"

I looked at her, searching for what she was asking about.

"What were we talking about in the living room?" she repeated the question.

"We kissed, and then you just pushed me away like I was some kind of teddy bear."

She looked at me with a smile and said, "Teddy bear, good analogy. Where were we before that?"

"You said the Americans are so free."

"What a country they live in! America must be a strange place and a nice place to live in at the same time."

"Why do you say that?"

"They dress in a strange way, with brightly colored clothing. The men have long hair and beards, the women wear all kinds of weird jewelry and flowers on their heads; some of them play music, travelling from New York to Los Angeles. Apparently, hitchhiking is the easiest way to travel across the country."

"Oh! You're referring to the hippies. They pass out flowers to strangers."

She passed the rice pan to me. I took it, scooped two spoons, put it on my plate, and passed the pan back to her.

Then we started talking as we ate our dinner.

"Yes, the hippies. As I read, it's a movement against the current norms of society. They're free to do what they want; they're free spirits."

"Is it nice to be free like that?" I wondered aloud, sipping my wine. It tasted better than the previous sip. I started to enjoy it. Chantal was also looking pretty relaxed. "That's why you put on such bright colors like the hippies, you're against tradition tonight!" I said to her.

"We are going to break all the traditions," she replied, smiling coyly.

"I like the spirit of freedom, just enjoying life."

"The hippies marched and protested against the war," Chantal went on, "This was to show how much they valued peace and harmony."

"Absolutely. The weird thing was that they destroyed themselves by using marijuana, LSD, and stuff. In the end, they did not contribute as they should have, or could have, to society."

We sipped our wine. Then I filled our glasses and emptied the bottle.

"Actually, the movement has spread all over the Western World," Chantal said.

"I read somewhere that there were hippies in Russia as well. But I don't think the movement will last long. How can they survive without working?"

"You are probably right. At least they're free, though."

We smiled and sipped our wine.

"I love you very much, Chant."

"I love you too."

I grabbed her hands in mine and pulled her toward me. Through the wide collar of her blouse, I could see her firm breasts; she was not wearing a bra. Pretending not to look, I pressed my lips against hers with passion. Our tongues touched, and she caressed me with her foot.

"You like them?" she whispered in my ear, mischievously.

"Yes, they are beautiful," I replied. "Let's go to the living room."

Without a reply, she stood up. We walked into the living room, where I sat on the long sofa. She walked briskly to the TV set, turned it on, and came back to me, throwing herself in my arms as though afraid of losing time.

We lay in each other's arms on the sofa, our bodies melting and tongues twisting against each other. I rolled over on top of her and kissed her neck. She murmured in my ears, "Put your hand on me, baby." I looked her in the eye and watched as her mouth fell open a little in anticipation.

Pressing my lips against hers, I put my hand in her blouse and caressed her soft, firm breasts as her body moved under my touch. She was so beautiful; it was absolutely worth dying for. I took her blouse off and kissed her, every part of her. Every inch of her was sweet and wonderful. I whispered in her ear, "Baby, I can't stand it anymore." She pressed my head against her breasts and said, "Just do it if you want to."

"I love you baby," I murmured, as her moans rose. I pressed my lips against hers and kissed her everywhere, moving inside her until, finally, I exploded. At that moment, she let out a sharp, piercing scream; but it was a joyful scream. It was the most beautiful moment of our lives. We were both exhausted, clinging to one another as though we feared separation.

"You're wonderful, but still we should not have done it," she said softly in my ear.

"Do you regret it?" I asked.

"No, I've waited for this moment for three years, since the day we met."

"Really?" I was shocked.

"You were so cute back then, and you're cuter now."

"You know, I kept thinking of you since the minute I bumped into you that morning. My love for you grew each day."

"I know. I could see it in your eyes. Now that I'm in your arms, what will you think of me tomorrow?"

"I'm a lucky man. All I want in life is to be with you, making love to you."

"It's so sweet. Let's go upstairs, and you sleep next to me. None of this downstairs nonsense."

"I like that better," I replied dreamily.

It had been the first time for both of us. The clock on the wall showed nine o'clock; it was too early to go to bed. We straightened ourselves up, as the image of B-52s dropping bombs from the sky flashed across the TV screen.

"It's war, honey. Don't try to justify it. We are losing this war," Chantal said. I said nothing.

She walked to the kitchen to get fruit from the fridge. As she walked away, I felt strange. I felt I was a new person. I was part of her. Her natural smell had absorbed into me. I could smell her as she was in the kitchen. I could only hope that she felt as I felt. She would be my future wife, we would have many children, and I would bring a lot of money and happiness to her as a famous lawyer one day, I thought to myself. I stared at the TV screen without blinking, as the image of bombs dropping from the sky flickered. She came back from the kitchen, put the fruit on the coffee table, and switched the channel.

"Thanks, honey," I said.

She sat next to me, put her arm around my shoulder, and kissed me gently on the lips.

"I love you," she said.

"I love you too."

Sophie

Chapter Ten

The next morning, I awoke to the cries of roosters. I opened my eyes and found Chantal laying on top of me and smiling in the soft light. We were wrapped in a blanket and my arm was gently draped around her soft, beautiful body.

"Good morning, baby," I said softly in her ear.

"Good morning," she replied, brushing her nose against mine and kissing me. "It was wonderful," she said again, tracing my lips with her finger. "You know something?"

"Tell me."

"I watched you when you were asleep. I looked at your face and realized you're so young! You're only 19 and I'm 23. You could be my younger brother, and yet you were all over me last night. I was completely under your spell. How did you do that?"

"Don't know. Am I demoted now to your young brother?" I replied and kissed her lips. As we were kissing, her eyes closed and our tongues met and twisted against each other. The feeling was so good, so wonderful; it was out of this world. "Chant," I murmured in her ear.

"No baby, I am your girl. Love me as you want."

"I know," I replied softly.

We kissed and stopped for a brief moment. She eased up a little onto her shoulders, gently pressing her breasts against my face. I bit her nipples gently, first the left, then the right. She writhed, moaned, and screamed with pleasure. I held her tight against me. Soon, we were lost in love again, melting into one another and coming together at the same moment. We fell in each other's arms again, deeply satisfied.

"That was very good," she murmured in my ear. "I felt the earth move."

"I love you, baby," I said, barely audible.

We held each other and fell asleep again, and when we woke for the second time that morning it was nine o'clock. We held one another in the blanket for a while and then showered together, brushing each other's backs, caressing each other with pleasure and excitement, kissing over and over again. It was love. It was wonderful.

We dressed and walked down to the kitchen.

"Let me whip you up some eggs," I said.

"That's a good idea. You wore me out," she said with a smile.

I filled the coffeepot half-full with water from the faucet, scooped three heaping spoons of coffee grounds from the jar and laid the pot on the stove to boil. Meanwhile, I heated the pan with a spoon of margarine in it, cracked two eggs, and fried them over easy. Chantal came from behind, put her arms around my waist and leaned against me, her breasts pressing gently against my back. Her scent hit my nose, making me lose myself in another world again.

I shut off the stove and turned around slowly in her arms, putting my arms around her, and kissing her deeply. We held each other for a while. It was a wonderful feeling.

"The food is ready," I said softly in her ear.

"Ok. I don't want to let you go. You make me feel so good," she said.

We ate our breakfast: eggs over easy, with two slices of bread. We sipped our coffee and looked at each other, smiling. It was the perfect morning for the two of us.

"You know something?" Chantal asked and leaned toward me.

"What's that?"

"I feel," she said with a smile, "your sperm tickling inside me as if you're making love to me this very minute."

"I'm happy, baby. I want to please you every minute of my life."

"You're pleasing me now. Do you think they'll be tickling inside me like this all day?"

"Don't know."

"They are moving inside me now. I love you, baby."

"I love you too."

"It's too late for school."

"I don't feel like going to school today."

"Me neither."

"What do you want to do?" I asked.

"I don't know. We can hang out in the city," she replied.

"That is a good idea."

After finishing our breakfast, we went to the living room. We sat on the sofa, the place we made love the night before, as soft music from the phonograph played in our ears. She rested her head in my lap as I stroked her soft hair. She looked up at me and smiled.

"I love you Savy. But…"

"But what?"

"I'm older than you, four years older. In a few years, you will find someone younger and more beautiful than me, and then you'll regret we met."

"Why? Are you thinking of an older man to marry?"

"Ok, Socrates, I cannot win your debate. You had me at 'Hello.' "

"You were in my dreams, even before I met you. How could I stop loving you?"

"In most couples, men are older than women. Some are even ten years older! Do you think people would laugh at us?"

"Let them laugh, see if I care. I'll be marrying the most beautiful woman in the world."

"You know you're my first. You took my virginity," Chantal said.

I leaned in to kiss her.

"Were you with someone before me?" she asked, looking at me in the eye and touching her fingers to my lips.

"Last night was my first."

"You seemed so experienced!"

"Why do you say that?"

"Your kisses and the way you touched me and made love to me... you knew how to please me."

"It's not difficult, you're so beautiful," I said with a sincere smile.

"So you could do that with every beautiful woman who comes along, all the time?"

"No, I couldn't possibility do that with just anyone, simply if she was good looking. I've wanted to do this with you since I was seventeen years old, the first time I met you. It actually took two years for my dream to come true."

"How did you learn to talk like that?"

"Honey," I said softly with a smile, "should I confess in front of Buddha's statue to prove my love to you?"

"No, I believe you, but I think you were crazy to shield me with your life when the bomb exploded last year at the university."

"Only one reason: I love you."

"What if I'm pregnant?"

"You think we will have a baby after last night?"

"Probably. Are you worried?"

"No, absolutely not."

"I want your baby!"

"We'll make lots of babies."

"I'd like that," she replied softly with a smile.

Life is wonderful when you wake up in the morning with a beautiful woman in your arms to caress and kiss, I thought.

"I'm a very lucky man," I said softly.

As I leaned against the sofa, she rose slowly and moved onto my lap, facing me and pressing her lips against mine. I held her tight in my arms, and she said, "Make love to me again, darling." I said nothing; just let her have her way. We kissed again and again until our clothes were stripped off. We made love again on the sofa in the living room.

Sophie

At eleven o'clock we left the house. We drove along one of the east-west high ways leading to the Central Market, then turned right, going straight, towards the lakefront. Along the lakefront, we drove north for twenty minutes, dodging traffic until we got to the bridge, which we crossed to the other side of the Tonle Sap. When we reached the other side, we headed south for less than a quarter of a mile and then turned into the driveway of my house.

Chantal stayed with us awhile, chatting with my mom and then sitting at my father's bedside, holding his hand and talking with him as much as he could manage. At one o'clock, I walked her to the car, kissed her goodbye, and promised to see her at school on Monday.

Once she drove out of sight, I went inside and sat next to my dad, who lay hopelessly in his bed. My dad looked me in the eye, grabbed my hand tight, and closed his eyes with great disappointment. He knew that Chantal and I had broken our tradition the night before. There was no need for me to confess.

We sat in silence and then, suddenly, I heard a bomb burst outside; it sounded close. Immediately, I ran outside to see what was happening. Black smoke was coming from the direction of the bridge.

"Oh, no! God, please save her life!" I cried out. Without a thought I ran to the bridge as fast as I could. When I arrived, the scene was completely secured; the military police had taken over. I asked people who had been there when the bomb had exploded. They said a red car had been thrown into the air before it plunged into the river.

"No, it can't be true!" I cried out. I ran to the river, ready to jump into the water to find her, but people from the crowd pulled me back and held me tight. I yelled her name from the top of my lungs until I lost consciousness. When I opened my eyes, I saw my mom, tears streaming down her cheeks, holding my hand.

"I'm so sorry," she said.

"Mom, it couldn't happen. She's alive, right?"

My mom said nothing. I stayed in my room all day. There were no tears left, nothing in me. I was finished. The next day it was confirmed. Chantal was missing. Two weeks later, my father passed away, leaving this world, along with three small children, my beautiful mother, and me.

How can it be, I asked myself? I lost two people whom I loved so much within two weeks of each other.

After that point, my schoolwork deteriorated, and I didn't care. The agony in my life was immeasurable. I went crazy; I couldn't sleep or eat for months. I wanted Chantal back. I wanted to trade places with her. If I could have, I would have.

Sophie

Chapter Eleven

The sun was rising in Koh Kong. I woke up, got out of bed, and walked to the window with my eyes half closed. I shoved it open. The morning light fell into my room, blinding me with its brightness.

I walked back and sat on the edge of the bed, resting my feet on the floor and interlacing my hands behind my neck. Outside, two birds were singing to one another on a tree branch. I sat idly on my bed looking outside for a long while before walking to the bathroom to shower and brush my teeth. I put fresh clothes on and headed into town.

As I walked, I thought of Sophie and the night before, when Khemerin and I had had dinner at her place. An image of the two of them sitting awfully close together kept flashing in my mind.

Khemerin knows I like Sophie, I thought to myself. He should not have come between us. But after all, it is her choice.

A breeze brushed my face as I walked along the seafront. When I arrived at the center of town, I paced up and down along the sidewalk and then leaned against the wooden fence that stretched for half a mile along the walk.

The city was not very crowded. From where I stood, I saw a few fishing boats floating far away under the vast blue sky. I crossed the street, walking to the shore, and went north, following the coastline and enjoying the beautiful morning, the fresh air, and sunshine. As I walked, I kicked at the smooth sand on the beach. I was enjoying the simplicity of the moment, when my eyes caught a man and woman standing under a palm tree, talking and laughing. As I came closer, I realized that it was Khemerin and Sophie. I was shocked. My throat swelled and my heart froze.

"Hey you, come here!" Sophie called out to me.

I stood still for a second, unable to decide whether to walk away, or to join them. Finally, I walked to them.

"Good morning, you two," I said.

"Hi, it's a great morning!" Khemerin replied.

I looked from Sophie to Khemerin and back to Sophie with a forced smile.

"We just had breakfast, and we came here for some fresh air," Sophie said, looking at Khemerin, smiling.

"We ate at the restaurant next door to Thansour. The food wasn't too bad," Khemerin added.

"It's good to know. I haven't eaten, for I'm still full from dinner last night," I replied.

"What's wrong? Are you ok?" Sophie asked me.

"I'm ok," I replied.

"You look very pale, like you've seen a ghost or something," Khemerin added.

"Am I?"

"Yes, you are," Khemerin replied. "What's on your mind?"

"It's nothing, Khem." I said. "I probably came down with something, maybe the flu."

"We're going to the zoo," Sophie said. "There's a small zoo on the east side of town. Do you want to join us?"

I gave Khemerin a knowing smile and turned to Sophie, saying, "I have another commitment this afternoon. You two go ahead." I paused for a second and added, "Look guys, I need to go now."

"What have you to do this afternoon? Can't you hang around for lunch?" Khemerin said.

I looked at Khemerin and said, "I have to go, buddy. I'll see you later, ok?" I turned to Sophie and said, "Good to see you."

I walked away from them and kept walking, wandering, not knowing where I was heading. In my mind, the beautiful morning had become cloudy, the bright sky dark, and the fresh breeze of the sea hot and awful. I walked back to my hotel room, my mind restless, wandering.

Inside, I took a long shower to cool off and then read until I fell asleep. When I woke up, I put on shorts and running shoes and went out running toward a nearby village. I ran slowly at first and then faster down the road, passing small houses made of bamboo and palm. Children playing in their front yards waved at me and I waved back. Dogs barked to scare me off.

In front of each house was a well of water. Clotheslines hung from tree branches and poles stuck into the ground. Chickens, dogs, and pigs were let loose in the yards, and fresh fish and other seafood lay across large, flat palm-leaf baskets, drying under the hot sun.

I ran a long way to the end of the village and then returned. By the time I got back to my room, the sun had gone down. I took another long shower and headed out for dinner at a nearby restaurant.

I sat at a table in the corner near the exit. Sitting there, I caught the eye of a woman sitting alone, two tables away. She smiled at me and I smiled back. She wore a long skirt and a blouse with an open collar, which revealed her generous cleavage and the brassiere that shaped her breasts. Her blouse hugged her curves snugly. She had thick, white powder on her face, red lipstick, black pencil on her eyebrows, and thick, black mascara. She reminded me of a female giant from a traditional Chinese opera I once had attended with my cousin Sarah in Phnom Penh.

"Are you alone, young man?" she asked as she walked toward me.

"Yes."

"Come and join me if you want," she said.

I looked at her with a smile and said, "Thanks."

"I can see you are very sad," she said. "When did you come to town?" she said, pulling a chair over to sit facing me.

"Is it that obvious?"

"I know almost everyone in this small city, and I don't know you."

"My name is Savy," I said.

"I'm Kim," she introduced herself. "I am twenty-nine years old and have never been married." She paused for a second and asked me, "How old are you?"

I looked at her and wanted to tell her to go away, but I didn't have courage to chase away a stranger.

"Why?" I asked.

"Just wondering," she replied. "There is no age restriction for a business transaction."

"What age restriction? What business are you talking about?"

"Don't pretend that you are naïve, young man," she said, and then, "Can I join you? At least I'll have someone to talk with. It's been a rough day for me."

"Ok, but I want to make sure we have no business together. I don't like your line of business, in case you want to know," I replied and looked away from her.

My food came as we were talking and she asked me to go ahead and eat.

"I'm guessing you have a broken heart," she said.

"No, I'm just far away from home and it's making me unhappy."

"Good lie."

"Look, I don't need a prostitute to tell me how I feel," I said, groaning.

"You're very rude, young man," Kim replied. "Do you want a good time? I can show you a good time."

"What do you mean?"

"You know what I mean."

I looked at her and shook my head.

"Why? Am I not beautiful enough?"

"No, it's not like that. You are beautiful," I lied. "First of all, I am not in a good mood, and second, I don't feel comfortable." My tone was soft, just to show some respect to the woman.

"I can make you feel comfortable, just go to my place after dinner."

"I want you to know I don't sleep with prostitutes, and also we're not eating dinner together. I'm eating my food and you're eating yours."

"You are very rude."

"I'm sorry. I don't mean to hurt you. I cannot do what you want me to do."

"Would you pay for my dinner then?"

I looked at her and said softly, "All right."

"Thanks."

"You're welcome."

"Look, just forget about her. It is not worth it. You know something? She hurt you and she went off with another guy richer than you, or more handsome than you, because she thought she is beautiful. When she is my age she will not be as pretty as she is now. Then she'll know how difficult it is to find a man."

"Kim, stop talking like that. I don't have a girlfriend, and no one dumped me."

"Come to my place. You are a nice guy! I won't charge you. I just want to have a good time tonight for a change."

"No, Kim. I cannot do that. It's just not like me. Besides, there are a lot of prostitutes where I come from," I said. "Most of them lived in mansions and were guarded with uniformed soldiers."

"Those women are not free. They make money for their pimps," she said. "I am free to do as I choose."

"If you put it that way, I have nothing to say."

I finished my food, got up, and told her, "I have to go. Don't worry about your food. It's on me."

"You are not coming home with me?"

"No. Goodbye, Kim."

I walked out, and at the door and I heard her shout at me, "You loser!" I did not turn around, but kept walking. I came back to my room, thinking of Sophie. I really missed her. Kim was probably right.

She was probably a beautiful young woman once and now she is an ugly prostitute. An angel turns out to be a monster, I thought.

That night, I took a shower again before I went to sleep. I read a few pages, but I just could not concentrate. I couldn't sleep. I tossed and turned in my bed until very late, past midnight.

The next morning, I left my room at seven o'clock and went running down the same road as the day before. I kept running to the end of the village, back and forth, to keep my mind off Sophie. I went swimming in the afternoon, but couldn't spend much time at the beach because it was too hot out.

Instead, I walked toward the sacred ground of a Buddhist temple, a mile south of my hotel. I stood in the shade of a Bohdi tree, looking at the majestic temple and the surrounding area, which reminded me of Watt Phnom, where Chantal and I had spent a lot of time together. While I thought back to my past, three monks passed by and I bowed at them. They nodded back with smiles in return. I sat against the Bohdi tree, thinking back to when I was thirteen years old.

It was early 1963 and I could remember of that particular event clearly. I am late for my morning class—half an hour late, as all the students are out of their classrooms and in the courtyard when I arrive. The principal and his staff are inside one of the classrooms; two policemen guard the door. The four buildings of the school have been secured, and all the students are crowded together in the courtyard. Some are standing in groups and seeming engaged in earnest conversation, while others pace back and forth in silence. When I inquire to my friends, no one knows what is going on.

As I stand in a crowd listening to others speak about the event of that morning, Heng, my close friend, leans over behind me, puts his arm on my shoulder, and whispers in my ear, "Son of a bitch, you're late for your class." As he says it, I feel him slip an envelope into my pocket, and then he says, looking me in the eye, "Be careful! Don't be a smartass!" He slaps me on the back and walks away.

That morning, when students went to their classes, they found Communist propaganda flyers in their drawers. At this time, any political movements, other than the Sihanouk party, were considered to be illegal. It seemed that some students or someone in our school was trying to recruit students to join the Communist party. Most students were scared because they did not want to be involved in any illegal activities.

I realize then, Heng has taken a chance and secretly stirred up our school; the envelope he put in my pocket contains none other than the flyer distributed in the classrooms early that morning.

I slowly stroll out of the school compound and head toward the refreshment stand, the usual place where I hang out during recess. I grab a table at a corner where I can have privacy, and I order a cup of coffee. The one-page flyer Heng gave me has very convincing arguments in support of the Communist movement. I read it several times until I remember every word of it and then I tear it into small pieces and throw it away. I am then convinced that there is a better choice for our society.

I am not too happy at home at the time, for I feel that my parents do not care for me; we fight nearly every day. I need attention and love, which I do not have at home. I think hard about every word I read on that flyer, and I believe I will find love, respect, and hope in the Communist party, as it promised. One week later I leave home, go to the bus station, and buy a one-way ticket to a village in Kandal province, where the Communist movements are active. I have decided to join the Communist movement and become one of them.

I arrive at the bus station at two in the afternoon, and half an hour later the bus leaves the station, rolling slowly in the streets and out of the city toward the southern part of the country. The bus is full and I sit by the window, looking outside. Tears start rolling down my cheeks, for I think I will not see my parents, little brother, and Sarah again. It makes no difference to my father and mother whether I live or die or disappear forever, I think to myself. The bus moves slowly on the national highways, going over some rough parts and holes in certain areas. I sleep most of the time, and I don't care where I will end up. Goodbye, Khemerin. Goodbye, Sarah.

Two hours later the bus pulls into the station in Khoki, a village in Kandal. The last station is two more after this one. Everyone gets off the bus for a short break as I sleep. I open my eyes and see a policeman standing beside me; he has tapped me on the shoulder lightly to wake me up. He asks me to get off the bus and takes down my name, the date and place of my birth, the names of my parents, my destination, and asks many more questions. I answer most of his questions, but I cannot give him a good reason why I am traveling alone. He then takes me to a police station and charges me as a runaway boy.

At the police station I am asked more questions, and after the interview, a guard brings me a bowl of rice and fried chicken, for it is dinner time after the interview has finished. When night falls, I'm taken into the courtyard toward two bunk beds, one of which is supposed to be mine, set under a big tree. The night is beautiful. Soft winds brush my face once in awhile, and the sky glows with a full moon and thousands of scattered, bright stars. A guard comes to me and sits on the bunk bed next to mine, one cup of tea in each hand.

"Chamran is my name," the guard says, handing me the cup. "Do you like hot tea?"

"Thanks," I reply, taking the cup from him.

"I thought so," replies Chamran. We're silent for a moment, and then he says, "So, you decided to run away."

"Chamran," I say.

"Yes?"

"Do you have children?"

"Yes, two boys and one girl. My oldest is about your age."

"Do you like them?"

"Yes, they are my children," says Chamran. "You are running away, but why?"

I do not answer and drop my gaze to the ground.

"You think your parents don't like you; am I right?" Chamran asks. "And so you ran away. You don't have to tell me how you are treated at home, but I am sure that all parents love their children."

"I believe that I have been punished excessively for my faults, but I don't think I have done anything wrong," I tell him.

"I have heard a lot about child abuse, but again we live in a society in which parents know very little about child psychology. They send you to school, right?"

"Yes."

"Raising children is a big responsibility for any parent. Since your parents have cared for your education, it means a lot. They love you. You need

to listen to them and obey them. Don't think too much—just do what you are told. I hope you understand what I am trying to tell you," Chamran says. We are silent for a while, and then he continues, "You need to think back to a time they stood by you when you needed them most."

I am silent and take a breath, looking into the sky, illuminated by the moon and stars' dim light, as the crickets chirp all around us. "Can you remember?" Chamran asks me again.

"When I was ten years old, I was very sick. They took me to the Calumet hospital, the French hospital and the best hospital in the country, you know. They spent all their savings on my medical bills," I say. "But now they don't care. They stopped loving me."

"Your brain is messed up, my young friend," Chamran says. I say nothing, just look at him sadly.

"There are a lot of kids your age running away to join the Communist movement simply because they have problems at home. You think that joining the Communists will make you happy and will gain you some respect, because you want to be loved and accepted.

"The flyers that you've read and the speeches you've heard are propaganda, simply deceitful lies. They say that children are subjects of the state, in this case the Communist Party, since it is not the government and it never will be, I hope. This is nonsense.

"In general, all parents love and care for their children; it's a law of nature. Do you understand? All parents always want the best for their children." He pauses for a moment and continues, "If you join the Communists, they'll teach you to fight for their cause. You'll be lucky if you stay alive. You're wrong if you think you'll find equality and justice in Communism. All you read about them is simply a deception and a big fat lie."

I'm silent. I stare at him, without blinking.

"They recruit young men and women who have small brains, kids in college and high school, to die for them, people like you," Chamran says.

"Sometimes I feel that my parents love me. Most of the time I don't think so."

"You belong to your father and mother. Right now, they're worried to death because you're not at home," Chamran says. "We found your parents and we know where you live. When they come to pick you up tonight, you'll *know then that they love you."*

"Did you find them, my parents?" I ask.

"Yes, we telephoned the police station in your district. They said they could find your family easily. Go to sleep. It's almost midnight."

"How about you?" I ask.

"Not now. My shift is coming. I need to go to my post. You'll be ok. Someone will sleep here to keep you company while I am on duty," Chamran says, pats my head with a smile, and walks away.

"Can I ask you another question before you leave?" I say.

"What is that?"

"What do you think of religions?"

"There are a lot of religions out there, and Communism is one of them. You can believe in Buddha, Mohamed, Jesus, Moses, Brahma, Mao Zedong, or whatever; it's up to you but you need to think hard. But beware the bastard who comes to you and promises you Heaven, but takes away your freedom. Freedom, kid, is important in life. Being free to think for yourself and being free to do what you want to do."

"Are Jesus and Moses the same person, but just different names?" I ask.

"You're probably right. I don't know. Go to a library and check it out," Chamran replies, standing up and adding, "I know now why you have a problem with your parents. I have to go. See you in the morning."

That night I sleep on the bunk bed, a guard on the bed next to mine, soft breezes caressing my face. In my deep sleep I hear a conversation far away. It's my father's voice, and then I open my eyes, looking around, and murmur, "Dad, is it you?" but there is no answer. I sit up, listening carefully. "Is it you, Dad?" I say again. As I sit on the bunk bed, half asleep, a guard walks in my direction. He comes to tell me that my father is with the Captain, processing paperwork to take me home.

On the way home, my father and I do not say a word. Our emotions are so intense that we just cannot find a word to say to each other. When I get home, my mother embraces me, tears rolling down her cheeks, and says softly in my ear, "I was so worried; don't ever do that again."

I just cannot utter a word, finally knowing that they love me. It is everything to me. I go to bed at four in the morning. My father comes to tuck me in and I manage to say, "Dad! I'm sorry!" He nods and gives me a smile, a sign of forgiveness.

The soft winds brushed my face and rustled the Bodhi leaves nearby, making soft rattling sounds overhead. My eyelids grew heavy, and I fell asleep with my book as a pillow under my head. I took a long nap, and when I opened my eyes it was sunset. I felt good and fresh. I stood up, dusted off my pants, and walked to the street with a good feeling.

I took a deep breath to let the fresh air into my lungs. I thought of Sophie. I tried in vain not to think of her. I'm in love with her but it's Khemerin she's interested in, I thought to myself as I walked down the road back to my hotel.

In the hotel, I walked through the front door and to my room on the first floor. As I put my key in the keyhole to open the door, I noticed a neatly folded piece of paper folded tucked under the door. I picked up the note and walked inside. Sitting on my bed, I read it: "Meet me in front of Thansour at noon tomorrow. Take me swimming. Sophie."

My heart beat with joy. I glanced at the clock on the table; it was seven o'clock. The evening was quiet and I was hungry. I was thinking of Sophie.

I thought to myself, when I see her tomorrow, should I kiss her? Hold her hand and let her know how much I miss her? No, none of these should come from me. She will let me know and I will go along.

That evening I went to Thansour for dinner. Sitting at the smoky bar with a bottle of beer in front of me, I stared at the TV screen on the wall, watching boxing aired from Thailand. I was thinking of Sophie, imagining the wonderful afternoon we'd spend the next day, when Khemerin pulled up a chair, sat next to me, and slapped me on the back.

We looked at each other but exchanged few words. Khemerin ordered beer and we ordered a big bucket of boiled crab for dinner. We watched the boxing match on the TV screen without saying anything for a while, and then gradually started chatting. I enjoyed watching boxing, but I knew nothing about it; Khemerin seemed to know much more. Gradually, the topic shifted to the past two days, and how Khemerin hadn't seen much of me. He expressed his concern, and I thanked him.

"Sophie is a very beautiful woman," Khemerin said.

"Let's not talk about her," I replied. I paused for a second and added, "I feel guilty for planning to leave the country while our friends are fighting."

"I see, so you want to go back and get killed," Khemerin replied. "I'm worrying for my family. They may not be able to get out."

"I never thought that the history of our country would change this way," I said.

"I don't understand why they want to turn the country into a Communist state. What's special about Communism, anyways? There are no Communist states in this world that are better off than those in the free world, either economically or morally," Khemerin said.

"The only thing I can say about the Communist state is that the government controls everything in the country, whereas in the free world, the free market drives the economy, creating competition, which creates an incentive for people to work hard and produce more," I said.

"The Communists want to eliminate the bourgeois and the capitalists."

"If they kill all the rich and the intellectuals, it leaves only the poor and uneducated."

"They're fascist!"

"You are right!"

"We're just parasites, based on their views."

"We need to get out of here before they kill us."

"The Governor has set up tight security along the border. No one can cross it without his permission."

"He's an asshole."

"There will be a band performing in front of the Governor's mansion on New Year's Eve, the evening of the 12th. Would you like to come?" Khemerin proposed.

"That'd be fun."

"Maybe it's the last performance in the city, the goodbye and farewell to the country," Khemerin said.

"How is the situation in Phnom Penh? Do you know?" I asked.

"You know as well as I do. We're losing the war."

"My guess is that we may be lucky enough to have the New Year's celebration next week. The Communists may come sooner."

"You'll come to the performance at the Governor mansion? It's free and is a public event," Khemerin said.

"It'd be fun." I sipped my beer. We finished our meal and ordered a third round of beer.

"We can ask Sophie to join us," Khemerin said.

"Ok, maybe she can join us," I replied.

"She could introduce us to the Governor," Khemerin said.

"What do you mean by introducing us to the Governor?" I asked Khemerin, searching his face.

"You know Sophie is very hot," Khemerin said. I glared at him, right in the eye, and he continued, "Ok, she's very attractive. The Governor may like her, and then she could introduce us to him. If I were in front of him for five minutes I could ask him for permission to cross the border to Thailand. We'll be safe, we'll all be safe."

"You want to be her pimp, turning her into a night girl? That's what you want to do, Khem? You cannot do that. I won't allow it!"

"Oh. Are you serious? I am not so sure she loves you…"

"Don't do that. Leave her out of this."

"I'll ask her anyway," Khemerin said, and gulped his beer.

"I'll tell her not to go, and I think I'm starting to not like you now."

"Are we fighting because of her?"

"No, I just cannot let you use her, that's all," I said. "I have to go. I'm tired." I got up and walked to the door.

"What are you doing tomorrow?" Khemerin yelled out as I opened the door.

I turned around and said, "Nothing."

"You want to hang out, do something?"

"I have plans tomorrow." I left the restaurant, went to my room, and went to bed.

Chapter Twelve

We met in front of Thansour the next day. Sophie walked toward me from a distance, wearing tight jeans and a loose, blue t-shirt, her hair flowing down her back. She carried a small, elegant bag.

"You look great," I said as she arrived.

"I'm sorry! I'm late," she said, smiling.

"No, you aren't. I thought I'd show up early."

"Let's have some fun," she said.

We headed toward the beach, walking side by side along the shore under the hot afternoon sun.

"Where were you yesterday?" Sophie asked.

"I ran for a few miles and went to the temple on the hill."

"Did you go there to pray?"

"It was beautiful up there. I fell asleep under the Bodhi tree."

We walked close to each other and I felt her hand brushing mine.

"I love to swim."

"Thanks for the note," I replied softly.

Sophie looked at me with a smile and said, "Good to see you!"

"Me too!"

"Have you found anyone to help you cross the border to Thailand?" Sophie asked, eyeing me sadly.

"We have to get out from this city all together," I said.

"Do you mean it?"

"Absolutely."

"When you arrive in Thailand, what will be next?" Sophie asked.

"I don't know."

"Dad said we will go to America when we get out of here. We have a lot of connections in Thailand."

"That's good," I said, lowering my eyes and kicking the sand.

"We'll keep in touch. I have to find a way to bring you with us to America."

"Thanks, Sophie. It means so much to hear you say that."

"I mean it!"

"Thanks."

"Do you think Sihanouk is a Communist?" Sophie asked.

"I don't think so," I replied.

"Why is he in China supporting North Vietnam and the Vietcong in the fight with our government?

"I think he had no choice. He's trapped."

"I think he loves himself more than the country," Sophie commented.

"You're probably right."

"Is the place we're going to swim far from here?" Sophie asked again.

"No, it's not far. Probably a ten-minute walk from here," I replied.

"Let's run then. You want to race?" Sophie said and looked at me with a smile. Then she started running, leaving me no choice but to run after her.

We ran for a couple of minutes and then she slowed down and dropped on the smooth sand, pulling my hands to sit next to her. We sat next to each other, shoulder to shoulder. She took my hand and said, "This is fun!" We looked each other in the eye for a brief second. As our eyes met, I felt there was a secret message being exchanged between us. We turned away, looking out to the vast sea.

"You were upset when you saw me and Khemerin the day before yesterday," Sophie said without looking at me. I did not answer.

"Why?" she asked.

"No, I was not upset," I replied.

"Don't lie. You disappeared off the face of the earth yesterday."

I did not say anything and looked down at the sand. We looked each other in the eye without saying a word. She leaned to kiss me on the cheek and said, "Happy now?"

"Yes," I said softly in her ear.

"You can kiss me quick before someone sees us if you want to," Sophie whispered in my ear. I leaned to kiss her on the cheek, my heart beating fast. She smelled so good. It was a natural smell, sweet and beautiful. We looked at each other and giggled.

"Do you think I am beautiful, Savy?"

"Absolutely."

She smiled and said, "Let's go. I love swimming." She stood up, dusted the sand off her jeans, and reached for my hand to pull me up. We walked southward for a little while, until we found a beach where the sand was smoother, and where children were running and playing with joy, their parents watching them nearby. We walked a little further, hand in hand, and sat a few inches apart on a rock with our feet dipping in the water below.

"Koh Kong is beautiful, don't you think? After all, our stay here feels more like a vacation," Sophie said. "Mom and Dad sold everything, including our house. We are leaving the country. It was Dad's idea, and Mom refused to go along with the plan at first. Then she turned around and agreed with him. We won't ever be going back. Dad did not tell you everything the night you had dinner with us."

"Your relatives in Bangkok should be able to help you," I said.

"Yes," Sophie replied. "Do you think Dad is overreacting to the current situation?"

"I don't think so," I replied, "unless you're prepared to live with the Communist government."

"I think Dad is right. When the Communists take over, they will kill all the educated people. It's just like the other Communist revolutions in China, Cuba, and the Soviet Union. Many people were killed,"

Sophie commented. She paused for a second and said, "Most people think Prince Sihanouk will come back and we will live in peace once more."

"The Communists have fought this war for a long time," I said. "The movement started secretly the day we got independence from the French. Since they'll win the war now, I don't see any reason why they wouldn't change the political leanings of the country towards Communism. There will be a revolution and a lot of killings," I added.

"If Prince Sihanouk is part of the Communist revolution, I don't foresee any killing in our country," Sophie replied.

"I don't think he cares for people as he said. Remember when we were kids; the scenes on the TV and movie screens, the exhibitions of executions of the people whom he accused of being traitors and CIA agents?"

"Yes, I remember that. It was sad."

"He executed those people in cold blood."

"But he seemed so good and caring towards the Cambodians. How come we didn't see his evil side?" Sophie asked.

"I don't know, Sophie. Dictatorship works well in a third world country like ours."

"Dictator is a horrible word. I cannot imagine that Prince Sihanouk is one of them. He was very popular! Even now he still has a lot of supporters," Sophie said with a sad expression, looking far away to the horizon. "If the President of a country lies to his own people to advance his own agenda, without caring for its own people's welfare and the future of the country, is he classified as a dictator?"

"I don't know about that. However, if he tries to control both the legislative and judiciary branches of the government, he is absolutely evil, and if he achieves this goal, he's absolutely a dictator," I replied.

"The world is full of evil."

"Of course," I replied. "The most important role of a government is to protect people who cannot protect themselves. A President who fails to see this role as important is a bad President. If he intentionally does things that are harmful to the people of the country, he is simply a traitor to his people and to his country," I said.

"We judge a person by his or her actions," Sophie added. "In the U.S., a President is in office for only four years; it is impossible to harm the country in a period of four years."

"You are right. But if he was an evil genius, he could get reelected for a second term. In an eight-year period, he could bring down his country, even a country the size of the United States."

"There is no perfect world," Sophie replied. "My uncle John said that the press has the right to criticize the government in America, and yet they are protected by laws."

"It's true," I said, "but if you had a lot of money, you could buy everything."

"I hope there won't be such horrible Presidents in America. I don't want to live under a dictatorial government, directly or indirectly. John will take us to America as soon as we get out of this country," Sophie said.

"You are lucky," I said.

"You'll come with us. Dad really likes you," Sophie said.

"Thanks," I replied, "but my future is in the air right now."

"No more talk about politics," Sophie said. "Let's race to that rock over there." She pointed to a big rock in front of us.

Sophie slowly took her t-shirt and jeans off, and I politely looked at the horizon. She had her swimsuit on underneath her clothes all along. She was ready to jump into the water.

"What, have you never seen a woman in a swimsuit?"

"Yes! No, I just forgot that you were surrounded by Western culture as you were raised. Swimsuits and bikinis aren't normal outfits for most Cambodian women."

"I hope that's a compliment," Sophie said, winking.

"Of course it's a compliment. You never cease to amaze me," I said with a smile.

I turned in her direction and then had to look away a moment. She was very beautiful. The shape of her body and her smooth, white skin made my heart beat faster. I heard her say, "Look at me, stupid boy." I turned toward her again, gave her a smile and said, "Let's race to that rock over there." I took off my Polo shirt, stood up, and said "Are you ready?"

"I'm ready," she said, standing up.

She counted to three, dove into the water, and the race started. I did not care if I won the race, as long as I swam alongside her. We kicked the water very hard, both of us swimming as fast as we could. I fell behind a few inches, because I glanced at her often to make sure she was ok. Within five minutes, we reached the endpoint of our race. Sophie reached the rock first and won. I climbed up on top of the rock, grabbed her hands, and pulled her up. We sat on the rock, shoulder to shoulder, breathing fast.

She smiled at me and said, "That was fun."

"Yes it was."

"You won. You're a good swimmer," I said.

"I was on the swim team in school. I practiced every day. How about you? Where did you learn to swim? You swim pretty well too," she said and put her hand on my shoulder. My heart raced, but I tried to keep calm.

"In the lake behind my house," I replied.

"Oh."

I glanced over at her. She was very beautiful. I leaned to kiss her on the cheek.

"Let's go back," she said.

"We just got here."

"It's too hot, let's go back. I want you to do something for me."

I looked at her. She stood up and said, "Let's go! We'll race again!"

"Ok."

"I want you to be serious. You cannot let me win the race or I'll stop talking to you!"

"You are good, Sophie! You beat me on your own!"

She looked at me, bent her back a little and said, "1, 2, 3, and go!" We both dove into the water and started to swim as fast as we could, racing back to the shore. She was very good and beat me again in the second race.

We walked out from the water and back to the rock where we had left our stuff. At the rock, I sat on the edge, dangling my feet. Sophie handed me a tube of cream.

"What is it?" I asked.

"Sun lotion," she said. "Go ahead, put it on your arms and legs. It protects you from sunburn."

I squeezed the tube into my left palm. I rubbed my palms against each other gently, and spread the lotion, rubbing my hands on my arms, legs and body, as Sophie watched me. I felt sticky.

"Put some on my back, would you?" Sophie asked, turning her back toward me.

"You want me put the lotion on my hands, and then put the lotion on your back, rubbing it?" I said.

"On my shoulders too. Don't pretend that you've never touched a woman," she replied.

I did as I was told, putting the lotion on my palms and then rubbing her back and shoulders. "You have soft skin, Sophie," I said.

She turned toward me and said with a smile, "Thanks, I feel better now. I just don't want to get sunburned. You have soft hands, too!" She took my hands and turned them up, examining my palms and saying, "You have beautiful hands. I don't think these hands have ever done any hard work."

"Can you read palms too?" I asked.

"I want to know more about you."

"Like what?"

"Like your childhood."

"Ok, if you want to know," I said, smiling.

I was born one year after my parents got married. It was a marriage arranged by their parents as part of our traditions. My parents seemed to be happy together. I had never seen them quarrel, argue, or raise voices to each other. It was possible that they fell in love after they became husband and wife.

I was not a happy child for many reasons, but one of them was that I did not care for the rules in the family. I don't think I was close to either my father or mother until my high school year.

During the first year of elementary school, my father paid much attention to my school work. Most evenings, he taught me to read and do basic arithmetic. Before I started first grade, my father taught me the song of our national anthem to pledge allegiance to the country and to our kings. The song was all about our King, whom we prayed to the Angels in Heaven to protect at all times. All kids should know our national anthem before entering the first grade.

I knew my father cared for me, which meant so much to me. I do not remember him spending much time with me during the later years of my schooling, but school was easy for me anyway. I liked very much to spend time with him, but it seemed he was busy with work all the time. Actually, I don't think my father was very happy.

As I spoke I felt Sophie take my hand in hers and press it hard. I felt very comfortable with her. I paused, looking at her with a smile. She said softly in my ear, "Keep going."

I was a good student. I never had any problems with school. Not only that, I participated in extracurricular activities when I was in fifth and sixth grade: I ran cross country and played soccer. Each morning before class started, we lined up in front of our classroom for school uniform inspection: white shirts and khaki pants for boys, and white blouses and blue skirts below the knees for girls. We had to observe other school rules and policies, such as keeping our hair short, our fingernails trimmed, and having good behavior. Teachers had the right to punish students who misbehaved. The punishment could be of many forms; beating a student with a stick was normal.

Every morning at seven-thirty, before class, we gathered in front of our school and sang our national anthem when our national flag was up at the top of the flag pole, after having been raised slowly by two students, a boy and girl, who were selected by our principal. This procession repeated in the afternoon at five o'clock before school closed at the end of the day. When we finished singing the national anthem, the flag was dropped down slowly. We were taught to love the country and our King since we were in the first grade.

"Did it work?" Sophie asked.

"Pardon me?"

"Patriotism? Do you still love your country and your King?"

"No, the widespread corruption in our government destroyed everything in me. Our King sold our country to the Vietnamese."

Sophie said nothing, looking at me sadly.

I grew up in a society that separated boys from girls. Boys and girls did not play together. We were in the same school and the same class, but we were separated because of our culture and traditions, which considered it inappropriate for boys and girls to be too close.

Khemerin and I have been friends since we were in junior high. We were in the student commando in the same unit when the war broke up in early 1970. I skipped one year in junior high and one year in high school. For this reason, I am two years ahead of Khemerin.

Sophie looked at me and said, "I don't understand."

"What part don't you understand?" I asked.

"You did not have really close female friends."

"In the last year of high school, I met Chantal. Later, we became very close friends, but she died last year on her way home after she dropped me off at my place. I killed her, Sophie." I said, looking away to hide the tears rising in my eyes.

"Khemerin told me about you two," Sophie said and added, "Do you miss her?"

"Her life was too short. We never found her body. Yes, I miss her, but I cannot live in the past. I need to move on. I know she loved me. If there is a Heaven, she's there. I know she would be happy for me to move on and to be loved again."

We paused for a second. Sophie held my hand tightly and my heart beat faster.

"Tell me about your life," I said with a smile.

"Mine's very dull, not like yours, which was full of adventure," she said. "Dad and Mom had maids to care for us. I went to French school from the first grade onward. We took vacations in France almost every year. We went to San Francisco twice to visit my uncle. I really like

America, it's very clean and the people are very nice. At school I have a lot of friends, both boys and girls. It's healthy to have friends of both sexes."

"I know. You and I are living in the same country, but in completely different cultures and environments."

"It seems you are doing fine dealing with me."

I said nothing, just looked her in the eye and smiled at her.

"You liked Chantal very much. I can see it in your eyes."

"Like you, she came from a good home. She was well educated and very intelligent."

"You were hurt very much, weren't you?" Sophie said.

"I am over it now," I said and forced a smile.

We were silent awhile and then, at the same moment, we both noticed the reflection of a thick cloud in the water. Gradually, the sky grew dark and a few rain drops fell.

"Let's go back," I said. "It'll rain soon."

She threw her t-shirt and sarong on top of her swimsuit, took my hand, and said "Let's go." I stood still, numb, looking at her, lost in her beauty. "Don't look at me like that. You're making me nervous!" she said, kissing me on the cheek. "Come on, it's raining!"

We ran back together, hand in hand, as the rain started to come down more heavily. The wind blew harder, and the rain drenched us through.

"Your place is closer," she said, over the roar of the wind.

When we got to my room, we were both soaked. I pushed the door open, and we scrambled in. We stood there, facing each other, and then starting laughing at how drenched we both were.

"Make yourself at home," I said. "You can go ahead and take a shower, ok?"

She nodded, walked away, and entered the bathroom, closing the door behind her. Outside it was raining and storming. I sat by the window, watching the dark sky, the flashes of lightning, and the trees swaying back and forth from the violent force of the wind. Then I heard

Sophie's voice calling from the bathroom, "Hand me one of your shirts."

"What did you say?" I asked.

"Give me one of your shirts, please," she repeated.

I walked to the closet, pulled out one of my shirts and tossed it to her through the door.

"Thanks," she said.

A few minutes later, she walked out from the bathroom, wearing her blue jeans and my loose white shirt, which looked good on her. Of course, everything looks good on her, I thought.

"It's my turn. It's raining and storming pretty bad outside," I said, walking toward the bathroom. After showering, I came out from the bathroom with a fresh set of clothes on.

"Mom and Dad must be worrying about us," Sophie said.

"I know. I need to bring you home as soon as the storm stops," I replied.

"It's comfortable here. I don't mind if it rains all night," she replied. I looked at her, frowning in disagreement. She smiled in response and then sat on my bed.

"You're reading *Les Miserables*?" She had found the book on my bed.

"Yes," I replied. "Have you read it?"

"Only for a school assignment, not the entire book though," she said. "What page are you on?"

"380."

"Come sit next to me and read for me," she said. "I want you to read for me."

I sat next to her, my heart pounding as I took the book from her. She gave it to me with a smile. I opened to page 380 and started reading.

"The dawn of the next day found Jean Valjean again near the bed of Cossette. He waited there, motionless, to see her wake. Something new was entering his soul. Jean Valjean had never loved anything. For twenty-five years he had been alone in the world. He had never been a father, lover, husband, or friend. At the galleys, he was cross, sullen, abstinent, ignorant, and intractable. The heart of the old convict was full of freshness. His sister and her children had left in his memory only a vague and distant impression, which had finally almost entirely vanished. He had made every exertion to find them again, and, not succeeding, had forgotten them. Human nature is thus constituted. The other emotions of his youth, if any such he had, were lost in an abyss...."

Sophie leaned on me, her head resting on my shoulder, her eyes half closed. I kept on reading.

"...And, in truth, in the mysterious impression produced upon Cosette, in the depth of the woods at Chelles, by the hand of Jean Valjean grasping her own in the darkness, was not an illusion but a reality. The coming of this man and his participation in the destiny of this child had been the advent of God...."

At this point, I stopped reading because Sophie fell asleep, her head drooping on my shoulder, her body completely leaning on me. I looked at her. She was an angel, the most beautiful of God's creations. I could smell her natural beauty. I took a deep breath, kissed her forehead gently, and laid her down on the bed. Then I walked away from her, toward the window, looking outside.

The rain was still coming down hard and the storm was still menacing the city. I sat by the window, watching Sophie from a distance for some time. She was an angel. I pledged in my mind to protect her, to seek happiness for her as long as I lived. Love is crazy, but truly wonderful, I thought to myself.

"Savy, how long have I slept?" Sophie's voice interrupted my thoughts.

"An hour, probably," I said and looked at her. Sophie sat up on the bed, looking at her clothes, and realized that everything was in proper order. She stood up and said, "What happened to Cosette?"

"I'm happy you had a good nap. The rain and the storm are over now. I should take you home."

She walked toward me and put her arms around my neck. For the first time, I felt her moist lips against mine. I was lost in a deep dream. I felt her soft body against mine. It was the most wonderful moment of my life. I whispered in her ear, "You are very beautiful, Sophie. I love you very much."

"Let's go home. It's our secret."

We left the room. It was six and already dark. The joy in my heart was immeasurable. I felt like a new man. I felt I now lived with a purpose; I wanted to live to please the woman I loved. We walked briskly along the seafront, across town toward her place, knowing that her parents were probably worried to death. When we arrived at her place she went inside, but her father blocked the door, preventing me from stepping in. Standing on the stoop, I heard the commotion from inside.

"Where were you, young lady? We were worried to death!" It was the voice of her mother, I assumed.

"We were caught in the storm and went to his place," Sophie replied.

"You went to his place," her mother retorted, "What is it you are wearing?"

"Everything was soaked, Mom. I'm wearing Savy's shirt," Sophie replied.

"What? You are wearing his shirt! What's come over you?" The voice of her mother was even louder.

"Mom!" Sophie yelled louder, "He read for me and I fell asleep."

"You slept at his place! It's not like you. Did he put a spell on you or something?" Her mother shouted with anger.

"No, Mom! I was tired and I fell asleep. When I woke up, he was by the window, not even looking at me. Are you happy now?" she replied, breaking into tears. "You want to hear more?" Sophie added.

"Shut up! I don't want to hear any words coming from your mouth," her mother shouted at her.

"Mom! I'm nineteen years old now, not nine."

Her father, still standing by the door, looked at me and said, "You should go. I'll talk to you later."

Chapter Thirteen

Two days later, Khemerin came to my room in the early morning and knocked on my door while I was still asleep. I walked to the door with my eyes half-open. Seeing it was Khemerin, I invited him in and then walked back to my bed, covering myself with the blanket from head to toe.

"Hey man, you want to come out for a while in the fishing boat with Khom and Sambat?"

At first I told Khemerin I would rather sleep. Then, with a little convincing, I changed my mind. Knowing Khemerin all these years, I felt he was very unhappy and needed to get away from people and enjoy a little time with friends. He needed to talk.

Once we were in the fishing boat heading away from the shore, Khemerin and I sat at the stern against the gunwales, facing each other and sipping our hot morning coffee. The engines hummed as the boat moved steadily. We were silent, seeming to have no words to say to one another. Above us, white clouds scattered here and there, and flocks of birds flew north under the vast blue sky.

"You've avoided me for the almost a week, and you walked out on me the last time we talked," Khemerin finally said.

I did not reply. I looked out at the horizon; I had so many things on my mind.

"You're so quiet. What is bothering you?" Khemerin asked again.

"Nothing," I replied. "I was just thinking it would be nice to live in a country like America, where the government is elected by the people for the people."

"Theoretically, it's very good, but it's impossible for the public to really know the candidates' true character. They tell you only good things about themselves," Khemerin said.

"Each party selects only the best person for the public to vote for. Isn't it a wonderful system?" I said and sipped my coffee. "Why does our country not have a system like that?"

"Yes, we did once in the early '50s, and Prince Sihanouk replaced the two parties with one party, his party, which was the Sakhom Resniyum."

"Yeah, I forgot the history behind that. He's an asshole."

"Why is there a two-party system in America?" Khemerin asked.

"The two parties should debate for the good of the people."

"Why not more than two parties, like a third party?"

"I can understand having a third party, but I believe the Americans have created a good system with just two parties. When you have an issue to debate, you only need one opinion to oppose the other. At the end of the discussion, the two parties should come to a conclusion that is good for their people."

"It is complicated. There is no perfect world," Khemerin said, sipping his coffee and continuing, "So, you really like her?"

"Yeah, we went swimming yesterday," I said, just to let him know.

"Good, she's very hot."

I looked Khemerin in the eyes, but said nothing.

"Oh, I forgot our pledge when we were kids," he said. "We will not fall in love with the same girl."

"No, forget about the pledge, it was fun back then. You feel free to do what you want. It's not my choice, it's hers."

"And you won't kill me if I take her out?"

"No, absolutely not. Like I said, it's up to her."

"I'd rather stick with our pledge, old buddy," Khemerin said.

"Thanks, rich guy," I replied. "Let's not talk about her."

"Fair enough," Khemerin replied. "There was a storm in the afternoon. How could you two swim?"

I did not reply to his question. I rose and walked to the bow, where I could be alone. I looked down into the water, which was dark blue. How deep the water is, I thought to myself. And then I thought of my cousin, Sarah.

I am six years old and Sarah is seven. At the lake behind our house, we play together every day, collecting shells and rocks along the shore, running up and down the hillsides, catching butterflies and dragonflies. Sometimes we spend all afternoon fishing. We use an old mosquito net cut in a big triangle shape to scoop the fish that swim close to the edge of the lake.

One afternoon as usual, we are fishing for a while, and we are tired. We take a break, sitting under a tree next to our clay fishing jar. We watch the fish swim and talk about everything that comes to our minds. The breeze brushes against our faces and rustles the leaves overhead.

After a good rest, I stand up and run toward the lake. Sarah watches me, wondering where I am going and what I will do next. I climb into a canoe, pick up the oar lying in it, and start to paddle. The canoe moves in a semi-circle, but goes nowhere because it is tied to a nearby tree.

"Come on Sarah, let's go to the other side of the lake to see the naval base," I cry out to her. The lake extends eastward toward the back of the naval base, a huge base on the Mekong River.

"No, you can't do that! The canoe is not our property, first of all, and besides, we may get lost," Sarah replies, running from the hilltop toward me.

"We're going nowhere, just pretending that we're crossing the lake. Come on!" I cry out louder to her.

Sarah steps in the canoe, picks up another paddle, and rows it. We are laughing, giggling, and splashing water at each other, as the canoe moves backward and forward in a semi-circle. We row the boat for a while, until we are tired. I put the paddle on the floor and look into the distance on the other side of the lake, lost in thought, remembering when I was five years old.

I had a beautiful goldfish then, which I put in a glass jar. I used to spend hours and hours each day watching it swim in a circle in the jar. If I put two of its kind together, they would fight each other. My friends wanted to put their goldfish and mine together to fight, but I refused because I didn't want to hurt my fish.

Very often, I would use a mirror to reflect its image to trick the fish into spreading its tail and beautifully multicolored fins as it saw its reflection. It died one day, floating in the jar as I pulled it from under the table in the living room, where I used to keep it.

I emptied the jar and laid my fish on a banana leaf. Kneeling down on my knees, I closed my eyes and prayed, "Lord, please bring my little goldfish back to life. I like it so much."

I opened my eyes, hoping for a miracle, but the fish would not move. Again, I closed my eyes and prayed, and again, God did not perform a miracle. Then I took my goldfish to the river in front of my house, where I tossed it in. As soon as the little fish dropped in the water, a big wave hit the shore and took it away. It disappeared in the blink of an eye. I stood watching the miraculous wave for a few minutes, and climbed the bank back home with the comforting thought that my fish had gone to Heaven.

"What? Are you daydreaming?" Sarah yells at me, startling me out of my reverie.

"Yes, I'm thinking of my goldfish. It's in Heaven now, don't you think?"

"Maybe! Maybe not!" Sarah cries out.

"What do you mean?" I'm surprised by Sarah's answer.

"Grandpa said dogs go to Heaven. He said nothing about fish going to Heaven."

"Really?" I asked, doubtful.

"Yes."

"Ok then."

I had no thought of questioning Sarah. I accepted the statement without questioning or searching for any logic behind it. This was the way I grew up, just believing everything I was told by someone I loved and trusted, especially the elders in the family.

I look into the lake through the clear water, and within my reach I see a beautiful plant swaying left and right at the bottom of the lake. For no particular reason, I reach out to grasp the plant through the clear water, but it is not within my reach, so I stretch a little farther and farther and suddenly fall into the lake.

I can't swim, so I yell out for help. Sarah jumps in after me to save my life, but she can't swim either. She grabs hold of me and together we sink to the bottom of the lake. We are drowning. Water flows through my mouth into my stomach; I know we are going to die. Miraculously, our neighbor who lives by the lake sees us drowning and runs as fast as she can to rescue us. She jumps into the lake and pulls us out. She lays us on the ground and sucks the water out of our mouths.

This was an act of love from one human being for another, saving grace in a time of need, I thought to myself, as I sat on Khom's fishing boat. Yet people are able to kill one another in a war, whether the war is waged for political or religious beliefs. I was saved that day simply by the grace of God and the goodness of one woman's heart.

I thought back to another face from my childhood: Chhamren, my best friend since elementary school and throughout junior high. When the war broke out, he joined the Navy and got killed three years later on one of his missions in search for the enemy in a village not far from Phnom Penh.

It was a shock and a horrible blow when I heard the news; my mother woke me up at one o'clock in the morning to tell me. He was not just a friend, but also part of our family. We had so many memories together: running cross country when we were in sixth grade, hanging out after school, and other good times.

We spent a lot of time walking together in the woods behind our village, where tall trees reached straight up into the sky and bamboo grew wild. There were no wild animals there, but there were poisonous snakes. In these woods we walked through tall grass that reached up to our knees in some places, and we shot birds with our slingshots. Sometimes we sat at the edge of a pond, talking and watching the fish swim in the clear, deep water. One Sunday, we found a honeycomb in a big tree and managed to chase the bees away by blowing smoke slowly into it so we could get at the honeycomb without danger of being stung. It took us two to three hours to successfully get all the bees out.

Another friend, Bin Salem, whom I considered a best friend and big brother, was five years my senior and lived close by. We were not really friends until I was in junior high, the first year I attended school in a town far from my village. He looked after me and took interest in my school work. He joined the army a year after the war broke out and got killed the following year.

Reflecting on my childhood friends, I thought to myself, soldiers die with honor in a war because they sacrifice their lives for the country and liberty of the people they left behind. There is nothing in this world more precious than life, yet Chhamren and Bin Salem sacrificed their lives, fighting for something they believed in: their country. It hurt me deeply in my heart. It hurt because they were too close to me.

As I was in deep thought, I felt a hand slap my back. It was Khemerin.

"Are you ok?" he asked.

"Yeah, I'm all right," I replied gloomily.

"You're sad. What is bothering you?" Khemerin asked.

"Do you remember Chhamren?" I asked.

"Yeah, sorry man. Move on! He's gone."

"He died honorably. Do you think he has a place in our history?"

"I don't think so. He was on our side, and the bad guys are going to win the war."

"He died in vain," I replied softly. "Remember Bin Salem?"

"Yeah, he was your big brother or bodyguard, something like that as I remember," Khemerin replied.

"They all died in vain."

"Remember Hun?" Khemerin asked.

"Hun who?"

"Hun Sen!"

"I've heard about him. When the war broke out he was in the same grade as I was, 11th grade, but in a different classroom. We never met, actually. He was one of the few people who quit school and joined the Communists."

"I know, we all heard the rumor about him," Khemerin said.

"I don't understand how people chose Communism against freedom and liberty," I said.

"Hey, people have their own minds, why do you care?"

"You are right, why should I care?" I replied and looked at the horizon. "I've heard," I continued, "that the Americans evacuated a lot of people out of Phnom Penh yesterday. Most of them were employees of the U.S. embassy and important people in our government. Your family is probably on the plane to America by now."

"Where is the news from? There was no report in the radio or papers about it."

"Last night, I went to Thansour and heard a group of soldiers talking about it."

"This country is going down."

"Think. We need to get out of this country fast."

"The Governor has ultimate power in this province. He is the person who put tight security on the borders for the past couple of weeks," Khemerin said.

"Do you have a lot of money?"

"No, not much."

"Don't worry, we'll do something," Khemerin said. "Tonight we'll have a couple drinks at Thansour. I hope these people will come back. I'm sure they can help us one way or another."

"Ok, let's try. We meet at eight," I said.

The sun was directly above our heads; it was hot. I stood against the gunwale and looking down below, I saw the reflection of a flock of seagulls flying above. Up into the sky, fifty or more birds were flying north in a V-shape formation. The waves beat the boat as it moved steadily toward the shore, and the breeze brushed my face gently. I took a deep breath of fresh air as the smell of salt hit my nose.

Soon, the boat slowed down and docked neatly at the quay. Khemerin and I jumped down off the boat. We said goodbye and thanked our friends for their hospitality. We walked to a restaurant nearby to grab some lunch.

In the restaurant, halfway through our meal, Khemerin looked at me with a smile and whispered, "Look who is coming!" I followed his eyes toward the entrance and saw Mr. Lopez walking toward us.

"Finally, I caught you two at the same time," Mr. Lopez said. We raised our heads, Khemerin smiling and I just looking him in the eyes, knowing for sure that we were in trouble with him. He stood upright, looking down at us sternly with his hands on his waist.

"May I talk to you two for a second?" Mr. Lopez said.

I rose, pulled up a chair for him and said, "Please, sit down. We are having lunch."

"I can see that. I will not take much of your time," Mr. Lopez replied.

Khemerin and I caught each other's eyes.

"Mr. Lopez," I said, "I am sorry. We got caught in the storm. I walked Sophie back to your place as soon as the storm was over."

Khemerin looked at me, seeming at first to disbelieve what he heard, but he kept calm and smiled at me.

"Stop, don't mention it," Mr. Lopez replied. "I want you two to stop seeing my daughter. If I catch you talking to her again, I will put bullets in your heads. You understand?" Mr. Lopez finished his sentence, looking from me to Khemerin.

"Sir," Khemerin said, "I had nothing to do with him and the storm. It is my first time hearing about it." Then Khemerin turned to me and said, "What was wrong with you, Savy?"

"Nothing wrong with us," I replied, and turned to Mr. Lopez. "Does she know about your warning, Sir?" I paused for a brief second and added, "She's my friend and I cannot walk away from her, just because you say so."

"What does it mean that she's your friend? She's my daughter. I take good care of her. There is no 'we' between you and her, over my dead body!" Mr. Lopez looked me straight in the eye with anger. He turned to Khemerin, "You too. Stay away from my daughter. Who do you think you are? You spent all afternoon with her the other day. What do you think she is?"

"We did not do anything. We went to the zoo and talked," Khemerin said, looking at me in shock.

Mr. Lopez rose up, pushed the chair aside, and said, "You two stay away from my daughter if you want to stay alive." And he walked out of the restaurant, red-faced.

"You stay away from her, understand!" I said to Khemerin.

"You are in trouble, buddy," replied Khemerin.

"Over my dead body," I mimicked Mr. Lopez. "I am not scared of that old man."

"What did you do with her during the storm in your room?" Khemerin asked inquisitively.

"Nothing. She took a nap while I was by the window watching the storm."

"It's very romantic. You expect me to believe that? Now I understand why Mr. Lopez was so angry," Khemerin said with a big smile.

"Look Khem. I didn't do it," I said in a loud voice.

"Ok, ok, I believe you!"

"Thanks, it's not funny," I replied.

"Ok let's be serious; what is next?" Khemerin asked.

"I don't care about her old man. If she wants to see me, I'll keep seeing her. The old man lost control of his daughter and got angry at me," I said.

"At us!" Khemerin repeated.

"You keep out of this and away from her."

"You're crazy!" Khemerin said.

After lunch Khemerin and I went our separate ways and promised to meet again at Thansour in the evening. On the way to my hotel, I thought of Sophie. Did she know that her father threatened me? What would her father tell her in order to break up our relationship? I did not blame her father for keeping me away from her, because he had every right to protect her, probably not legally, but morally. I lived in a society that treated women as sexual objects. My love for Sophie was real, true love, from my heart, the love of a man for a woman. But her father didn't see it that way.

Back in my room, I turned on the radio to listen to the news from home. It was another way to keep Sophie off my mind. The news did not say anything about the American evacuation of their Embassy's employees and key members of our government. However, the newscaster announced briefly that the U.S. Air Force had temporarily evacuated several thousands of children from the orphanages in Phnom Penh.

This news did not make any sense to me, but nothing made sense any more. The images of the orphanages where Chantal and I worked as volunteers in early 1971 came to my mind. The children are safe, I thought.

I drifted away, thinking back to my past and ahead to my future. Then I fell asleep. After a long nap, I woke up to the sound of the radio playing contemporary music. It was seven-thirty in the evening. I got up, went to shower, put on fresh clothes, walked out of my room, and closed the door behind.

At the restaurant, Khemerin was waiting for me at the bar when I walked in. He had a bottle of Tsingtao in front of him, and I ordered the same. We hit the bottles and he said, "Friend!"

"Friend!" was my response back. We smiled to one another.

"What's on your mind?" Khemerin asked.

"Nothing," I replied.

"Don't lie, it's the woman."

"I am not leaving without Sophie," I said and sipped my beer.

"That's ok. You could elope with her if you think it's the right way to do it."

"Thanks, Khem. You always have such brilliant ideas."

"Hey, I'm trying to help!"

"Let's find a table in a corner where we can see the traffic going in and out of the restaurant," I said.

"Do you remember the guy you saw last night?"

"Absolutely."

Khemerin turned to the bartender and said, "Can we move to the table over there? We would like to sit at a table; we're talking business."

"No problem. Just go ahead. Your drinks in the bar go with your dinner."

"Good idea," Khemerin replied, and we moved to the table in the corner, from where we could see people going in and out of the restaurant. We ordered two grilled fish and a pint of beer. I finished the bottle and poured the beer from the pitcher into two mugs, one for me and one for Khemerin. We raised the mugs, toasting to our friendship, and we gulped the drinks at the same time, "Cheers!" Khemerin said.

"Cheers!" I replied.

"Tomorrow evening is New Year's Eve," Khemerin said. "Would you come to the festival at the Governor's mansion? It's a public event."

"Of course," I replied and added, "What year is it?"

Khemerin looked at me and said, "Pig or cow, doesn't matter. Maybe pig."

"It's hard to keep the years with animals."

"How many animals are there in our calendar?"

"Twelve, I guess."

"Can you count them all?"

"Nah."

"You know in India some people worship cows?"

"Would you shut up?"

"They call them holy cows," Khemerin insisted.

I looked at the fish and said, "Khemerin, what is this, big heads? Where is the meat?"

"They're called dragon fish."

I looked at the pitcher, noticing it was empty. We asked the waiter to fill our pitcher and then continued our dinner.

"They're expensive. Have you seen the prices on the menu?"

"I'm damn hungry," I replied. "There's no meat, Khem."

"Just suck the bones and drink your beer," he raised his glass, and I did the same.

"Do you think all women are beautiful?" Khemerin asked.

"You can save the question for tomorrow, you know," I replied.

"Tell me now."

"Ok, I think all of them are beautiful. Don't you think so?"

"Are you sure?" Khemerin replied with a smile.

"Absolutely."

"How many women have you actually fallen in love with?" Khemerin asked.

I was silent.

"Come on, spit it out, buddy!"

"Ok, five not counting my first grade teacher."

"Wow, five, and how many times you have sex, one or twice?" Khemerin said and sipped his beer.

I was silent.

"Did you do it?"

"Do what?"

"You know, with Sophie, in the storm, in your room."

"I told you we did not do it."

"Why not?"

"Because we are not pigs!"

"You are a lousy liar, you know that, don't you?" Khemerin said.

"Let's not talk about it," I replied.

We were silent for a while, sipped our beer and looked at the entrance to make sure we did not miss anyone walking into the restaurant.

"Do you think he's coming?" Khemerin asked. He was referring to the soldier I had met the night before, who had information about the evacuation of the American embassy employees, and possibly key employees of our government, out of Phnom Penh.

"Don't know. We just have to keep our eyes open," I replied.

We continued to talk as we ate and drank. The dragon fish actually wasn't too bad, except that there were a lot of bones and not enough meat. The restaurant was dim, noisy, and smoky. Even though I enjoyed my conversation with Khemerin, my mind was on Sophie, wishing I was with her instead.

As we were almost done with our dinner, four people in military uniforms walked in; it was the company we were expecting. I looked at Khemerin and said, "Our guys just arrived." We continued our conversation and dinner as though nothing had interrupted us. Khemerin signaled to the waiter to come over.

"You see that table there," Khemerin said when the waiter arrived, winking at him, "That table is on me, everything for the New Year's celebration."

"Yes, sir," the waiter replied and walked away.

Soon, one of the four guys in military uniforms looked in our direction and waved at us with a welcoming smile. Khemerin stood and said, "Let's go, we have business to discuss."

When we arrived at the table, Khemerin said, "Allow us to buy your dinner tonight," Khemerin said.

"Come and join us," one of them said.

"We just finished our dinner, but we'd be happy to have a few drinks with you," Khemerin said.

We introduced ourselves by shaking hands and exchanging names. The leader of the three soldiers was a lieutenant named Vichey.

"Why are you so generous? What do you want from us? Cut the crap, would you?" Vichey said, suddenly suspicious.

"Last night, I overheard you say the Americans evacuated a lot of Cambodians out of Phnom Penh. Maybe you can tell us more," I said.

"You're the one who sat next to our table last night; I remember you. How did I know?" one of the soldiers added. "I only heard some important officers in our government were among them. It's a rumor. We know nothing about this."

"My dad was probably on that plane," Khemerin said.

"What does this have to do with me?" Vichey said.

Khemerin looked him in the eye and signaled to the waiter for more drinks.

"Look kid," Vichey continued, "I don't care how rich you are, but if you have something to say, just say it now. The four of us are very close friends. We keep no secrets amongst ourselves."

"Can you help us?" Khemerin asked, cutting to the chase.

"Help you do what?"

"Help us cross the border to Thailand," Khemerin said. "When this country falls, they will kill us all. They'll probably kill you guys before they kill us. It's the truth. Don't pretend that we're safe. You and I both know better."

The three soldiers looked at their officer, seeming surprised by what Khemerin just said, because people generally did not dare to talk about the fate of our country so openly.

"You want to get out," Vichey said. "The Governor gave orders to close the border. No one is getting out under his watch."

"You are close and have access to him, right?" Khemerin asked.

"Who the hell are you?" One of the soldiers cried out, and Vichey signaled him to calm down.

"Look, we have money," Khemerin said. "How much do we need to spend in order to cross the border?"

"Look, kids," Vichey tried to say something, but Khemerin pulled a bundle of money from his wallet and put it in Vichey's pocket and said, "This is a present for our friendship. Keep it."

"Look, kid," Vichey continued, "the Governor's order is strict. No one is allowed to cross the border without his permission. I promise I will talk to him, but that's all I can do. I will not see him tomorrow or the next day because of the New Year. I'll talk to him when I can. Can you meet me for lunch here on the 16th, when the New Year's celebration is over?"

We agreed to meet again after New Year's and continued on with our conversation, to different topics. We shook hands for the last time that evening after the four soldiers finished their meals. Khemerin threw some money on the table for the tip.

"Khemerin, how much did you put in his pocket?" I asked when we were alone.

"Oh nothing, it's the price you pay for information. You know that there's nothing for free," Khemerin replied.

"I know, but how much?" I asked again.

"Why do you care? It was my money."

"You're insane. You spent too much money on those guys," I said.

"It's a lot because you don't have it. It's the Americans' money," replied Khemerin.

I looked him in the eyes and said, "This money should go to the Cambodian people for medicine and food, but it's piled up in your dad's bank account instead."

"He gave it to me, and you shut up. We're leaving the country, remember?" Khemerin replied.

Chapter Fourteen

Iawoke on the morning of April 13th to the sound of traditional Cambodian music playing on the radio. It was the first day of the three-day celebration of the Cambodian New Year. I sat on my bed for five minutes, rubbing my eyes and yawning, and then walked slowly and lazily toward the bathroom with my eyes half closed.

While I was in the shower, the music on the radio stopped and a news broadcast from Phnom Penh came on: "The city has been hit badly by enemy rockets and our troops have withdrawn from their defensive positions as the Communist troops advanced into the city. The government is calling for student commandos to assist in protecting civilians and to restore order to the city, which has been in chaos for the last twenty-four hours. The fighting has intensified."

I got out of the shower and put on my blue jeans and white polo shirt, the one with the emblem of two Americans walking on the moon on the left pocket. I thought of my family, who were surely trapped in Phnom Penh. The Communists are absolutely going to take over the country, I thought to myself. It is only a matter of days.

It was ten-thirty in the morning. I walked out of my room toward the seafront, where everyday business was conducted, and where I had hung out nearly every day for almost two weeks. It was a beautiful day, but I was despondent, troubled inside. I missed Sophie and wanted to talk to her. I missed her kisses and the hug that she had given me in the evening after the big storm, three days earlier. She had made me feel so good inside.

The market was more crowded and lively than normal. There were rows and rows of gambling tables set up in the market and on the sidewalks of the seafront. There were crowded tables for poker, blackjack, backgammon, roulette, baccarat, and more. Gambling had been illegal until 1965, the year Prince Sihanouk opened a casino in Phnom Penh and legalized gambling for the three days of the New Year, and since then it had become part of our traditional New Year celebration.

I strolled from one table to the next, trying to enjoy myself and not think of Sophie. I stood by one of the roulette tables, watching the dealer spin the wheel, the small ball flying with it. When the wheel slowed down, the ball jumped from one number to the next and then dropped on one of the 36 numbers on the wheel. The dealer announced the winning number, the crowds burst into a loud yell, with some cheering, others scorning, and still others quietly betting again.

In one section of the market, it appeared that the games were played on a smaller scale. The players were children and women, most likely. The dealers sat on stools two inches above the ground, rolled dice, and howled for passersby to bet on their games. Each had a piece of board the size of a regular chess board; on it six animals were drawn. The winner was the one who bet on the picture of the animal that was face up on each die. Because three dice were rolled at once, the chance to win the game was 50 percent.

Deep in the trenches of the market was a small, dark corner completely obscured by the belligerent and screaming crowd that gathered in front of the cockfights. I walked out from the crowd and back to the seafront, my mind still on Sophie. I sat on a bench under a palm tree, looking at the horizon above the vast sea.

"Hey, you!" It was Khemerin's voice. He emerged from the crowd and walked toward me.

"Good morning," I said.

"You look like shit," Khemerin said, sitting down next to me.

"I am not feeling well."

"Take your mind off her, man."

"I just can't."

"Forget it. It won't work," Khemerin said. "We need to get out of this place alive. Now you're involved in a romantic relationship. It just complicates things."

"I miss her very much. It's not easy to lose a beautiful woman like her."

"You're crazy," Khemerin said. "Did you play any of those games?"

"No, maybe I'll play later," I replied. "Did you enjoy the games?"

"Yes, I won some," Khemerin said, gesturing toward the crowds. "It was fun. I spent nearly two hours in there."

"I dodged through the crowds earlier, but didn't see you."

"I know, there are a lot of people."

"What did you play?" I asked.

"Blackjack."

"Congratulations for winning," I said.

"It was nothing, but thanks. It was lucky for sure."

"Sounds fun."

"They don't play only during the New Year. They play year-round, except not publicly. You know that, right?"

"Of course," I said. "What do you think about gambling?"

"I don't think gambling is bad. Gambling is legal in Nevada and everywhere, why not here?"

"I think gambling should be controlled by the state. It absolutely affects society in a bad way. We just cannot confirm it because we have no studies to support the claims," I argued.

"We are living in a society which lacks an understanding of the concept of free speech and using information to make a better society."

We were silent for a while, looking at the crowd.

"Do you remember when our superintendent and his administrators busted into our history class, checking for cards hidden under our drawers? Most of the students at the time played cards with their lunch money. They played before school and during recess. It was wild back then," Khemerin said.

"Yes it was scary; we threw the cards out the window just before the raid," I said.

"How did you guys know they were coming?" Khemerin asked.

"I don't know. It's human instinct, kid instincts," I replied. "Someone saw that they were coming, so we just passed notes and whispered to one another. The cards had all been thrown out the windows before they got in."

"I remember you played quite often."

"Yes, I played quite often," I said sadly. "I not only played in school, but also in my neighborhood. Mom caught me playing cards with friends in my neighborhood one day and punished me severely. Since then, I've stopped playing. She was afraid that I would get addicted and sidetracked from my school work, or that I might steal money for gambling."

"She might have been right, but we cannot say that gambling is all bad. Everyone gambles in life, one way or another. Risk-taking is a part of life. We are risking our lives, running away from the Communists, leaving our homes and families behind. We don't know what tomorrow will bring," Khemerin said.

"We are taking a risk, but to some extent we control our fates and destinies. Risk on a gambling table is uncontrollable."

"Don't forget, there are some pros out there. These people sure can make money on gambling tables."

"You are right. I forgot about that."

"I would put money in a good company's stock. It's a good risk. Sometimes people panic when the price of stocks drops."

"I'm not sure."

"What do you mean?"

"You are talking about a perfect world. Stock prices drop during economic downturns. You forget that the CEO of a company could bring his or her company down and pack money away. "

"I think you are wrong about this. A CEO has responsibilities to stockholders. The CEO's job is to improve the financial position of the company and to make sure the company's stock value goes up," Khemerin argued.

"You really think that these CEOs care for the interests of stockholders?"

"You are probably right, but your life would be fucked up if you do not take any risks."

"We have to take risks sometimes in life, but the risks have to be carefully studied."

"Talking about risks, we need to get out of this fucking country soon before they fry us alive," Khemerin said.

"I know," I said. "Do you trust him? Mr. Vichey, the officer who promised to help us for our escape to Thailand? I only hope he can help."

"He's the only one in town who wants to take our money. Trust me, I would put bullets in his mouth if he tried to cheat me," Khemerin said.

"Ok, tough guy. Just don't let people know what's on your mind," I said and patted his back.

"You have an emblem of two Americans walking on the moon on your pocket. What the hell is that?"

"It's a symbol of human achievement. You know that," I replied and tapped him on the shoulder.

"The Americans won World War II, beat the Germans and Japanese at once, sent men to the moon, but lost the war in Southeast Asia. Unbelievable!" Khemerin replied.

"The Americans are strange, don't you think? I can't understand it. During 1967 and 1968, they dropped bombs on Hanoi. No one thought Hanoi would survive the bombs. Hanoi was going to be crushed onto her knees. Then there was this actress named Jane Fonda who went to Hanoi, showing her sympathy for the Vietnamese and the Vietcong and blaming her own government. The U.S. government should have revoked her citizenship, along with her driver's license, don't you think?" I said.

"Yeah! Fucking cunt!" Khemerin replied. "You want to go to the pagoda? Your girlfriend may be there. Then you can take her to your room and do whatever you dream up with her."

"It's a good idea, Einstein, but your last comment isn't funny," I replied.

We walked to the pagoda on the south side of town. As we

approached it, we heard traditional Cambodian songs echoing through the speakers attached to the Bodhi trees in the compound. When we arrived in the pagoda, we saw men, women, and children, some playing traditional games in the courtyard, most of them children and young adults. The older people sat in the house of worship, listening to the preaching of the monks in the pagoda, reciting in Sanskrit, an ancient language that no one could understand, except the monks themselves.

It is a tradition to go to the house of worship on New Year's Day. I was told that New Year's Day was originally a time for remembrance of the night of Buddha's enlightenment. The fact that groups of Buddhists celebrate their New Year's Day on different dates is still a mystery to me – Thailand, Burma, Sri Lanka, Cambodia, and Lao celebrate their New Year, three days, from April 13th through April 15th, as Chinese, Korean, and Vietnamese celebrate their New Year Day's in mid-February. We decided to hang out in the courtyard instead of going inside the pagoda. We walked in the courtyard and watched people playing traditional games.

There was a crowd of men and women playing a game of tug-of-war. I liked this game because it was very active. We later joined the game—Khemerin on one side and I on the other. We had a good time with this game, and then we walked away and joined another group tossing seashells into holes.

The players were divided into two teams. Each team tossed sixteen seashells into eight holes. The winning team was the team that first filled the eight holes. We watched that game for a while, but found it to be too slow and boring. We soon scurried over to another area, where we heard loud yells and screams.

A crowd of people surrounded a man with a baton in hand and his eyes covered with a piece of cloth. Above him was a clay pot filled with water and hanging from the branch of a tree. The objective of the game was for the man to hit the clay pot with his eyes covered. As we stood in the crowd watching, the man swung his baton a few times, right, left, forward and backward, until finally the pot was smashed and water poured down on him. The crowd burst into laughter.

It was fun to watch, but we did not play because we didn't want to get wet. There was a band playing traditional music and a throng of people were dancing, cheering, and laughing on the other side of the compound. We joined the crowd. I danced to a few songs but then left the stage after a while. Khemerin was still onstage, dancing and courting women, but I couldn't enjoy myself because I missed Sophie. She was nowhere to be seen.

I walked toward a small bamboo house next to the pagoda, where I met a young monk who was not much older than me. We introduced ourselves; his name was Sokha and he had resided in this temple for two years. His came from a small village in Kompot, a province in the southwest of the country that had been controlled by the Communist troops since shortly after the war had broken out. Sokha had joined the monkhood when he was ten and had spent his life learning the history and philosophy of Buddha and classic Cambodian literature. He said he had to leave his home town when the Communists had taken over.

Sokha said the monkhood had given him peace of mind, no anxiety, and no passion for sex. I wondered if it was all true, especially the part about sex. He also believed that Prince Sihanouk would eventually be back and that Cambodia would once again become a peaceful country.

As we carried on our conversation, Sokha poured hot tea into two small cups, one for me and the other for himself. We clicked the cups together to celebrate our New Year.

"You seem to be sad. What is bothering you?" The monk asked.

"I miss my family," I replied.

"I can see it is deeper than that," the monk replied, looking me in the eye.

"I fell in love with a woman I met on the plane two weeks ago," I said, sipping my tea.

"Does she love you?"

"Yes, but her father has forbidden me to see her."

"We have a tradition and you need to respect it."

"Great!" I said. "Preah Ang (which means "Father"), have you ever fallen in love with a woman?"

"No, never. And I never will," the monk replied.

I looked at him, sipped my tea again and said, "You've never been in love with a woman in your entire life?"

"No, never," was his reply.

"Preah Ang, how about your mother?"

"Yes I love my mother, but it's a different kind of love," the monk said. "Buddhism has deep roots in Cambodian society. It is the core of our traditions and culture."

"Her family is not even Buddhist. They are Catholic," I replied.

"It's irrelevant. Culture has deep roots in each one of us."

I was quiet for a while and then said, "To me, Buddha's teaching is complex. I could never understand it."

"Sometimes we believe what we don't understand. We believe because it is the religion of our ancestors and passed from one generation to the next," the monk said.

"Don't I have to think before I believe?"

"Why should you think?"

"Buddha was not God. He was simply a great teacher. Do you think the real God will throw us in Hell because we do not accept Him before we die?" I asked.

"Who is the real God in your mind?" the monk asked irritably.

"I don't know. I'm just scared of Him sometimes at night when it's dark." I answered.

"Buddha taught us about the recycling of life."

"I really don't know about my previous lives. I like this life and I don't want to go on to the next life," I said.

"Buddhism plays a big part in our lives and society. It shapes our government's functions. Buddhism and the pagoda have been the center of culture and literature in Cambodian society," the Monk said, making sure I was on track.

"People living in Cambodia are free to practice any religion, without threat from our government; regardless Buddhism is the only official religion of the country," I said.

"It's true. Buddhism is the official religion of the state," the monk repeated proudly. "Our government does not threaten people who practice other religions."

"But the government controls them," I said.

"What do you mean? I don't think our government controls them. There are all kinds of religions in Cambodia: Islam, Christianity, Taoism, and more," the monk said, smiling and sipping his tea.

"We have the Ministry of Religion," I said. "What does this ministry do anyway?"

"You are talking too much," the monk said. "I don't want to discuss government and politics."

"Preah Ang, people do not gamble only during the three days of the New Year, they play after the New Year, year-round," I said.

"What has this to do with religion?" the monk asked.

"I think our government should add controlling gambling to the duties of the Ministry of Religion. After all, practicing religion is simply a gamble for our next life. If our government controls the destinies of people in the next life, why not control gamblers who may need help in this life? The name of the ministry should be changed to the Ministry of Religion and Gambling, don't you think so Preah Ang?"

"I think you are talking too much. Now I understand you should leave the country before the new government comes in," the monk said.

He poured me some tea in my cup and we continued to talk. We talked about our culture and Cambodian literature, which I had read. The monk is well read and educated.

"Excuse me," the monk said, "it's time for Athma (which means "I") to go to the great temple for meditation. It's been nice to spend time with you."

"Can I come back again, Preah Ang?"

"Any time. I'm sorry to cut our conversation short, for now it's time for me to meditate."

We said goodbye and I walked back to my room. Khemerin was nowhere to be found. Sophie's image had been on my mind all day. I missed her terribly.

Lying on my bed, I drifted far away into the past until I heard a knocking on my door. At first I thought it was Khemerin. I needed to be left alone. I walked slowly toward the door. Surprisingly, as I opened the door, Sophie stood there with her beautiful smile. Without a word to each other, we threw ourselves into each other's arms.

"I miss you so much," she whispered in my ear.

"I miss you more," I said softly. We embraced each other, afraid we would be separated again.

I loved her so much. I embraced her in my arms, her soft body pressing against mine, and felt her wet lips against mine. We kissed passionately. She stroked my hair and caressed my face. Was there any moment in life better than this? We were both lost in a deep love and half asleep.

I slowly opened my eyes, realizing that we had somehow migrated to the bed and were lying in each other's arms. Sophie's eyes were half closed, her sweet lips smiling at me.

"My darling, you are very beautiful," I whispered in her ear.

"Really?" she said dreamily.

"Absolutely," I said.

"I'm glad you think so," she replied.

She lay on the bed and I rolled over to lie on her. I kissed her lips and then slowly kissed her soft, beautiful neck up and down, continuously. I felt her arms around me and her soft hands gently scratching my back. I was lost in love.

"What are you doing?" Sophie whispered in my ear.

"I don't know," I said softly.

"Don't stop," she said dreamily. I pulled the blanket over, hiding us beneath it.

"No, baby …what are you doing?" Sophie asked me softly. I couldn't answer, and she said again, "No, it's not right and you know that, right? It's a sin, right? But I do love you, baby."

Then she drifted into a deep dream. I held her in my arms with love and passion. Our love was everything. We kissed again and again. Our bodies melted into one. We woke up from our dream, realizing we both wore nothing. I held her in my arms, caressing her soft beautiful body.

"Sophie, you are very beautiful," I whispered softly in her ear. She touched my face and traced her fingers around my lips, saying, "It was wonderful. You're wonderful."

We were in bed, talking, holding each other and kissing each other over and over again, and we made love again.

"Savy, I'm coming with you when it's time to leave this city," Sophie said, rolling over on top of me and kissing me on the lips. I said nothing, just put my arms around her soft body and kissed her over and over.

"What about your dad?" I whispered in her ear.

"I'm coming with you," she said again and this time her tone was even more serious.

"Your dad, does he have a plan to leave? We need to leave this country very soon. The country is going down."

"I don't know, I think he is looking for someone to get us out."

"Look, I will give you the name of a guy who can help. Tell your dad to contact him soon. I am not leaving unless all of us leave," I said to Sophie.

"He does not like you," Sophie said with disappointment.

"He protects you and I completely understand that," I said and leaned to kiss her again.

We lay in bed, staring at the ceiling, exhausted. She turned to face me with a smile.

"Tell me more about your life in Phnom Penh."

"I thought I told you everything," I said in a low voice. "Nothing more to tell. I did not have a luxurious life like yours."

She seized my hands, pressed them tight against her chest, and said, "Have you killed anyone with these soft hands?"

"No, never killed a soul," I replied and leaned to kiss her on the lips.

"I like your hands," she said.

"You are so sweet," I said.

"Savy, make love to me again."

I rolled over and kissed her. We made love again. I felt the earth move each time we made love; it was absolutely wonderful.

We kissed and cuddled for a little while, and then I got up and went to the bathroom, put on fresh clothes, and came back, sitting next to her as she still lay in bed, hidden under the blanket.

"That is the name of the guy," I pointed to the folded paper on the table, "who will help us get out of this city. Give it to your dad. I will not leave this country without you, Sophie." I leaned to kiss her lips and whispered in her ear, "I'll take you back to your place. It's time to face the music."

"I'll come back to you tonight if Dad doesn't want me," Sophie replied and kissed my lips as I pressed mine against her passionately.

"You do that," I said.

We spent four hours in bed holding each other that evening. It was eight o'clock when I took her to her place, dropping her off by the door but not going inside to face her parents. I came back to my room and waited for her return, but she did not come back that night. It was a good sign, I thought; Mr. Lopez has to be nice to her, or he will lose her. Sophie is no longer her daddy's little girl.

Sophie

Chapter Fifteen

When I woke up, the rays of the morning sun were creeping in through the narrow gaps of the unfitted walls and the edges of the windows. Even in such small measure, the light was blinding. I stretched out to reach the radio beside my bed and turned it on.

The news from home was not good. Communist troops were approaching Phnom Penh from the west and there was a ferocious fight at the navy base. My instincts told me that my family back home was not safe. I got out of bed and walked with my eyes half closed toward the bathroom. Once out of the shower, I put on fresh clothes and looked at the clock on the wall. It was ten-fifteen. I sat on the bed, stared at the wall, and thought of Sophie.

I had been alone in my room all day the day before. I read and wrote in my diary to pass the time, but deep inside I just wanted to see Sophie and hold her in my arms. I missed breathing in her wonderful, indescribable scent.

To go to her place on a whim was not possible now that her father had warned us not to see each other. I looked at the clock again; it was eleven o'clock. I thought I ought to go to town, maybe find Khemerin and play a few games at the market to take my mind off Sophie.

As I was sitting on my bed in a daydream, I heard a knock on my door. I walked to the door and opened it. Sophie stood there with a smile and then threw herself into my arms. She stepped inside and I closed the door immediately.

We did not say many words to one another, but rather fell into each other's arms. I kissed her cheeks, neck, and face as though I had not seen her for years. Our lips pressed and our tongues touched. I dropped her on my bed and continued to kiss her passionately. I took her clothes off in a hurry; she unbuttoned my shirt, her hands shaking. We threw our clothes in the corner and fell in each other's embrace. Next thing I knew, I was deep inside her as she held me tight against her body with both hands, my lips against hers.

When we were done love-making, we lay naked in each other's arms. We were exhausted but satisfied. I loved the feeling of her soft skin against my body.

I've missed you so much these past two days." I whispered in her ear.

"I missed you too," Sophie replied gently.

She caressed my face. Her hands were so soft. I kissed her lips and she returned my kiss; she excited me immensely.

"Darling, hold me tight. I want to sleep in your arms," Sophie murmured in my ear. She seemed tired, as though she had not slept in days.

I held her in my arms, and she closed her eyes and fell asleep. I kissed her forehead and curled her soft, beautiful hair around my fingers as her eyes closed and her mouth opened a little. She was very beautiful, one of God's angels fallen from the sky, now in my arms. When we woke up from our nap, we decided to go out and walk toward town.

As we walked, I could smell her sweet, natural smell absorbed by my body.

"I'm sorry I couldn't come yesterday," Sophie said as we walked on the sidewalk on the seafront, side by side, toward town.

"I missed you so much these last two days," I replied.

"I didn't want to upset Mom too much, so I just stayed in my room all day and cried alone."

"I'm sorry."

"Not your fault; I just missed you."

I put my arm around her shoulder. She glanced at me and said, "Don't do that. People may laugh at us."

"What the hell! Let them laugh!"

"This isn't America. They'll laugh at us, you know that."

"How'd you get away from your mom and dad today?" I asked her and took my arm off her, just to please her.

"I told Mom that I was going to see you. She didn't say anything."

"What's your dad going to say?"

"He is my father, but he does not own me… He's an asshole."

"He has every right to protect you," I said, trying to ease her temper.

"No, he controls me. He thinks I'm still nine years old."

We took a late lunch and decided to join the crowd at the gambling tables, for a change. We moved from one table to the next, Sophie holding my hand, seeming afraid to get lost in the crowd. We stopped in front of a roulette table. Sophie looked at me and said, "Let's put some money on the table." She pulled two five-hundred bills from her purse and handed one to me.

"No, you play if you like. I'll watch," I said and tucked the money back into her purse.

"Ok, we'll leave quickly if we lose these two bills," she said as I pulled her close to me and wrapped her in my arms, standing behind her. She said nothing, but leaned her back against me while everyone concentrated on the game. The dealer spun the wheel clockwise, and the ball rolled in the opposite direction. He called out, "Bet time." Everyone laid their money on the table.

Sophie put a five-hundred bill on red. The crowd cheered while the wheel slowed down and stopped. The cheer was even louder when the ball was bouncing from one number to the next. Finally the ball dropped on number twelve, which was red. Sophie won five hundred.

She handed me the winning money and said, "Please, spend it for me." The dealer spun the wheel again. As the wheel spun, I put the five hundred Sophie had just handed to me at the intersection of numbers eight, nine, eleven, and twelve.

"You bet on high risk slots," Sophie said and dropped her money on black.

"It's the only way to spend it as fast as possible," I whispered in her ear.

"Don't be so charming," Sophie said and pinched my bicep with her sharp fingernails.

The ball dropped on number nine: black.

"We won!" Sophie yelled with excitement. The dealer pushed 3,000 in my direction and 500 to Sophie.

"Now, we have more money to spend than I thought," I said and we looked at each other joyfully.

"It's your money, just do what you want," Sophie said.

I looked at her and extended my hand toward her with my palm up. "What? You want my prize?" she asked.

"Let's put 4,500 in one place and call it a day," I said.

"OK, darling, if you say so. I'll do anything to please you," she handed me her money and added, "Put everything on the odd." I kissed her gently on her lips and did as she said.

The ball dropped on number twenty-one this time. We both jumped with joy. Now we had 9,000. I pulled her out from the crowd.

"You keep it," Sophie said.

"No, you keep it. It was your money to start with," I said and pressed my lips against hers.

"You keep the money. You need it more than I do," she said in a serious tone. I said nothing, and went along with her suggestion. It was Cambodian money, after all, which did not hold much value, if it were converted to the U.S. Dollars.

"It's crazy. It seems like I've known you for years, even though we just met a little more than a week ago," I said and pulled her close to me.

"It's called love. True love should not be too difficult," Sophie said. "We were just lucky out there."

"Absolutely, we got lucky," I replied.

"Don't push your luck, darling," she said, looking me in the eye and leaving it at that. We both smiled at each other.

"You want to check out the pagoda? There are a lot of activities there," I said.

"Of course."

We walked toward the pagoda. When we got there we toured the sacred grounds, watching people playing traditional games and dancing. Sophie seemed to lack interest in the festival, so I took her to meet my friend, the monk.

"You've come back, my son, and welcome," the monk said.

"Preah Ang, I want you to meet my friend. This is Sophie."

"Oh, my daughter, are you Cambodian?"

"Not really, her great-great-grandparents came from France a long time ago," I said as Sophie held my arm tightly.

We walked to the place where the monk lived. We climbed the stairs and went inside. When we were inside, we sat on the floor and the monk served us tea. And then Sophie stood up to ease her circulation, for she was not used to sitting on the floor. She walked up and down, surveying the small room of the house and pictures on the walls. As she stood in front of an altar where a statute of Buddha was set behind six burning candles, I walked toward her and stood behind her.

"He's not that much older than us and he calls us son and daughter!" Sophie whispered in my ear.

"We have to address him as Preah Ang, meaning 'Father,'" I warned Sophie politely.

Sophie turned to the monk, who stood not far from us and asked, "You have a nice place; I like it very much. I love the pictures on your walls. You really have good taste for art," she paused and added, "Is that where you sleep, inside those curtains?" Her eyes fixed to the thick curtains hung as walls to separate an exclusive area of the house.

"Yes," the monk replied with a smile, and added, "You are lovely, my daughter."

"Do you think so, Preah Ang?" she responded, smiling at the monk.

She walked toward the monk, who backed up a few steps, as though afraid that Sophie was going to bite him.

"Have you ever fallen in love, Preah Ang?" Sophie asked, as she stood facing him.

I pulled Sophie back and said, "Preah Ang is doing fine without women. We talked about it two days ago. I'll explain to you later when we have time."

"You two seem very close. How long have you known each other?" The monk asked.

"Two weeks," Sophie replied.

"You two move awfully fast. Slow down, my children," the monk said.

"You can tell, Preah Ang?" I asked.

"Only a blind man cannot tell, but anyway, it is not my business and I don't want to think about it," the monk said, glancing at Sophie and then back at me with a sinister grin.

"Do you think about it sometimes?" I asked the monk.

"I think I talk too much. You only bring trouble," the monk said.

"You are not much older than us. You cannot call us children," Sophie said and touched his hand. The monk seemed to recoil from her touch.

I pulled Sophie close to me and whispered in her ear, "Don't bother him. He is a Holy man." Sophie said nothing, just looking at me with a smile.

"Preah Ang has a nice place. We would like to come back to visit Preah Ang again." Sophie said, looking the monk in the eye.

"Come back at any time," the monk said, looked at the clock on the wall, and added, "Athma have to go to the great temple for meditation. It's wonderful to meet you."

Soon, we said goodbye to the monk. Sophie gave him a hug before we parted.

"He's cute, isn't he?" Sophie asked as we walked out from the sacred ground of the temple.

"Why? You like him now?"

"For God's sake, he's a monk! Are you jealous?"

"No, I am not."

"Good. Do you agree that he's cute?" Sophie asked again and took my hand.

I looked at Sophie and said, "No, I didn't find him cute or handsome. He's just a good monk with a pure heart," I paused and said, "Do you love him?"

"Love is too strong, but I found him cute. Not like you, but cute."

"Can we drop it?"

"Ok!"

We walked back downtown quietly, barely talking to each other. I was in deep thought, thinking about Sophie's behavior towards the monk, and her words about him. It was hard to believe that she wanted to hurt me, but anything was possible. She obviously found the monk attractive.

It was hard to understand her, because I had only known her for two weeks. No question about it, our relationship moved awfully fast. Too fast. I was very uncomfortable with it all, on some level. Sophie could change her heart, leave me in the cold, and there would be nothing I could do to bring her back.

Something I had once read said, "If you love her, let her free." Deep inside, I loved her. I was not selfish, but I needed to let her know I loved her so much. It would be a disaster for me if she went off with someone else.

As we walked, the wind blew in our faces. I took a deep breath, letting the fresh air flow in my lungs. I glanced at Sophie as we walked, and she tossed me a smile. She was so beautiful. At that moment, a line from a song hit me: "Oh palm tree, oh palm tree, so tall and thin. You sway with the wind like a woman's heart."

I looked at Sophie again; again she gave me a smile, but said nothing. We walked side by side in silence. Today she loves me, but tomorrow she may not, I thought. She's young and beautiful like a rose in a garden, and she knows so well that her beauty is a gift from God to her. Her beauty has a power that brings men to her knees.

When we got downtown, we sat on a bench underneath a palm tree, looking at the horizon above the sea. The breeze brushed our face once in while.

"Savy, you are so quiet," Sophie said and took my hands. I looked at her and gave her a smile, but said nothing.

"You're upset with what I said earlier," Sophie said again. She paused for a second and continued, "I'm sorry if I hurt you."

"I just want you to know I love you very much," I said sincerely.

"I know you do, and I love you too," she replied. "What time is it?"

I glanced at my wristwatch and said, "It's four o'clock." I paused for a moment and asked her, "Do you need to go back?"

"Yes, it's better for me to go back. Mom and Dad are probably wondering where I am. Mom knows that I'm with you, but I need to go back."

"Ok," I replied softly and leaned to kiss her on the cheek.

"Ok, I have to go. See you tomorrow."

And we parted.

The next day, April 16, 1975, Khemerin and I met with Vichey at Thansour, where we had lunch and discussed the plan for our escape to Thailand. We were sitting at a table in a quiet area, as we had requested, and were waiting for Vichey to come, worrying that he would stall us.

"You think he'll keep his promise?" I asked Khemerin.

"He'll come. Besides, I know where he lives. We'll go to his house tonight if he doesn't show up," Khemerin replied. "I saw you two sitting on a bench on the seafront yesterday afternoon."

"Oh, why didn't you stop by and talk to us?"

"I thought you two needed privacy."

"Yes," I said faintly.

"What's the matter?" Khemerin asked.

"Nothing. We had a good time and were at the pagoda for a while," I said.

"Do you mind telling me everything, just between us, friends?

"It's a private matter between me and her."

"Private matter! Way to go, my friend! Congratulations!"

"Thanks."

"What's next?"

"Time will tell."

"It is very complicated, my friend," Khemerin said.

As we spoke, Vichey stood at the door, looking for us. Khemerin waved at him and he came toward us.

"Good news," Vichey said, pulling up a chair and sitting down.

When the waiter came, we ordered a pitcher of beer, some curried chicken, and a plate of fried fish for lunch.

"What's the good news?" Khemerin asked.

"Oh, my guys are on duty, in case you want to know."

"Thanks," I said.

Vichey looked at us and said, "News from Phnom Penh is really bad. It's going to fall any day." He paused for a second and said, "The Governor wanted to help."

"Oh, it's very kind of him. How much?" Khemerin asked.

"We, my friends and I, will hire a boat and let all of you out."

"All of us! Who else is there?"

"There were more people who have come to us for help. We already have a boat ready and will let you out all together tomorrow night," he paused and added, "You'd be lucky if we could get out by tomorrow night."

"What's the price?"

"Thirty U.S. dollars per person."

"Thirty dollars is too much," I said. Khemerin and I looked at each other.

"Look, there are lot of people involved in this, including the Governor, the border guards and the boat. Thirty dollars includes everything. You don't have to worry about a thing. We guarantee that we'll get you out of here, safe and sound."

"That's a lot of money and we don't even know what will happen to us when we get to Thailand," I said.

"You're right," Vichey sipped his beer and smiled.

"Can you tell us who was in the rescue planes with the Americans three days ago?" Khemerin asked.

"The Governor told me, but please do not spread rumors. The Americans evacuated U.S. Embassy personnel and some key members of our government."

I said to Khemerin, "Maybe your family is in New York by now."

"I'm in," Khemerin said, looking at Vichey and then at me. "How about you?"

"I'm not sure, Khem. I cannot leave Sophie behind!"

"You need to make a decision for your life, buddy. You can't even go to her right now. Her father will kick your ass!"

"Sophie?" Vichey repeated the name.

"Do you know her?" I asked.

"She's on my list," Vichey replied, taking a piece of paper from his pocket, unfolding it, and checking it to confirm the name on his list.

"Yes, she is on the list, travelling with her father. There are a total of five people in the family and all are paid in full," Vichey said, looking from Khemerin to me. "There's a hundred and fifty dollars in my pocket. He's a nice guy, the father." He looked at me and said, "So, you're mixed up with his daughter, huh? She's very beautiful; everyone knows who she is in the Governor's mansion. We talked about her."

I did not say anything, just looked at Vichey uncomfortably.

"You in or not?" Khemerin said to me.

"I need sixty dollars now. The boat will be leaving at eight p.m. tomorrow," Vichey said.

Khemerin opened his wallet and handed Vichey thirty dollars. He looked at me and said, "You have thirty dollars?"

"Yes," I said and pulled from my wallet one twenty dollar bill and one ten. I handed them to Vichey and looked at Khemerin with a smile.

I thought to myself, I only have twenty dollars left for the rest of my adventure, out of the fifty dollars my mother had given me at the airport. Fifty dollars: her whole life's savings.

"Thanks for helping us," said Khemerin. "Here, keep another five dollars for yourself, but you need to take good care of us until we're out of this hell," Khemerin said.

"You got it! Thank you!"

We touched our glasses in a toast to our friendship and our mutual endeavor. We were finally about to leave the country of our birth.

We split after lunch and I went to my room. I worried about my family back home; I was concerned about their safety and when I would see them again. Listening to the news on the radio left me more worried. I was relieved, though, to know that Sophie would be in the same boat on our escape night.

Night came and darkness covered the city. The sky was illumined only by the stars and the full moon. Khemerin came by and we went outside. Sitting on a bench, having a few beers, we talked about our past, present, and future.

"Hey buddy, can I ask you something?" Khemerin asked.

"What's that?"

"I don't want to pry, but if you need help let me know."

"About what?"

Khemerin looked at me and said, "Money and stuff."

"Thanks, I'm ok," I replied.

"Freedom! Freedom is wonderful," Khemerin said, sensing how uncomfortable I had become speaking about money.

"What are you talking about?" I asked.

"America is a free country. When I'm out of here I'm going to find my family. I hope they are in New York. America is a free country and the Americans are free people. They travel everywhere and they speak their minds freely."

"Khemerin, don't talk about that freedom crap unless you have money. You know and I know that without money you have no freedom," I said.

"I know," Khemerin replied. "It's a beautiful evening. I think it's the last evening of our lives in this country."

"You're right."

We talked until eleven o'clock and then said goodnight to one another.

The next morning, Sophie came and knocked on my door. When I opened the door, she threw herself in my arms hysterically. Her voice was trembling as she spoke, telling me that the Communists had taken over Phnom Penh.

"Turn on the radio and hear the news for yourself!"

I turned on the radio and what I heard was a shock to me. There were tunes of songs I had never heard in my life. They were the songs of the Revolution, new Cambodian songs and a new Cambodian government replacing the old. As I listened to the news on the radio, Sophie held me tight, her head on my shoulder, tears streaming. The news and the songs combined were despicable to my ears, so I turned the radio off. It was the most frightening moment of my life.

That morning, the city of Koh Kong had not yet fallen into Communist hands, but it was quiet, like a ghost town. No one left their homes. There was no one on the streets, save for our soldiers, still quietly patrolling.

Sophie took a chance coming to see me one last time, wanting to make sure I had planned to escape. She was relieved when I told her we all would leave the country on the same boat. At noon, Khemerin stopped by and I checked out, paying the bill and saying goodbye to the innkeeper for the last time.

We walked Sophie back to her place. Her father was easy on us this time; perhaps he was influenced by the day's news. That afternoon, we hung out at Sophie's place and helped her family pack. Mr. Lopez shook our hands and thanked us for the information I had given to Sophie two days earlier.

At six in the evening, we all walked downtown together. At the shore, a boat was waiting for us, with three soldiers for security. Only people on their list were allowed to embark on the boat. Meanwhile, we'd all heard a terrifying rumor that the Communists were evacuating all the people in Phnom Penh to the countryside and killing everyone who had worked for Lon Nol's government, along with university students and intellectuals. Today, though the Communists had taken over Phnom Penh, the Koh Kong Governor was still in power and his soldiers were still fighting to provide security for people in the city.

I climbed the boat, went inside, and took my seat without a word to anyone. Some crowds on the shore were fighting their way to the boat, and others just stood there and watched us preparing to leave the country. Sokha, the monk whom I met on New Year's Day, waved in Sophie's direction as I watched from the boat. People who had paid their fee came aboard, and soon the boat was crammed with people. The boat was floating no more than two inches above the waterline.

The Captain, who was also the owner of the boat, had asked everyone to take no more than three suitcases per family. There were approximately a hundred people on board that night. At first, it appeared that the passengers paid no attention to the baggage restriction until the guard came to reinforce the rule. There was chaos, as passengers struggled to decide what to keep and what to go without. There was yelling and arguing among wives and husbands. A woman in her mid-thirties was yelling and crying hysterically; she was not willing to give up her valuable belongings and had been asked to get off the boat. I was reminded of the crowded flight I had taken from Phnom Penh just ten days earlier.

Everyone was on board around seven. The boat moved offshore and anchored half a mile away, as the Captain had to wait for further instruction from the coast guard. While we waited for the boat to leave the shore, we had full protection from three uniformed soldiers, for a portion of our fare went to the Governor, who had promised to protect us until we escaped the country.

Night fell in the city. To my right were streets and rows of trees with their tall silhouettes cast along the shore, houses, and small buildings; on my left was the vast sea, extending off on to the dark horizon. The boat swayed mildly with the waves. I sat four or five feet away from the Lopez family, and Khemerin was at the stern with the Captain.

It was a pivotal moment of my life; there was no turning back, even though I knew so well that tomorrow would be another day of challenge and uncertainty. I thought of my mother, brothers, and sister. Where were they at this moment? I asked myself. I glanced at Sophie once in a while and we smiled bravely when our eyes met. I was so relieved she was on the boat with me; I'd never have left without her.

I leaned against the gunwale, looking out at the vast sea. It was calm, and the breezes brushed my face once in a while as I sat there, deep in thought.

Everyone in this boat is leaving the country they love dearly, for they are frightened of the Communists and of losing their freedom. Our lives are uncertain, even though we will successfully cross the border tomorrow. Nothing is left for us, except hope. Once, famous 19th century French novelist Alexander Dumas said, "Hope is the best of things, and the best of things will not die. Hope is all we have."

I began to pray, "Oh God in Heaven, please protect us, protect everyone in this boat, guide us with your invisible hand to freedom and safety. God, please shield my mother, brothers, and sister from all harm, as they are now forced to leave home to flee to the countryside and unknown places."

Tears rolled down my cheeks because I realized I would not see my family again for a long time, or maybe forever. A soft hand touched me; it was Sophie. She came and sat opposite me, stretching her legs on my lap. She smiled at me, but she seemed tired. I grasped her ankles and massaged her feet gently for a while until I, too, was tired and fell asleep, my back against the gunwale. I slept awhile and when I awoke, she was alone at the bow. I walked toward her and sat beside her.

"Are you ok?" I asked her.

"This is crazy. I never thought my life would come to this," she answered sadly.

"Too crowded," I replied.

"Not only that. Where do we land in Thailand? And what are you going to do there?"

"I don't know. You have relatives waiting for you on the other side of the border, which certainly must relieve a lot of pressure for your dad," I said.

"I'll come with you," Sophie said. I was silent, looking out at the horizon.

"It's scary out there. The sea is so vast. We're lucky there's no storm tonight. I hope the weather remains calm and we'll be safe during our trip. This boat would be flipped over if a big wave hit it," I said flatly. "We're in God's hands. All we can do is put our trust in Him."

"I didn't know that you were so religious," Sophie said and looked at me with a smile.

"No, it's not a religious thing. God is real and He is our Protector," I said and continued, "You seemed to be very sad. Will you share with me what's on your mind?"

"What is the fate of our friends whom we left behind?"

I did not reply, just remaining silent, and Sophie added, "You know, our families and friends in Phnom Penh."

I nodded and said, "I prayed for the safety of my family in Phnom Penh and everyone on this boat."

"I don't understand why the Communists are forcing people out of the city. What do they want to achieve? And why are they killing so many people?"

"The killing is not difficult to understand, but forcing people out of their homes is completely insane."

"What do you think about the killing?" Sophie asked vaguely, adding, "I hope my uncle was on the plane with the Americans last week."

"They are killing people like you, me, and your uncle, people who refuse to live under their oppressive regime. There are a lot of killings, for sure." I said and looked her in the eye.

"Why can't we leave now? What's holding us up?" Sophie asked.

"Don't know. Something's weird."

Khemerin came from behind and sat facing us.

"Are you two ok?" Khemerin asked.

"Do you know when we leave?" I asked him.

"I don't know," Khemerin said. "The Captain said we might be leaving around midnight. He's waiting for the coast guard to give the ok. Something's holding us up."

"What if we can't leave tonight?"

"We'll all die."

I looked at Sophie and we held hands, tightly.

"Hang in there, man. We'll be ok. Go and get some sleep."

Sophie leaned her shoulder against mine and whispered in my ear, "Let's go back in. I need some sleep."

"You go first."

She rose and walked into the crowded room. I watched her beautiful body moving slowly and then disappearing inside. The soft breeze brushed my face and the boat rocked gently left and right on the waves. I stood up, slapped Khemerin on the shoulder and went inside.

Sophie

Chapter Sixteen

Around midnight, the boat started its engines and moved north, the stars and moon illuminating the vast sky. The sea was calm, and light, cool breezes passed through the air. The boat moved slowly at first and then sped up to about five knots. We were packed in closely and couldn't stretch out our legs without touching others sitting nearby.

I sat with my back against the gunwale and Sophie lay on a blanket stretched on the floor, her head on her mother's lap, her feet resting in mine. I caressed her feet gently and then fell asleep. When I awoke, Sophie was in a deep sleep, her eyes closed and her mouth slightly open. I looked at her and then up to the moonlit sky. I thought of my mother, brothers, and sister. I was leaving the country for safety and my family was forced out of their home to the countryside, to places they had never known. Tears came to my eyes.

The boat was about one mile off the shore, moving slowly with its engine humming in my ears. On my right was the city of Koh Kong, the lost paradise where I had stayed for almost two weeks. Although I'd been there just a short while, I now carried with me a lot of new memories. The city was like a ghost town in the moonlight; people were sleeping as though nothing had changed from the previous night. As I looked to the shore from the slow-moving boat, the houses and trees appeared to move backward. I wondered whether the Thai authorities would allow us to enter their shores when we arrived in their country.

The boat rode along the shore. It did not make any difference to me at the time whether we were in the Gulf of Thailand, the China Sea, or the Pacific Ocean. The sea was an endless body of water. If the boat sank, all of us would die.

Onboard, it was surprisingly quiet, except for the humming sound of the engine in the background. I heard some low, soft conversations from the back; some people were still awake. I looked in the direction of the Lopez family, but they all had fallen asleep.

Slowly and gently, I lifted Sophie's feet up off my lap and laid them on the floor. I stood up, stretched my arms, and walked toward the bow. I sat with my back against the gunwale, stretched my feet in front of me, looked into the sky, and lost myself in thought.

After my father passed away, my mother worked very hard to keep us alive and the three of us in school. My youngest brother is with her wherever she goes. She has sacrificed so much for us. I should not have left my family at a time like this.

My mother was tough on me when I was very young, but her rules were simply to ensure I was disciplined and focused on what was important. She gave me life and educated me. At a time like this, she was concerned about my safety and encouraged me to leave the country. She handed me fifty dollars, her life savings, two weeks ago when I bade her farewell at the airport.

I felt a mosquito bite my arm. I slapped hard but missed it. I was deep in thought, thinking of my ten-year-old-brother and the time we had an accident that nearly got us killed on a street in Phnom Penh a few years back.

I am on a motorbike, riding in the busy streets of the city, with my brother behind. It's the middle of the afternoon. We ride from one section of the city to the next, enjoying ourselves very much, passing bicycles, tricycles, taxis, buses, and cars in the streets under the hot sun. The streets are small and busy, and traffic conditions allow us to ride no more than 15 miles an hour.

I maneuver left and right to get through the traffic as my brother holds me tight around the waist, our hair flying. We stop at a red light, my two feet on the ground, hands on the handlebars, moving the adjustment gear back and forth to rev the engine, just for the fun of it. When the green light flashes, I speed up, going ahead of everyone.

As I weave in and out of traffic, a car cuts me off by surprise at one intersection; it comes from my right. I slam on the brakes and my bike stops instantly, sliding to the left and throwing us on the street.

Sophie

Immediately, I stand up and look for my brother; luckily, he is unhurt. We brush the dust from our clothes, and I pick up the bike while its engine is still running. As we gather ourselves together, a man comes out of his car to inspect the side of his vehicle and then turns to me, saying, "I could have killed you, you know."

I look at him and smile, "Why didn't you?"

Since there is no damage to his car, our conversation ends and we go our separate ways. We come home and do not mention the accident to our father or mother, ever.

As the boat moved slowly on the sea, I closed my eyes, thinking of my past in a country I loved dearly. Prince Sihanouk had isolated the country from the Western world for nineteen years during his leadership. It was a deadly mistake for the nation, for he had simply sealed the Cambodians off from technical progress and the Western civilization. The second big mistake was, in my opinion, that Prince Sihanouk had secretly formed an alliance with Ho Chi Minh, the head of Communist state North Vietnam and the Vietcong.

He had constantly reminded us to beware of a Vietnamese invasion, yet he had formed an alliance with the enemy, trusting the enemy, which was not very smart. He had spoken as if he had always loved the country and the nation. The truth was that he loved himself a lot more. During his leadership, the opportunities and hopes of people had been crushed in Cambodia. In the last five years of war, Cambodia had been torn apart, and it was a losing war to the Lon Nol government and the Americans.

I was in the boat on the way out of Cambodia, but I had no real destination, no clear sense of where I would end up at the end of my adventure. When I was thirteen years old I had run away, but I was shielded by the love of God. He protected me from all dangers. He brought me back home safely. Now, for real this time, I was leaving my country, knowing for sure that I wouldn't be able to return home for a long time, or ever.

My hope was in God's hands, hoping that He would take me to a new land, a place where I wouldn't have to live in fear, and where I would find hope and opportunity. I knew then that God would not abandon me. I was on a small boat on the vast, midnight sea. In His invisible hand, He would guide me out of Cambodia, carry me out of danger.

Khemerin sat down on my right and handed me a bottle of beer, which I took. We looked at each other with fear in our eyes and quietly sipped our beer.

"Thanks for the beer," I said, looking at him, and added, "Where's it from?"

"There are a few packs at the back in the Captain's cabin, and I thought you may need it. Are you ok?"

"I'm ok, but worried about what tomorrow will be like."

We were silent. The salty breeze hit our faces as the boat moved slowly through the dark water.

"What's next? What will tomorrow bring?" I asked.

"Nobody knows. We would have died for sure if we had stayed and fought, pal."

"Why is this fucking boat moving so slow?" I asked.

"Who knows? He is a stupid ass, as you can imagine."

"Who are you talking about?"

"The Captain," replied Khemerin.

"I think your family was in that plane of Americans that left the country before the New Year. They are probably in New York by now."

"I don't know. I don't know how I can find out."

Our conversation was interrupted when we saw Sophie standing in front of us. I handed her my beer and she sipped it. Then she handed it back, bent her knees, and squatted facing us.

"You two are like two brothers," she said, brushing Khemerin's hair and smiling at us.

Khemerin grasped a short stool within his reach and pushed it in Sophie's direction.

"Here, sister, this will be easier on your circulation."

Sophie took the stool and said, "Thanks. What did you just say?"

"How can I find out whether my family got out with the Americans last week?"

"The American Embassy in Thailand might know where your father is," Sophie replied.

Khemerin looked at me with a smile, then back to Sophie, and said, "Thanks! I never thought about that."

"Is there anything else you two are hiding from me?" Sophie asked.

"No, nothing," I replied as soon as she finished her sentence.

"Khemerin, you can tell me. You two have something hidden from me. I could tell when you two were looking at each other."

I looked at Khemerin and said, "You tell her."

"Sophie, they killed everyone who worked for the old regime. Your uncle has no chance if they found out who he is."

"He knew that, but he did not want to leave the country," Sophie replied. "It's such a beautiful night," she said, changing the topic. "The sea is calm and the sky is so clear with the bright stars and moon." She was obviously reluctant to talk about her uncle.

"That one is the North Star, the biggest and the brightest," I said, pointing to the sky. "You see, the stars in the constellations are divided into six groups, based on their brightness. Each one has its own personality. Generally, the North Star is brighter than the rest and always positioned to the north."

"Where did you learn all this stuff?" Sophie asked.

"From my dad," I replied.

"Tell me about your father."

"Yes, tell us about your old man."

I looked at Khemerin and back to Sophie.

"Yes, tell us about him," Sophie added.

"My father passed away last year from multiple cancers. He was extremely intelligent and lived a good life. When he was our age, he lived a rich life since his father a wealthy businessman who owned an import/export company. But the business went bankrupt in 1957." I paused and sipped my beer.

"Back then, education was not viewed as very important in our society. My dad spoke and wrote French very well. I was born a year after he married my mother. It was an arranged marriage, you know." I paused and looked at Sophie and Khemerin in silence.

"Go on…" Sophie said.

"My mother said he was very shy, being a father at such a young age. He did not hold me or come into contact with me until I was five. It did not make any difference to me. All I remembered was that he loved me and that we had done so many things together."

"Why'd your mom tell you about your dad not having loved you when you were a baby?" Khemerin asked.

"I really don't know." I said, looking at Khemerin. "I know he loved all his children and provided a comfortable life for his family. He highly valued education. We went fishing together a few times at the lake behind our house in our little canoe, parked under a big tree by the lake. He fished for fun and to escape his normal life. He worked for our government all his life, but I don't think he was very happy with his work or with his life. I think he was trapped in his career and he had no way out."

Khemerin looked me in the eye.

"What? You want to say something?" I said to Khemerin.

"Everyone wanted to work for the government but then felt trapped. It's normal," Khemerin replied.

"You are absolutely right, Khem."

"In life we need to have freedom to do what we want to do. It would be awful to feel trapped in one place or in one job," Sophie said.

"We live in a society depending too much on government; it produces nothing except useless paperwork," I said.

"Did your mom and dad get along well?" Sophie asked.

"I don't know, but I never saw them fight or quarrel. Then again, Mom was a good wife to him until he passed away. I don't think my mother was very happy either during her marriage. The tradition of arranged marriage is sick."

"It's different in our generation," Sophie said.

"I'm not too sure," Khemerin replied.

"I don't think we will liberate ourselves completely from traditions, but I think Sophie is right. Things have improved a lot in our generation," I said, and then, looking at Sophie directly, added, "Hey baby, you are very beautiful. I love you more than anything in this world." I handed her my beer, which she took and sipped.

"You're so sweet. I love you too."

"You two cut it out," joked Khemerin, "I'm starting to get tired of your romance."

I continued with the story of my father.

"One day, my father woke us up at one in the morning and led us to the front porch. The sky was bright and full of stars; it was the most beautiful night I'd ever experienced. He pointed out a comet extending in the vast sky. Its bright head was far to the southwest, and its tail extended across the sky to the northeast. It was the most beautiful thing I had ever seen. We looked at it for a while and then we went inside. My dad explained the comet to us.

"He said a comet is an orbiting object consisting primarily of ice and dust. It is a reflection of the bright light from the sun when it orbits nearby. Sometimes, it has two tails instead of one and, as he said, 'There is an old saying, my son: what we saw tonight is a sign that the country will be at war.' We knew so well that that old saying was simply a myth. However, a few years later, this war broke out in our country."

"Myth and the interpretation of a star have played important roles in primitive societies," Sophie said.

"The stars guided the three wise men to the manger where Jesus was born," Khemerin added.

"Thanks, Khem, for your comment," I replied. "Tell me about your old man, Khem."

In the distance, we saw red lights flashing. They appeared to be coming closer and closer.

"Khem, what is it?" I asked. Three of us looked in the direction of the flashing lights. Sophie grasped my hand, terrified.

"Some kind of signal for us," Khemerin said. "You two go inside. I have to help the Captain. Like I said, he is not very bright and could get us in a lot of trouble.

Fifteen minutes later, our boat headed toward the shore, escorted by a coast guard boat. As our boat entered the dock and was properly tied to the quay, three military guards with flashlights in hand jumped into our boat, shining the lights on our faces for inspection. At the stern, Khemerin, the Captain, and other two soldiers in military uniform appeared to be having a serious conversation. Then they climbed the bank up to the coast guard station. Everyone in the boat was quiet and worried.

Half an hour later, Khemerin, the Captain, and another soldier descended the bank. I could not make out who the soldier was, as it was too dark out. They got to the boat and jumped in. The Captain went to the stern to take the wheel, and Khemerin and the soldier worked their way through the crowd in the boat toward my direction. It was then that I realized the soldier was Vichey, the lieutenant who had arranged our escape the day early. We shook hands when he arrived.

"You're hiding and letting your friend do all the work?" Vichey joked.

"He's good with people," I said. "What's going on up there?"

"Everything is all right. You are free to go. Like you said, my friend, we are losing this war."

"Why don't you come with us?" I said.

"It's not that easy," Vichey said, looked in Sophie's direction, and then back to me with a smile. "I just wanted to say goodbye and good luck. From here, you will be on the open sea, sailing to Thailand for approximately six more hours. The Captain knows where he is going from here."

He shook hands with me and Mr. Lopez, who was standing next to me as we talked. Vichey left us, climbed up the bank, and disappeared. He had been on our boat at the stern with the Captain from the start of our journey—all this time. Khemerin did not say a word to me about it.

Our boat left the quay for the open sea toward Thailand at four-thirty in the morning on April 18, 1975. Half an hour later, the Cambodian shore disappeared and ahead of us was only the vast sea and sky. The morning sun came up behind us.

The boat moved northward at five or six knots on the boundless water, as small waves lapped and splashed all around us. It was a beautiful morning and the sea was calm. It was hard to move from place to place since the boat was crowded, and sometimes one had to make room for others to pass by.

The engines ran smoothly and the propeller pushed the boat forward slowly. I extended my hand down to feel the surf. At first, the heat did not bother us much, but later it got hotter and hotter. The radiation of the sun was intense, and the reflections from the sea made it all the worse. It was incredibly hot and dry onboard. I was thirsty and so was everyone around me.

We drank and passed bottles of water to one another. Small children cried, and some threw up over the side. The boat started to reek. We needed more drinking water. I looked at my wristwatch. It was only nine-thirty.

The boat began to rock up and down, left and right, shaken by the wind. Even though the weather was calm, the waves were big enough to rock our boat. Everyone was scared. I looked in Sophie's direction. She was tired and her lips were dried from thirst. I drew out a small metallic container in which I had some drinking water, and handed it to her. She opened the lid, took a sip, and handed it back to me.

I said, "You keep it. I'm ok." My voice was husky from thirst.

I leaned against the gunwale, stretched my feet out in front of me, book in hand, and tried to read, but it was impossible to concentrate. Khemerin stood in front of me and handed me a can of beer, which I took. I noticed he only had shorts on now. His shirt was wrapped around his head and he was wearing his Ray-Ban sunglasses.

I said, "Thanks pal! You look like an American pirate in a Hollywood movie."

"No, the Americans are not pirates, never have been. How about a Brazilian pirate?"

"Whatever. Sit down!"

He sat next to me.

"Are you ok?" He paused. "It is the last can."

"Thanks," I said. "I'll make it last."

"It's too damn hot."

"I remember my old man," I said, looking to the horizon. "When I was fourteen years old, I went hunting with him, one of his brothers, and one of his friends, who was a Colonel in the army. We flew in an army plane to a remote jungle of Ratanakiri, one of those provinces in our country where there were no roads leading in or away. It was an isolated province, as you know.

"The military plane dropped us at the base. It was a small base. We walked out of the base through a village. People in the village lived a primitive life, covering their intimate parts with leaves and nothing else. Children were naked, some playing with mud and some running from tree to tree, playing hide and seek. Women wore jewelry stacked up to their necks and huge earrings made of pieces of elephant tusks that dragged their earlobes to their shoulders. Then I realized that it's human nature that women love jewelry."

"That's funny. Tell that to your girlfriend," Khemerin cut me off.

"We walked through the village. Dad, my uncle, and the Colonel had rifles slung on their shoulders, and I walked beside Dad, holding his hand.

"Out of the village, we walked into a jungle, through big trees, up and down hills, around meadows and swamps. We hid behind big trees so as not to disturb herds of deer feeding on the prairies or drinking water from the ponds. Then, when the moment was right, my father raised his rifle to his shoulder, aimed at a large deer, and pulled the trigger. The blast came out of his rifle and the big deer fell on the ground. The rest just ran away.

"My uncle and the Colonel were also good shots and took a few more down. We hid the deer that we had shot under the trees, covering them with leaves to avoid leaving them in plain view. As I walked closer to my father, leaving my uncle and the Colonel behind, I heard a fierce wind coming toward us. We all looked in the direction of the sound and saw a large tiger running very fast in our direction.

"My father pushed me aside, stood straight, raised his gun, aimed at the tiger, and shot the tiger when it was just fifty feet away from us.

When the tiger fell to the ground, Dad turned around, seeing the Colonel behind him, ready to shoot if there were others coming. But the scene was quiet. We only saw one tiger that day.

"Hunting was fun but a dangerous sport. My father was almost killed that day by an elephant as well—a big one. We walked into another part of the jungle, my father ahead of us. I was walking behind with my uncle, but the Colonel was nowhere to be seen. As we walked, I saw my dad jump to the left, and his brother rushed to rescue him, pushing me aside. I hid behind a tree, not sure what was happening, but frightened. Not far from where my father lay on the ground, his rifle thrown away, a big elephant was walking step by step toward him. The creature's trunk thrashed branches and small trees as he walked.

"Dad yelled to his brother, 'Shoot! Shoot him!'

"The sound of gunfire came clapping from my uncle's rifle, and the elephant slowed down. His small eyes seemed to be searching for the source of the sound.

" 'It doesn't work! It's like shooting a building. It's too big,' my uncle yelled at his brother. The elephant stepped toward Dad, who lay on the ground, trying to stand up.

" 'Shoot his ear, shoot through his ear,' he yelled to my uncle.

" 'Daddy! Daddy!' I called out.

"Then, gunfire sounded from my uncle's rifle again. Slowly, the elephant stopped walking, turned to my uncle, and fell to the ground slowly, like a collapsing building. My dad stood up, and we walked slowly and carefully toward the elephant lying on the ground. It was alive, still looking at us with his small eyes, as blood flowed to the ground from his ears.

"Later, we brought home the deer meat and the elephant horns, leaving the tiger and the elephant with the people in the village. I asked my dad how he could shoot so bravely, and he said he learned how to handle a gun and to shoot in the army reserve. My dad was a brave man."

"I would like to hunt one day. Shooting tigers makes you feel strong and brave," Khemerin said.

"Dad was a brave man."

Sophie dodged through the crowd, coming toward us. She came and sat next to me, resting her head on my shoulder.

"I am not feeling well. I want to throw up," she said.

I handed her my beer.

"No!" she replied, barely audible. She closed her eyes.

"Your dad is going to kill me when we get ashore."

"If he kills you, he'll have to kill me too. I'm not a baby anymore."

I put my arm around her, trying to make sure she was comfortable.

"You are in big trouble, my friend," Khemerin whispered in my ears, making sure Sophie didn't hear.

"I hear you, Khem," she said it loud enough for both of us to hear.

Khemerin handed me a large cloth, which I used to cover Sophie from head to toe to protect her from the hot sun as she rested, her head on my shoulder. Most people in the boat were getting seasick by now.

"What time is it?" Sophie asked.

"Eleven o'clock" I said.

"I'm hungry and thirsty."

I gave her my beer and she took a long sip.

"Thanks," she said.

"We're landing soon, and then we can cook and have lunch." I tried to reassure her.

As we talked, our boat turned forty-five degrees, heading for the Thai shore. Everyone began to cheer, but then a loud voice from a megaphone echoed over the open sea. We were being intercepted by the Thai coast guard. Our boat slowed down and the engine whirred to a stop. The boat floated aimlessly on the sea, going nowhere, swaying left and right, up and down with the waves.

"What is it, Captain?" Khemerin yelled from the bow.

"We cannot go to the shore. They will shoot if we try," the Captain yelled back. People on the boat were frightened.

"We have to go back," a voice came from the stern.

"No, we cannot go back," another voice bust out.

A roar of voices burst out, arguing whether we should attempt to land the boat or return to Koh Kong. We floated there for some time, as the arguments raged. More passengers became ill, and the ones already sick became sicker. The children's cries rose higher and higher.

I glanced at my wristwatch. It was noon. The sun was directly overhead, beaming down upon us.

"What's going on? Why can't we land the boat?" Sophie asked.

"We have to do something. We cannot go back; they'll kill us all," I said.

"You think I'm going back?" Khemerin scoffed. "Let's do something."

He looked around and then at me. Taking a big paddle from the bottom of the boat, he handed it to me and said, "You take off your white shirt, tie it to this paddle, and wave to the coast guard. I'm going back there to bring the boat ashore."

"Ok."

Sophie sat straight against the gunwale and when she saw me tying my shirt to the paddle, she said, "What are you doing? What if they shoot?"

"They won't," I replied.

"It's dangerous."

Five minutes later, I heard a loud yell from the stern: "Oh my God, help. He is going to kill my husband."

Then I heard Khemerin's voice burst out: "Stay calm, everyone. We are going to land the boat. Captain, land the boat or I will blow your head off."

Khemerin had the Captain in his arm and a pistol pressed to the Captain's temple.

"What are you doing, Khemerin?" I yelled at him.

"You raise the white flag, Savy. We're landing this fucking boat. Captain, this is your last choice: you land the boat or you die." Everything fell silent.

"Khem, my God, don't do that," Sophie shouted and stood up from the bow.

"It's ok, we are going to get this boat ashore," Khemerin replied.

Everyone was quiet. They looked between Khemerin and Sophie.

"Sophie! Come here," Mr. Lopez yelled from the crowd. "You two are very dangerous," he added angrily.

"Dad! We're landing the boat. Can't you see?" Sophie cried out. Mrs. Lopez covered her mouth, shocked that Sophie would talk back to her father.

I pulled Sophie by the hand, told her to sit down, and moved to the very end of the bow, raising the paddle tied with my white shirt.

"You be careful!" Sophie whispered.

The engine started and roared, and the boat moved toward the shore, breaking the waves. Khemerin kept pointing the gun at the Captain's temple while everyone else remained silent. I stood at the bow, waving my white shirt. I had no idea what I was doing at the time. I had just seen it in movies—when you surrender, you wave a white flag.

The yelling from the microphone became louder, and more urgent, but it made no difference to me and Khemerin because we did not understand a word the coast guard was saying. When we were closer to shore, we were intercepted by three Thai coast guard boats. They escorted us safely to shore.

When our boat arrived, I was surprised by the warm welcomes we received from the people standing there. They offered us food and drinks as we got off the boat. Some passengers threw up, and most of us were still very weak and seasick. We sat and lay hopelessly on blankets spread all over the beach area. The drinking water was like nectar from the gods. I stood against a big rock, looking toward the vast waters extending to the horizon. We landed on the shore five miles inside the Thai border in the province of Trat.

That day, a few tents were set up on the beach, where the authorities interviewed us one at the time. They took down our names, addresses, and genealogical records. After the interview, we were transported to a refugee camp, which turned out to be an elementary school in a nearby village, with guards at the gates of the school to prevent us from going in and out of the camp freely.

We learned that the Koh Kong Governor who had taken our money had also left Koh Kong four hours before us that night. He had been immediately transferred to the American Air Force base in Thailand when his boat had arrived on the Thai shore. Everyone on his boat was transferred to the base and protected by the Americans.

Lucky bastard, I thought to myself. Now I know why you delayed our trip by leaving us in the boat until midnight. We also learned that thousands of Cambodians in Phnom Penh sought refuge in the French Embassy to avoid Communist persecution.

Chapter Seventeen

Cambodia collapsed on April 17, 1975, and the Communists took over the country and cut it off completely from the outside world. People who had the means to escape left the country for Thailand, where they were transferred to refugee camps set along the border of Thailand and Cambodia.

Our camp was located at the bottom of a chain of mountains on the other side of the road. To the west of the camp was a thick forest with hills, lakes, swamps and meadows; to the south approximately half a mile was the gulf; to the north was a village with small houses.

An unpaved road went through the village and the camp to the center of the province, fifteen miles from the border. At the edge of the camp, there were two deep wells on both sides of a passage that led straight into the village. The water could only be taken out by tin containers of no more than five gallons attached to long ropes hoisted through pulleys.

The camp was composed of two identical buildings, made of brick, and each had six rooms, where we were crowded into and took up small spaces to hang up our mosquito nets to sleep at night. We were allowed to occupy the building on the east as the one on the west was left empty. Outside the building, we made stoves on the ground to heat water and cook meals. Smoke and the smells of food wafted from these stoves from morning until midnight. On our first day, some people in the nearby villages came to visit us, bringing us food and clothes.

The next morning, as I stood leaning against a tree in the courtyard, watching children playing ball, Sophie walked toward me from a distance. She wore a light blue blouse, dark blue jeans, and white sneakers. Her hair was loose and flowing down her back, past her shoulders.

"Hey, you! Good morning!" Sophie greeted me when she arrived.

"Hey!" I replied.

"What are you reading?" Sophie asked, referring to the book in my hand.

"Oh this," I said, "*Three Musketeers* by Alexander Dumas."

"I read a few of his books. He was a good storyteller."

"I agree," I said with a smile. "Did you have a good night's sleep?"

"Not really. It's too crowded."

"Come here closer. I want to kiss you," I said softly.

"No, not in public," she replied.

"Oh, I understand. By the way, what time is it?" I asked.

She glanced at her wristwatch and replied, "Quarter past ten." She added, "I hardly slept last night."

"Tell me about it. There are six families in my room. That's seventeen people, including children. It's terrible!"

"We have no privacy. Absolutely none," Sophie replied.

We were silent for a moment. Sophie seemed deep in thought and sad.

"What's bothering you?" I asked Sophie, and added, "You seem to be unhappy."

"You know I am thinking of relatives and friends whom we left behind in Phnom Penh and in Koh Kong," Sophie replied and added, "What do you think of the killing in Phnom Penh?"

"Sophie, it's incomprehensible."

"Do you think North Vietnam is behind this mass killing?" she asked.

"Everything's possible, including Prince Sihanouk. The Communist victory in Cambodia was attributed to Sihanouk's popularity. He mobilized Cambodians to help the Vietnamese and Khmer Rouge in this war. He has the blood of innocent Cambodians on his hands."

We were silent for a moment, watching the children playing.

"Dad sent a letter to his brother about our current situation."

"Your uncle will take all of you to America."

"I know. I don't want to go if you are here."

"Go! I'll join you later."

"It's easy for you to say. America's far away."

"I know," I said softly. "Saigon is still fighting," I added.

"It won't last," Sophie replied. "Where's Khemerin?"

"Don't know. He might be hanging out with the girls in the back and learning to speak Thai. Practicing!"

Sophie looked at me with a smile and said, "He's a good friend and very brave. Without him yesterday, we might have had to go back." She paused and continued, "You too. You'd have taken some bullets if they shot at us."

"No, they wouldn't and I knew it," I shrugged.

"How about the gun?"

"He threw it in the sea just before the coast guard intercepted us."

"Did the Captain file a complaint?"

"I don't think so. They're getting along fine now," I said.

"How can they get along?"

"I don't know. It's an art that Khemerin has perfected—pissing people off and then making them feel good."

"Communism and any government in the form of a dictatorship, directly or indirectly, are terrible. They destroy everything, the wealth of the country, and especially the souls and freedom of the people they govern," Sophie said.

"Dictators get richer, and richer, and richer, and richer! Sons of bitches!" I said.

"Do you think one day there will be another revolution against the dictatorship in Cambodia?" Sophie asked.

"You know what I'm thinking?" I said, pausing a moment, "If North Vietnam has an agenda to occupy our country, another revolution would be very difficult."

"Why?"

"They'll control our country with force. You know how the Vietnamese work."

"Devils."

"By their nature, devils succeed in their little corner, doing sneaky things."

"You mean deception."

"Sihanouk just lost the country to the Vietnamese," I said. "Ho Chi Min outwitted him. The son-of-a-bitch is done."

"Maybe North Vietnam will take good care of him and his family."

"Probably. Like I said, he loved himself more than he loved the country." I paused and looked into the sky and then back to Sophie, "Let's go to bed, honey."

"Oh my God! How can you think about that? I can't even find a decent place to shower this morning."

"Oh no, baby, you can't be naked in the shower anymore. The shower's open for all to see!"

"I want to cuddle in your arms, baby," Sophie replied.

"You do?"

"Of course, if we had privacy." I looked at her and she gave me a faint smile. "Of course," I repeated.

Two buses drove into the camp, entering the front gate. Khemerin ran from nowhere toward us. As he came close enough he yelled out, "They're bringing more people in. Two boats just arrived this morning."

The refugees got off the buses and were guided by two policemen to the vacant building, as the three of us stood looking at them. Suddenly, Sophie grasped my hand and said, "Is it him? Sokha's here." She pointed to a man with shorts, a t-shirt, and a shaved head. She seemed to be very happy to see the monk among other refugees walking out of the buses.

"Yes, it's the monk all right," I said, turning to her and then to Khemerin.

"Who's he?" Khemerin asked.

"He's the monk we met in Koh Kong, but he's not in his yellow robe, you know, his uniform," I replied.

Sophie looked at me but said nothing.

"Maybe his robe got wet," replied Khemerin.

"Come on, let's find out," Sophie dragged me and ran toward the crowd. I let her go and we walked behind slowly.

"You, Sokha!" Sophie yelled. The man turned around, saw us, and walked toward us rapidly. Sophie gave him a hug, seeming excited to see him. The monk stood in front of us, staring at Sophie without blinking his eyes, smiling.

"I'm so glad to see you're alive!" Sophie said.

"I'm happy to see you too," the monk said and looked at my direction.

"Tell us how you got out," Sophie inquired.

"The new government troops came yesterday. They forced us out of the city into jungles."

"What're the people going to do in the jungles?" Sophie asked. Khemerin and I listened quietly.

"It doesn't matter as long as we're out of the city. They said that the Americans would bomb the city at any moment," the monk replied, "I walked along with the crowds and last night we hired a boat and drove out... and here we are now. We left Koh Kong in the middle of the night. The Communist troops are everywhere now. They took over the country. The war's ended and we're defeated."

"Oh, you haven't met Khemerin, my friend," I said and formally introduced him to Khemerin, who put both hands together under his chin, bowing to the monk. In our culture, this is an act of respect to someone with high authority. The monk extended his hand to Khemerin instead; Khemerin took his hand, hesitatingly.

"I left the monkhood," the monk said.

"You left the monkhood, just like that! After all these years of study and meditation?" Sophie said. "And since when did you leave the monkhood?"

"Just after you left Koh Kong that night," said the monk.

"Why that moment?" Sophie asked.

The monk looked at her, briefly, and then to Khemerin and I, saying, "You know! But I have to go before the spaces in the rooms are all taken." Then he walked toward the west building, following the crowd.

"How long have you guys known the monk?" Khemerin asked.

"We met on New Year's Day," Sophie replied. "Look, Mom and Dad have been rough on me again. I don't want to make a scene with them in this place. I'll see you when I can."

"Ok."

"I have to go," Sophie said again.

"Ok, see you later then," I said. She walked back to the building where she stayed.

"What do you think, buddy?" I asked Khemerin.

"About what?"

"The monk. He made me feel uneasy," I said. "Sophie and the monk seem too close."

"It's your problem, man. She's hot and you know that!"

"That's right! It's my problem."

We were silent for a while and then Khemerin said, "Come and have fun."

"What is that?" I asked.

"I am learning Thai. You have to come, the teachers are cute."

"Ok! See you around then," I replied.

The next day as the day before, in the morning, we stood in line for facilities and showers at the wells. Late in the morning, I strolled in the courtyard, eyeing the newcomers, hoping to see Khom and Sambat. I also hoped to see Sophie, but could not find her.

I went behind the building, in the woods, and sat under a tree for hours, reading alone. I thought hard about my future. I have to plan my life carefully; any decisions I make at this time will affect me for the rest of my life, I thought. I do not have much money, and I need to be careful of my expenses. How could I live without money? I asked myself. I missed Sophie and I felt uneasy knowing that she and the monk were good friends, as Sophie had told me.

In the afternoon, I asked the guard for permission to go outside the camp to a nearby market to buy some necessities, such as a few bags of rice, some dried fish, and pots and pans for cooking. The next day, I put up a stove in front of my unit and made coffee that afternoon. As I poured coffee into the cup I was holding, I saw a familiar woman walking in my direction. When she came closer I realized that it was Kim, the prostitute I once met in Koh Kong.

"Hi, Kim," I said when she arrived. "You made it. I'm happy for you."

"Yes, it's good to see you too," she replied.

We stood facing one another, two feet apart. I wanted to hug her, but I felt it was not appropriate, for in our culture, men do not hug women in public.

"They killed everyone who resisted them. I was so scared when those guys came with black uniforms, some with red bandanas around the necks and others wearing them around their heads, all with guns. They shot in the air to chase us out of the city and they killed people in cold blood. I was so scared," Kim said.

"You're safe now," I said and continued, "Do you want a cup of coffee?"

"If you have enough," she said.

"Here's your coffee," I said, handing her the cup. "Come on! Let's sit at the table over there. We can talk if you want."

"Of course, kid," she replied.

At the table in the middle of the courtyard, we sat opposite each other in the sunlight and sipped our coffee.

"Do you know anyone besides me in this camp?" I asked.

"No, all of us scattered out of the city. Most people I knew from my job were soldiers. They killed them all, if they were ever caught. Oh, those poor men."

"Do you know Vichey?" I asked.

Kim looked puzzled. She scratched her head and said, "Not sure!"

"Vichey, the lieutenant," I reminded her.

"Yeah, yeah! I remember him now," she cried out, and added, "He was a good man."

"What happened to him? Tell me now."

"They tied him up, bound his feet together and his hands behind his back. I don't know how they found out he was a lieutenant in the army. They shot him in the temple. He died instantly, in a pool of his own blood."

I was shaking, my heart trembling.

"Oh my God!" I cried out, looking at Kim, unable to blink.

"I really miss my family, Kim," I said.

"Were they in Phnom Penh when you left?"

"Yes. Now I don't know where they are."

"I'm sorry," Kim said.

In the distance, Khemerin walked toward us. He sat next to Kim when he arrived. He put his arm around her, but she took it off and moved a little farther from him.

"Hi! Sister, you made it," Khemerin said and looked at me. "You two know each other. Surprise, surprise!"

"Yes, I know Kim," I replied proudly.

"Oh, Khem! I'm glad to see you again. I was sort of expecting you in this camp, for I had seen you on the boat which left Koh Kong the night before the Communists took over. You walked up and down in the crowd as I watched from the shore, among others." Kim said slowly and smiled at him with joy, and continued, "Look, honey, I invited him to my place for tea and he said no. He isn't a pig like you." She paused and adding, "But thanks for the nice tip, baby."

"No problem," Khemerin said. "You and I need to get out of this place for a few hours, so we can talk quietly."

"Anytime and anyplace you want, handsome," Kim replied.

"Kim," I said, "you need to think about evaluating your trade."

"It's a noble profession, you butthead!" Khemerin said.

"Have you seen Sophie?" I asked Khemerin.

"You've lost your girlfriend to the monk and you're asking me where she is."

"No, I don't think she likes him. They're just friends."

"Good thinking."

"Are you talking about the same woman who tore your heart apart in Koh Kong?" Kim asked.

Khemerin looked at me with a smile.

"I think it's the same girl," Khemerin answered for me.

"Here's my advice to you, kid," Kim said. "Tell her that you love her, but you need to respect her and give her room. Be patient. If you lose control of yourself, I'm sure you'll lose her."

"Thanks, Kim," I said.

"Have you seen Khom and Sambat?" I asked Khemerin.

"I don't think they could make it," Khemerin replied.

"Do you have any idea where your family is now?"

"We can't even get out of the camp. How can I go to the Embassy asking about Dad?" Khemerin replied, then turned to Kim and said, "I need to lie down and discuss this with you quietly, so you can make me feel good."

"You're so sweet, baby," Kim replied.

Night fell, but the camp was not completely dark. The dim light in the camp came from the moon and the stars scattered across the sky. On the stairs of our building, Khemerin and I sat shoulder to shoulder talking. Kim had left us some time ago.

"Khem! Can we ever go home again?" I asked quietly.

"It's hard to say. We don't even know where we'll end up next week or next month."

"Remember camping in Takeo when we were kids?"

"Of course."

"The night was just like this, but only us. Now we have 500 people in the camp," Khemerin said.

"What will happen to our families back home?" I asked.

"Who knows? I need to get to the U.S. Embassy to find out, like Sophie said. The Embassy may know."

"I really miss Sophie," I said.

Khemerin patted my back and said, "Hang in there, buddy. You'll be fine. Let her know that you're serious. It's not your decision, it's hers."

"I'll kill myself if I lose her," I said.

"Do that, ok? I promise, I'll tell your mother that you died in a refugee camp because you lost a French girl," Khemerin said. "If you lose her, I am going to bang her like everyone else."

I did not reply, just looked at him sternly.

"Remember our pledge when we were camping in Takeo? We swore never to fall in love with the same girl," Khemerin added.

"Life was so much fun back then," I said. "Why do we have to grow up, get old, and die?"

"Don't ask me that question. I really don't care about philosophy and I'm no Buddha."

"Why war? Why fighting?" I said.

"You know as well as I do, Savy. The thirst for power! That's what it's all about."

"What did the Americans gain from this war?"

"I thought the war was to stop Communist expansion in Asia. It's a big deal. Now Americans are drawing out of the region. What's next?" Khemerin said.

"It's a complete mess. Saigon is still fighting."

"It won't last long. I give it another week. They cannot fight without Americans."

"Jesus. It's a complete mess."

"Let's go to sleep. It's late. We'll look for her tomorrow. I know you miss her. Don't let your emotions control you. Be strong. There are a lot of French girls out there. You just have to find them."

"Thanks, Khem. Please shut up," I said. "Good night, buddy."

The next day was the fourth day of our life in the refugee camp. As I sat under a tree, reading in the woods that morning, I heard a commotion coming from the inside the camp. I rushed over to find two International Red Cross vans parked in the courtyard of our camp. Soon, they set up a tent there to do their work: interviewing, distributing food and clothes, providing medical checkups to everyone in the camp, and taking care of the sick.

The next day, World Relief International came, and the following days other charitable organizations—some of whom I'd never heard of—came to help us. That week, we were exposed to the outside world. We had more food and clothes than we ever thought we'd have. I felt secure. We are not going to die without food and medicine, I thought.

Periodically, these organizations came to our camp, checking on us to make sure we had everything we needed. I volunteered to help people in the camp as a translator for these organizations and to help them distribute food and clothes to all refugees in the camp. The French language I had learned in school came handy, for these agencies brought along their personnel, most of whom could speak French. Many of them also spoke English.

April 30, 1975, was a beautiful morning with a bright sky. Fresh breezes blew into our rooms through the open windows. The wind blew off my mosquito net and left me lying asleep in the open air. Khemerin lay next to me, his mosquito net falling off like everyone else's.

We woke up, folded our mosquito nets and sleeping bags, put them neatly against the wall, and then walked to the well to refresh ourselves.

"I had an interview with the American Embassy yesterday," Khemerin said.

"Did they tell where your dad is?"

"Don't know, but they'll let me know soon."

"I'm going to America, Khem," I said.

"How?"

"Don't know, but I am going."

After brushing our teeth and showering, we walked back to our place, put on fresh clothes that we had washed the day before, and went out to the front of the building.

"You make the coffee, buddy," Khemerin said and walked away.

"Where are you going?" I asked.

"I'll pick up some wood in the forest for tomorrow."

"Thanks. It's thoughtful of you."

Khemerin walked away and disappeared in the woods as I made the fire to brew the coffee.

It was a hot day. After breakfast, I went to my usual place in the woods behind the building to be alone and read.

I really love Sophie, I thought to myself. She's everything in my life.

Under the tall, shady tree, I sat on the ground, leaning my back against the tree trunk, stretching my legs in front of me. I read a book written by Voltaire, the French author. As I was reading, soft hands covered my eyes from behind.

"Guess who?" teased a female voice. I grasped her hands and guided her to sit next to me.

"What're you doing?" Sophie asked.

"Nothing. I'm thinking of you."

I looked her in the eye and said softly, "I thought you'd never come. I was afraid I was going to lose you."

"Why would you think that?" She said.

"We haven't seen each other for almost a week. Are you hiding from me?"

"No!" She paused, looking me in the eye, and continued, "Dad forbade us to see each other. He said we are too young. He really liked you at first, but now he hates you. He said we're going to America. His brother is sponsoring us."

"The other day, you seemed too…" I said and couldn't finish what I wanted to say.

"…too close to Sokha," she completed the sentence.

"Not what I wanted to say."

"You can deny it if you want," she said. She paused for a second and added, looking at me with a smile, "I think he's cute and it's not a bad idea to have friends."

"He's cute," I repeated.

"Ok, you're cuter. Happy now?" she said and added, "Do you want to be my bodyguard, protecting me all the time?"

"I'd love to if you'd let me. I'll do everything for you," I said.

"Would you control me if we were married?"

"Married?" I said in surprise.

"Dad is right. We are too young to be married."

"I did not mean that, but it does cross my mind sometimes," I said. "No, I couldn't do that. I couldn't control you. Your happiness is mine." I leaned to kiss her.

"Don't do that. You cannot kiss me in public."

I said nothing and smiled at her.

"Saigon fell this morning," said Sophie.

"I know," I sighed. "A lot of Vietnamese are leaving the country, sailing into the open sea in small fishing boats as we speak. An American fleet is picking them up in the China Sea, millions of them."

"Didn't the Americans evacuate many of them from Saigon three days earlier?"

"You're right."

"There are so many of them. The fleet could sink. I've heard that the Americans dumped all their heavy equipment, trucks, jeeps, and helicopters in the sea to make room for these people."

Sophie looked at me and said, "What a nation, what people!"

"Sophie, I'm going to America," I said steadily.

"How?"

"I don't know, but I'm going. Will you come with me?"

"I'll come with you," Sophie said with a smile and added, "I'll go with you to the end of the world."

"No honey, we'll stop in America. I don't want to live in Canada."

"Don't be so charming."

"Look who is coming!" I said.

We looked to the edge of the woods and saw the monk walking slowly in our direction.

Sophie   209

"Come here, Sokha!" Sophie yelled out and motioned him to come over.

Chapter Eighteen

A week later, the Thai authorities moved us to another camp in the center of town to avoid any surprise attacks by the Khmer Rouge (new Cambodia, which was led by the Communist government), for our camp was close to the border. The Thai government and her people had been good to us; they not only welcomed us in their country, but also cared for our safety.

The situation in the new camp was much better, for it was in town and there was running water and a better place to shower in the morning. In addition, there were English and Thai classes that everyone could take, even though they were not mandatory.

I attended a few English classes, but I couldn't learn. I found that the English language was hard to learn, compared to French. Back home, I had English class an hour a week in junior high and high school, but learned nothing, because we simply did not understand how important the language was, nor did we have a good teacher.

We were grateful for the Thai people who volunteered to help us. I did not pay much attention to learn Thai either, though. Looking back, it was a mistake that I did not make more of an effort to learn other languages beside the French and Cambodian I had acquired.

There was a big temple within walking distance of our camp, and we were allowed to participate in services during religious holidays. There were guards at the gates of the camp at all times, but with their permission we could go to the market in the center of town. We had to cram ourselves in small rooms to sleep at night.

I had not seen Sophie for three days since we moved to the new camp and I missed her very much. The next morning, I decided to stop in front of Sophie's unit and happened to catch a glimpse of her by the stove, boiling water. My heart beat harder, just seeing her from a distance. An Angel from Heaven is boiling water in a refugee camp, I thought. I walked toward her and stood in front of her. She raised her head up to me and looked back inside the building to ensure that her parents were not nearby.

"What's up?" she said.

"I'm going to the beach to get some fresh air. Do you want to come?" There was a beach adjacent to the camp, and we could go there to walk along the beach, sit on the rocks, or swim at our own risk.

"Go ahead. I'll join you later," she said.

I continued my walk toward the beach area. At the beach, I walked along the shore, sat on a big rock, and read a book by Voltaire; it was *Candide*. The story was about love, hope, and material wealth that evaporated in a blink of an eye. The author's original name was Francois-Marie Arouet, but he changed it to Voltaire before he became famous. While reading, I started to think about my own relationship with writing.

I like to write and I write every day. The desire to write has been in me since I was thirteen years old, maybe even before that. I should change my name when I go America. I would like to call myself William Wheaton. William Savy Wheaton is a cool name. William is the name of a smart businessman whom I read about in a French book. Wheaton, Illinois, is a very nice, beautiful town 25 miles west of Chicago. I read about it a few years ago and about the students of Wheaton College protesting against the Vietnam War.

The students were angry with President Nixon. People in Wheaton voted for Republicans, yet they did not like Nixon. That did not make any sense, but it did not matter to me. Wheaton, Illinois, is a beautiful town with beautiful houses and churches on every street in town—that what was written in the article I read. It would be nice to live in a town like that.

Oh God, Creator of this universe, the sky, the earth, the moon, stars and the sun, take me to America and put me in Wheaton, Illinois. I want to call myself William Savy Wheaton. That will be my new name when I go to America.

Sophie

As I was daydreaming, Sophie walked briskly over and sat next to me. We looked at each other with happy smiles.

"You like the sea, don't you?"

"Yes, I do. It's beautiful."

"I agree. The sea is so vast."

We were silent for a while.

"What's wrong? You seem deep in thought, dreamy," Sophie said.

"Our ordeals were nothing to compare to those of the Vietnamese who are riding straight in the open sea. They put their lives at risk for freedom. We only rode for ten hours, five or six miles offshore."

"What do you mean? It was horrible on that boat. If the boat had sunk that night, we would have died."

"Sophie," I said softly, "people who came to help us in the camp, most of them are Americans. As we are sitting here, right now, the American fleet in the open sea is picking up every single refugee boat that's leaving Vietnam. The Americans give them food, clothes, new homes, and a new country." I paused, put my arms around her, and continued, "There are so many refugees from Vietnam in the open sea. The Americans are picking them all up."

"Amazing, but why?" Sophie asked.

"To save human lives," I said softly to her. "Who are these people? Ever since I was a little child, Prince Sihanouk taught us to hate the Americans. The U.S. is imperialist, he told us. Now we're seeing it with our own eyes. Bastard liar."

"Why did you bring him up again? I thought we had a deal not to talk about him and to forgive him for what he has done to us," Sophie asked.

"I'm sorry," I said. "I am disappointed and angry when people lie to me. Lying hurts."

"I know. Just put it behind you, ok?" she said and held my hand in hers.

"Sophie," I looked her in the eye and continued, "I am going to miss you terribly if you go to America. You are part of me. I love you more than everything in this world."

"My happiness is with you. Like I said, I am not going anywhere without you."

"America is a beautiful country. You should go. Soon you will speak English, go to college, and get a good job. Most importantly, you'll be able to speak your own mind. You'll be free."

"You have to stop talking like that. I am not going anywhere without you. I've said this to you more than once. I meant every word I said. I know America is beautiful, but my happiness is with you," Sophie leaned her head on my shoulder. I held her waist and kissed her soft hair.

"Savy! Do you miss Chantal?" Sophie asked.

"She is no longer in this world."

"I know. Did you cry when the accident happened?"

"Yes, but life goes on. I am sure she's looking at us from Heaven right now, and she is happy that you've come into my life."

"Why do you love me?" Sophie asked.

"You are beautiful and I am attracted to you. Besides, everything about you is perfect. I suppose I could ask you the same question." I waited for her answer.

"You make me feel beautiful every time I am with you, and you seem to understand me pretty well."

I pressed my lips against her and said, "I love you."

"Savy, I am not going to the U.S. with Mom and Dad. We need to think about us. Our next step is getting out of this camp together."

"I know, I am thinking of something. God still performs miracles for each one of us in a unique way."

"Will you take me out of this place for a few hours? I miss you so much; I want to be alone with you."

"I love you, honey. Let me know when you have time. We'll go shopping," I said. We sat on the rocks that morning as the sun rose higher and higher in the sky. Soon, it was uncomfortably hot, so we decided to walk back to the camp.

On our way back to the camp, we bumped into the monk, who was walking in the opposite direction.

"Hi, you two," he said.

"Hi," I said.

Ignoring me, he turned to Sophie.

"I've been looking for you all morning," the monk said.

Sophie turned toward me, looking me in the eye, and said, "Excuse me. I would like to talk to him alone."

She led Sokha to a tree far enough that I could not hear their conversation. Sophie did all the talking. Sokha looked at her and up to the sky and to the ground; he paced back and fort, seeming to be irritated and unhappy. They seemed to be arguing for fifteen minutes, which seemed to be a long time for me, watching them from a distance. Then Sophie walked back toward me, angrily.

"What was going on?" I asked her when she came back.

"It's over! I told him stop following me wherever I go," Sophie replied, and walked briskly ahead of me, and toward her unit.

"Sophie!" I called her as I walked faster to catch up with her. "What do you mean by 'it's over'?"

She turned facing me, looking me in the eye, and replied, "It means he will not follow me any more." She paused and added, "Take me out of this place; I hate this place."

She walked faster toward her unit, leaving me behind. I watched her until she disappeared into the building of her unit. Behind me, the monk stood under a tree, looking at me. I ignored him and walked back to my place. I thought I should probably get a haircut, but I needed to eat first. I went inside my unit and walked out with a small bag of rice and a package of dried fish—donations from the charitable organizations that had come to our camp a few days earlier.

I poured the rice into the pot, added water from a container, and put it on the stove. Then I made the fire in the stove to boil the pot. Half an hour later, I had my rice done. The meal was filling, but far from delicious. I hate being poor and miserable, I thought.

After lunch, I walked toward the gate and bumped into Khemerin on my way.

"Where are you going?" Khemerin asked.

"Out to get a haircut."

"Hey," Khemerin said, "Can I ask you something?"

"What's that?"

Khemerin paused for a second and said, "If you need money, let me know."

"What makes you think I need money?"

"Hey, I just want to help, ok?"

"Thanks, Khem. I'll let you know when I need it. I'm fine for now."

"Ok, promise!" Khemerin said again, "When your twenty-dollar bill runs out, let me know."

"How do you know that I only have twenty dollars in my wallet?"

"Your girlfriend told me."

"Thanks Khem. You talked about me behind my back," I said.

"I took her out for ice cream, and she told me you're dead poor."

"I'm going to get a haircut. I'll let you know when I need the money, and thanks for your concern. I'm ok now."

I walked toward the gate and told the guards I wanted to go out for a haircut. I needed their permission first. When I went outside the camp, I always brought something back for the guards, at least a few packs of cigarettes.

I had been in Thailand for a little over a month and was able to speak Thai enough to carry out a conversation, because Thai and Cambodian languages are very similar. Anyone who knew Cambodian could learn Thai easily.

"Good afternoon!" the barber said.

"Good afternoon," I replied. "I need a haircut."

"Sit down a minute. Let me finish with him first," he said, referring to the customer on his chair.

I took a seat in a corner, picked up a magazine, flipped a few pages, and put it back and picked up another one. I read a few pages, then put it back and tried yet another one. I flipped a few pages and laid it open on my lap, staring at the pictures of the models, lost in a daydream.

It's clear that Thailand is more advanced than Cambodia. Their roads are bigger and better and their towns are much bigger and cleaner—even towns and villages on the border in the province of Trat. People are civilized and nice. Thailand absolutely has more magazines than Cambodia, which reflects the freedom and education of the people here. We only had a few daily newspapers in Phnom Penh, and one was operated by the government itself.

I don't remember there being any magazines circulated in Phnom Penh, except during the Prince Norodom Sihanouk era. In fact, it was a magazine that was run by Prince Norodom Sihanouk himself. It was called "Pseng! Pseng!" which means "Extra! Extra!" It was a weekly magazine, but it did not have much to offer, other than trashing the U.S.

As the King and the chief of state, Sihanouk glorified himself and his government. He printed half-naked pictures of American models in the magazine and was proud of that. Prince Norodom Sihanouk was a piece of work. He was not only a politician who sold the country out to the Vietnamese, but he also played movies and sang.

As I was daydreaming, the barber called me to his chair for the haircut. I sat down and he put a big, white cloak over me and tied it around my neck. Then he sat down in a nearby chair, fixing his blow dryer without saying a word to me. I watched him fix his blow dryer as I sat in the chair, feeling very uncomfortable.

"The blow dryer wasn't working. I had to fix it. It is fine now," the barber said and came over.

I said nothing, but thought to myself: if you have enough money to run the shop, you should have enough money to buy more than one blow dryer. Fixing a blow dryer in front of clients is not appropriate. I was annoyed.

You're a Cambodian refugee," the barber said.

"Yes, I am," I said. "Thanks to your government and your people, who have helped us."

"We are neighbors. We have to help one another. You would do the same if Thailand fell apart."

I said nothing, because I knew our country wouldn't do the same.

"Are you from the first boat arriving on our shore?" The barber asked.

"No I am not. The Governor of Koh Kong came first. He took our money, left the country, and now he is in America. I was on the second boat, the neglected one," I said.

"Yes, you are among the rich refugees who come to our country," the barber said.

I said nothing.

"Had you been in this part of our country?"

"No, never."

"Do you like this area of the country?" the barber asked.

"Yes, I like it. It's very nice," I said.

"You want to live here? We could help you to get Thai citizenship, and you can marry one of our women!"

I said nothing.

"You don't like Thai women?"

"No, it's not like that. They are beautiful," I said.

"Are you married?" the barber asked.

"No."

"Do you have a girlfriend?"

"Yes."

We kept talking as he cut my hair.

"That's nice," the barber said. "Did you meet her here in the camp?"

"I met her in Koh Kong before we escaped," I said.

"That's nice," the barber said. "There's a beautiful woman in your camp," the barber said.

"I am not sure who you are talking about. There are many women in the camp."

"The beautiful one, you know whom I'm talking about," the barber said and went on. "She is very beautiful. She has an American look, with dark brown hair and green eyes. She is very hot. Her name is Sophie. Everyone knows her." He paused. "Oh! It would be nice to sleep with a woman like that."

I said nothing.

"Honestly, I want to go to bed with her when I see her. She walked by my shop a few times."

"Stop thinking about her, or I'll kill you," I said. "She's with me. She is my girlfriend. Stop talking about her, please."

"Oh! That's funny. She's your girl, ha."

I looked at him, silently confirming with my stern gaze.

"I've heard she has a visa to America. What will you do then?"

"She is not going anywhere. She'll stay with me here in the camp."

"You're funny. She won't stay here in this camp, my boy. You're dreaming."

I looked at the barber; he was old enough to be my father. I stopped talking and we were silent for a while. He concentrated on doing what he was doing.

"All done, young man," he said.

I looked in the mirror and said, "No, you're not." I added, "You made me look Chinese."

"What's wrong with Chinese?"

"Nothing's wrong with Chinese, but I'm not Chinese."

"You could be Chinese," the barber said.

"I don't want to be Chinese."

"What look do you want to have?" the barber asked.

"I want to have an American look," I replied.

"But you're not an American."

"I have to have an American look, because I'm going to America."

"How can I do that, if you are not an American?" the barber asked.

"Look, old man," I said, "the hair above my ears is too thick. Thin it up a little," I said.

He did as I said.

"The other side," I said.

He did as I commanded.

"That's set. You look like Humphrey Bogart now."

"No, I am not Humphrey Bogart," I said. "But it's much better than before."

"Thanks, kid, for the tip on new hairstyles for men," the barber said.

"Whatever," I said and paid the bill.

On the way to the camp, I was thinking of Sophie and how she was too hot and I was too damn lucky. I entered the camp, greeted the guards, and handed them four packs of cigarettes—two for each. I walked toward my building and found Sophie and Kim sitting at the table, the one directly in front of my unit.

"You two know one another?" I asked in surprise.

"We met a few days ago," Kim said. "Now I know why you're crazy about her."

"Ok, sister, you're right. I am crazy about her," I replied.

"You two want coffee?" I offered.

"It's a good idea," Sophie said.

"Do you have tea?" Kim added. I stood straight, looking at her without uttering a word. "Ok. Coffee is fine," she added.

As I walked into the building to get coffee and the coffee pot, Kim yelled out at me, "I like your haircut."

"You look like Humphrey Bogart," Sophie added.

I turned around, smiled, and said, "Thanks."

This haircut was a big mistake, I thought to myself. I am not Humphrey Bogart.

As I made the coffee, I heard a yell from the table: "Make one for me too." It was Khemerin's voice.

When the coffee was boiled, I poured it into four cups, one for each one of us, and brought them to the table.

As I put the tray of coffee on the table, Khemerin said, "You haircut is cool. You look like Humphrey Bogart."

"Thanks, Khem," I said, and looked at Sophie with a smile.

"Who is Humphrey Bogart?" Kim asked.

"An American movie star from the '50s," Sophie said. "He played in two of the best movies that I like the most: *The African Queen* and *Sabrina*."

"Audrey Hepburn was in *The African Queen* and Katherine Hepburn in *Sabrina*. I really like Audrey Hepburn," Khemerin said.

"You have them backwards, Khem. Katherine Hepburn was in *The African Queen*, not Audrey," Sophie argued.

"The two aren't related, right?" I said.

"You are right, they are not," Sophie said. "My parents bitched at me because I spent time with you at the beach this morning. I hate them."

We were silent.

"Kim, are you free this evening?" Khemerin asked.

"No, honey. I am resigning from my position. That trade is sinful. I am born again now in Christ. I am learning English, too."

"That's good, Kim," I said.

"What trade? What profession?" Sophie asked. "I'm lost in this conversation. What are you guys talking about?"

"Let me tell her. She's my friend and I've not been honest with her about my past trade," Kim said. We were silent and Kim continued, "I was an assistant whore for three years when I was in Phnom Penh."

"What does an assistant whore do?" I asked. Everyone looked at me with a surprise.

"It's a good question. Actually, I sat at the front desk, answering the phone and bringing customers to private rooms to wait for the whores. These whores were busy. We needed a schedule to make sure our clients did not waste their time in the waiting room."

"That's not that bad. It's like a nurse's aid job," Khemerin said. "And you became a whore when you moved to Koh Kong."

"That's right, rich guy. I met you in Koh Kong and you paid me big tips for my ass," Kim said, "It was a sin. I'm a Christian now. I am not doing that anymore."

"Oh God," I sighed and buried my face in my hands.

"How did you meet Savy? Did he pay you a big tip too?" Sophie said.

"No, he wanted to commit suicide, thinking that you and this rich guy were together. I invited him to my place for free tea and he refused, but he paid for my dinner though," Kim said. "But I've given up that trade now and I'm reborn in Christ."

"Good for you, Kim," Sophie said.

Three weeks later, Khemerin learned that his family had not been on the American rescue plane as he had hoped. He was devastated by the news. However, he was qualified to immigrate to the United States. The officials at the American Embassy would come to pick him up in two weeks. He was thrilled at the prospect of finding a new home in a new country but sad at the same time, for his family was trapped in Phnom Penh. He did not understand why his family could not get on the plane with the U.S. rescue team. He was terribly upset about the situation in Phnom Penh.

Nonetheless, there was good news, so we decided to have a small celebration for him among the four of us: Khemerin, Kim, Sophie, and me. We had lunch at a restaurant in the market in the town's center.

"Congratulations, Khem," I said.

"I'm happy for you," Sophie said.

Kim did not say a word, just smiled. We knew that she was also happy to see Khemerin go to America.

"The U.S. government will find me a sponsor in America," Khemerin said.

"What is a sponsor?" I asked.

"A sponsor is a person or a family who is willing to help me adjust to my new life in America. I will become an American citizen after five years. Isn't it great?" Khemerin paused, and continued, "I will ask my sponsor to find me a good English class, and then I'll go to college. I will become an engineer."

"What kind of engineer?" Sophie asked,

"I will be an electrical engineer," Khemerin said.

"Why do you want to become an electrical engineer?" I asked.

"Well, my friend, without electricity you live in the dark," Khemerin answered proudly.

"Lucky you," I said. I turned to Sophie and said, "You seem very unhappy. What is wrong?"

Sophie dropped her fork, looked at me, turned to Khemerin, then back at me, and said, "Yesterday we got a letter from the U.S. Embassy also. Khem, we are on the same flight to America. The letter confirms my uncle as our sponsor and says that we will be picked up on July 15. We leave this camp in two weeks. We are going to America."

"Congratulations!" Khemerin said and looked at me.

"Congratulations!" Kim said. "I'm very happy for you, but I'm going to miss you."

"I'm not going," Sophie said softly.

I said nothing. We were silent for a while. I just could not swallow my food. I said to Sophie, "You should go. You will be happy there in America."

"Ok, if you want me to go, I'll go." Then she threw her napkin on the table, stood up, and walked out of the restaurant, back to the camp.

"Sophie, stop, please!" I cried out. She did not even turn to look at me. I said to Khemerin, "I need to go after her. Will you let me know my bill and hers?"

"Of course I'll let you know. Go! She's very angry with you, Mr. Dumas," Khemerin replied. I ran after Sophie. I walked behind her, begging her to stop, but she refused to listen. To avoid a scene in public, I let her go. I walked behind, keeping a good distance apart. She entered the camp and went into her unit, and I went into mine.

For the next three days, I did not see her. I missed her terribly. I didn't want her to leave, but I didn't want her to miss a good life in America, either. I loved her so much. I only wanted the best for her. I was miserable.

Chapter Nineteen

I had not seen Sophie for three days since she walked out on us in the middle of our farewell lunch for Khemerin. I missed her terribly, but there was no way I could talk to her or let her know I was sorry. As I was eating lunch in the front of my unit, a little girl standing in front of me about three feet away caught my attention. She stared at me.

"What is your name?" I asked her.

"Sok," she replied.

"You want to eat, Sok?" I asked.

"No. Here, this is for you from Sophie," she said and handed me an envelope.

"Thank you," I said, taking two baht from my wallet and handed them to her. Smiling, she took them and ran back to where she had come from, as fast as she could. I tore the envelope, took out the letter and read it: "Meet me at Nonthaburi today at three o'clock. Don't be late."

Nonthaburi was the restaurant where we had eaten three days earlier. I glanced at my watch; it was one o'clock. I was anxious to meet her, so I finished my lunch as fast as I could, took a shower, and got dressed, leaving the camp at two-thirty. I arrived at the restaurant ten minutes before the hour. I selected a table in the corner of the restaurant and ordered a glass of Coke.

Sophie walked into the restaurant exactly at three, and the host showed her to my table. She pulled a chair and sat opposite me with smile on her face. She extended her hands to reach mine and leaned over to kiss me. I kissed her back passionately.

"I'm sorry for my behavior the other day," she said to me.

"No apology is needed, Sophie. I said things that I should not have. It was my fault. I should apologize to you."

"If you sincerely want me to go, I'll go. I just don't want to be in your way."

"It's not like that, Sophie. I've grown attached to you. I don't know how I can live without you. I thought you might be happier in America. I am a man without family. I'm poor and without destiny."

"You're wrong. I'm happy with you. I have faith in you. If I went to America without you, I would die before I landed in San Francisco. I am not going anywhere without you. If you really love me, please stop pushing the issue." I was completely silent, so she continued, "What? Say something!"

"I love you," I said softly.

"I love you too."

"What do you want to do for the rest of the afternoon?"

"It's up to you. I'm happy as long as I'm with you," she replied.

We were silent for a while, and then she said, "We can go inside and look around the market."

We paid for our drinks and walked out of the restaurant. We crossed the road and walked toward the market, an area under a big roof with no walls surrounding it.

Under this big roof, we walked in the crowd, passing department stores, shoe stores, bookstores, and stands with fruits of all kinds. The refreshment stands and restaurants were on the other side; we did not go there. Instead, we walked to the center of the area, to a place where they sold jewelry and expensive watches.

I was surprised to see that they had some expensive watches: Citizen, Seiko, OMEGA, and Movado. Sophie pointed out some beautiful diamond rings that she loved. She asked the merchants at the counter to show her necklaces, earrings, and wrist bands, all of which were made of pure gold.

"Look, aren't they beautiful, pure gold?" Sophie said.

Sophie

"Absolutely!"

In our culture, gold is valued the highest among precious metals. Some women won't wear jewelry unless it is made of gold, and most families keep their savings in gold jewelry. Sophie grabbed my hand and smiled.

"You are wearing a very nice gold chain necklace."

"Thanks," I said. "It was passed on to me after Dad passed away. The tradition was to pass it on to the first son in the family for generations."

Sophie gave me a smile and said, "Let's get out of here. We'll come back if we need to."

We walked out of the store and out of the area. On the corner of the market across the street, we saw a bus station.

"Where do these buses go?" Sophie asked.

"I don't know, but we can find out."

We crossed the street to the bus station to check out how far the bus went. At the ticket counter, Sophie asked the clerk because she spoke Thai better than I.

She turned to me and said, "The bus goes all the way to Bangkok."

We looked at each other, and she put her arms around my neck and whispered in my ear, "We still have hope." I said nothing and she whispered in my ear, pointing across the road to a hotel, "Do they have TVs there? I have not seen any movies since we left Phnom Penh."

I released her and said, hesitantly, "If I take you there, would you come with me?"

"Yes," she answered softly.

"Come with me, then."

We walked toward the hotel.

I checked in and we walked as fast as we could to our room, fearing someone would see us.

"I miss my bed at home. It wasn't too firm or too soft," Sophie said while I was turning the TV channels, looking for a good program.

"Hey Sophie, *Little House on the Prairie* is on TV, the American show," I shouted with excitement.

"I like that show. We used to pick it up from the American station in Saigon," Sophie replied, and continued, "Keep it low and come here." She motioned for me to sit beside her on the bed. I sat next to her.

"It's very complicated," I said and put my hand around her.

"It is not our first time, so why does it have to be complicated?" Sophie replied.

"You are very beautiful, Sophie."

"Kiss me, then."

I pressed my lips against hers. We fell into each other's arms, embracing with love and passion. Slowly I laid her down on the bed, dropped myself gently on top of her and continued to kiss her, our lips pressing against each other and our tongues entwining. Wrapping her arms around me, she kissed me passionately.

"Don't stop!" she murmured. I did not reply. Slowly, I unbuttoned her blouse and pressed my lips on her soft, white, beautiful chest.

"Oh my God," she murmured. I was lost in her beauty.

"Let me help you," she said, sitting up. I took her blouse off, throwing it on a chair nearby. Her breasts were hidden in the cups of her bra. I kissed her chest, around the upper part of her breasts.

"You are very beautiful," I said to her dreamily. I felt her hands stroke my chest as she pressed her lips gently against my torso, making me feel good.

She slowly loosened my belt and unbuttoned my jeans. As my pants dropped to my ankles, I kissed her hair, her soft, beautiful hair, with love and passion. I felt her hands in my boxers, which also dropped to my ankles. She stroked me gently until I was fully erect.

"Oh, my God," she moaned. It made me even more excited.

I felt her soft tongue licking my shaft, up and down, and then all around the head. From there, I was lost in a dream. I opened my eyes and saw her standing face to face with me. I pressed her lips against mine.

"Sophie, I love you so much," I whispered in her ear. She did not reply, but instead, pulled me down on top of her.

"Sophie, please let me kiss you more," I whispered in her ear.

"Take it off if you want to, I'm yours," She replied dreamily. Slowly, I removed her bra, kissed her breasts and gently bit her nipples. I kissed every inch of her soft, beautiful body, and slowly I unbuttoned her jeans and removed them. She was wearing panties, and I slipped them off without any resistance from her.

Her hands pushed my head against her even harder as she moaned. I could no longer resist the excitement. Slowly, I dropped myself on top of her gently, and we made love. Long after I released my energy inside her, I held her in my arms for a long while. We were both naked, lying next to each other while the *Little House on the Prairie* played on the screen in the background. We did not care about the show.

"Sophie, I am sorry for what I did just now. It meant so much to me," I said softly in her ear.

"Why are you sorry? It was not our first time."

"What we did was more than making love. It was crazy."

"Oh that," she replied, giggling. "Actually, I like it. I never imagined that you could do that."

"Me neither, it just happened," I said.

"I know. I appreciate it. It showed that you have no fear of me."

"You are right. You were good yourself," I replied.

"I did not know what came over me; it just happened. I hope you don't think I am a bad girl."

"Oh my darling, don't ever think that way. We belong to one another for the rest of our lives."

We made love once more before we turned off the television and returned the key to the clerk at the front desk. It was seven in the evening. We decided to have dinner at Nonthaburi. The evening was wonderful, the best evening of our life. I got back to my place at nine.

I was still in a good mood, when Sophie's father walked into my unit, looking for me. He stood there a moment, his eyes red; I could tell he was ready to eat me alive. Suddenly, I felt the force of two hundred pounds striking me in the stomach, and then a second blow in the same place. I fell to the floor and did not bother to get up. I lay there, my hands around my knees, my knees on my chin.

"You bastard, you're ruining my family." And he was gone.

I was hurt. I coughed a few times, my saliva mixed with blood. I tried to sleep that night, but the pain prevented me from sleeping. No one knew about the incident, not even Khemerin, because I did not want to make a scene in the camp. I only hoped that Sophie would not get hurt.

I'll kill that bastard if he lays a hand on her, I thought to myself.

Sophie

Chapter Twenty

It had been almost a week since Sophie and I had spent the afternoon in the hotel. I hadn't seen her since we parted that evening. Her father had laid the law down; she was not permitted to see me.

I received letters from her nearly every day. The first one was dated July 5, 1975, the morning after our day in the hotel.

July 5, 1975

My darling,

I had a wonderful evening yesterday; it was an unforgettable moment. I still feel you inside me. I don't know what it is, but it is a good feeling.

My father was angry with me yesterday when I got back. He did not talk to me or look at me, but I saw anger on his face and in his eyes. I was scared. Mom told me that I am not allowed to see you and not allowed to go five feet from our unit. My life is in a prison camp right now as my family is preparing to leave for the U.S. I don't want anything bad to happen to you, but there is no point in fighting with my father. I am always thinking of you and our plan to get out of this camp. I want to go to America with you. I do not belong here in this camp, and neither do you.

I miss you terribly. I cry alone because no one understands me. When I was young, I cried to my mother and she comforted me, but not now. Mom said that I'm too young to fall in love, beside the fact that we are refugees with no home, no country. She said my future will be brighter after we settle in America, where I can go to college and have a good career.

Oh America, it is a dream land for Mom and Dad, maybe for everyone in this camp. America is simply a Utopia without you. Love is what happens when two people are drawn to each other; how dare she say I'm too young to fall in love? My guess is that she never fell in love, and that is why she does not know what love is all about. The American spirit is in our hearts, even though we may not realize it, because we cannot be happy without one another. The two of us are pursuing happiness together.

Hope is the best of things, and don't give it up, darling. I've belonged to you since the evening I leaned my head on your shoulder while you read *Les Miserables*, the evening of the big storm in Koh Kong. I took sanctuary in your room and in your heart. The rest is just our love story. I do not regret that we made love. It means so much to me.

Love, Sophie

After reading this letter, I wrote back to her the same day.

July 5, 1975

My dear Sophie,

I understand your present condition and your tears, which are only symbols of our true love. My tears shatter because I miss you so much. Your father is capable of inflicting pain, both mental and physical, onto me, but I will never allow him to put his hands on you and hurt you. Our ordeal will not last long. It's simply a temporarily pain that we need to go through.

I adore you and will love you till the end of my life. I love you more than my own life. I am thinking about our future and happiness. Our future and destiny is in the invisible hands of our God, the God of love who created all things in the universe. You are beautiful, a replica of an angel of God, and His blessing, a gift for me. I am the happiest man in this world because you love me.

The plan to build our life and hope in America is not sealed, even though I (we, if you and I become one, which your parents will not recognize) am not qualified as a refugee to be sponsored by the U.S. government. There must be an alternative avenue for us to be accepted into the program. How can the U.S. government deny our fate while extending its generosity to millions of Vietnamese refugees who left Vietnam by boat into the open sea?

I believe that we would have a greater chance of success if we present ourselves to the immigration officer at the American Embassy in Bangkok. This is our plan and this is our last hope. Put our lives in His hands, our God who loves us. I love you. My heart is full of joy and happiness when I think of you.

Love, Savy

In front of me was the vast, dark blue sea, stretching far into the distance. On the horizon, the sky was painted gold and light blue. From my vantage point, the golden hue extended across the horizon from left to right, from the surface of the sea to the sky, glowing brighter at the center. Above this magnificent gold color, the sky was blue, and extended as far as my eyes could see.

The gulf of Thailand was a darker blue, in contrast to the light blue sky. Its gentle waves moved briskly under the soft wind, the waves rolling shoreward and then backward, again and again. The sea was dark because there was not enough light from the sky; it seemed that night had not yet left this corner of the universe. It was still sunrise.

"It's beautiful, isn't it?" a voice from behind me announced. It was Khemerin.

"Absolutely!" I replied.

"You woke up early today," Khemerin said.

"Enjoy the beautiful scene. It won't last long," I replied and turned to him. "It's your last day here, isn't it?"

We sat on rocks and looked to the horizon, breathless, gazing in awe at the beautiful sunrise appearing in front of us.

"Good luck with your new life and adventure in America," I said.

"I never thought that we'd come to this. We shared so much together, especially in these last couple of months during our escape," Khemerin said. "I am going to miss you."

"I'll miss you too."

"I've dreamed of America since I was little. I went to Paris a few times with Mom and Dad, but never to America. Dad always said he did not have time to take us there, to New York."

"You'll adjust well in America," I said.

"Do you know what I like the most about America?"

"I don't know." I looked at Khemerin and added, "Tell me."

"I like blond hair and blue eyes, don't you?" He paused and continued, "I also like red hair, auburn, brown, and dirty blond. Their eye color goes with their hair color. These women have long, beautiful legs and sexy bodies you have never dreamed of."

I looked at Khemerin with a smile and said, "Go on!"

"Why does God make them so fucking beautiful?" he replied. He put his hand on my shoulder and said, "Remember when I told you that I wanted to become an engineer? Not anymore. I've changed my mind."

"You've not yet started school, and you're already changed your mind," I said and smiled. "By the time you'll finish your college degree, you might change your majors two or three times, I guess. What is your goal now?" I asked.

Khemerin was silent for a while, looking to the horizon. Then he said, slowly, "I am going to learn English. Speaking perfectly in English, I will save money, marry an American woman, dirty blond, or auburn, or light blond, move to Montana, buy a pick-up truck, and live happily forever with my beautiful American wife. That is my goal."

I give him a big smile, and said, "It's a wonderful dream. You should be an author and write a romance novel."

"You think I'm joking, don't you? Let me tell you one more thing."

"What's that?"

"My American kids will not speak any language except English. Do you know why?"

"Why is that?" I asked.

"Their parents will be Americans, that's why."

"That's a wonderful plan, Khem. How about me? Will we be friends?

"Oh you, we're still friends, but you'll have to learn English fast. When I get to the States, I'll stop speaking or writing Cambodian. We'll communicate in English. Like it or not, that's what my life is going to be."

"Thanks for the information. I'll learn English so that our friendship won't die, regardless of how arrogant you are."

"You're my good friend, because you understand me," Khemerin replied.

"I understand you, all right."

"How is Sophie? What's your plan? She's also leaving today," Khemerin said.

"I don't know, buddy."

"Oh, and don't misunderstand me, ok? Sophie is beautiful, even if she isn't blond with blue eyes."

"I'm ok if you find her unattractive, Khem. You didn't hurt my feelings when you praised those sexy American women."

We looked at each other and smiled. The sun came up, the day broke, and we walked back to the camp.

Later, I stood under a tree, 50 feet from the camp entrance, where a green bus with a U.S. Marines license was parked. The bus was there to pick up Khemerin, Sophie's family, and four other families, including the monk, en route to the United States of America. The ex-Koh Kong's Governor had sponsored the monk, the lucky bastard.

Khemerin walked toward me. We shook hands, hugged, and said

goodbye and good luck. He walked toward the bus and climbed in, sticking out his head for the last time, waving at me and reminding me of the first day of junior high. The Lopez family and other families walked briskly toward the bus with smiles on their faces. They were going to America, their new land, new homes, and a new country, and the trip was being paid in full by the U.S. government.

Sophie glanced at me from a distance. She and her mother, sister, and brother walked behind Mr. Lopez, all of them carrying luggage. Sophie carried one travel bag and her purse, and she glanced at me often while walking toward the bus. They climbed into the bus, one by one. Sophie was the last one and stood there awhile, reluctant to climb in. And then, with one last glance back at me, she got in.

The doors closed and the engine started. My heart sank.

Suddenly, the door sprang back open, and Sophie hopped off with her travel bag and purse and ran towards me. Her mother jumped out after her and shouted, "Sophie! Come back, you cannot stay." Sophie stopped between me and her mother. Then she turned around and shouted back, "Mother, I am not going, goodbye."

Sophie ran to me and threw herself in my arms. I scooped her up and kissed her, disregarding the customs of our culture.

"I am not leaving without you," she whispered in my ear.

"I know," I said softly.

Back at the entrance gate, Mr. Lopez led his wife back onto the bus, which moved slowly out of the camp. We stood hand in hand, watching the bus carry our friends and loved ones off to America. The bus drove out of the camp, turned right at the entrance, and disappeared out of sight. I held Sophie's hands and saw tears rolling down her cheeks. Her eyes were puffed and red.

"You're crying," I said.

"Yes, I have been for more than a week."

"You're still crying," I said, wiping her tears away with my fingers.

"I love you. You will not disappoint me, right?"

"How could I?" I replied, holding her hands, and dropping to the ground on my knees. I looked up at her, held her hands a little tighter

Sophie

and said, "Sophie, will you marry me?"

Sophie stood still. My heart was frozen. Then she burst out laughing, as joyful tears rolled down her cheeks. She pulled me up and threw her arms around my neck. We stood there kissing, tears in our eyes.

She said, "Yes…Is it crazy?"

I whispered in her ear, "Yes, but love itself is crazy and beautiful."

She pressed her lips against mine and I kissed her passionately. Again she whispered in my ear, "We can make love anytime we like."

I replied, "No, honey, we marry first, and then we can make love every time we want." I took the necklace from my neck and put it on her.

"Oh, Savy…." Sophie said.

I put my arms around her, embraced her tight, and said, "Darling, it's my dowry for our marriage."

We heard loud applause. Apparently, the crowd had been watching this whole time. We had created a romantic scene in the refugee camp, a spectacle far beyond our cultural norm.

We sent a letter to Mr. Gene Richardson, our friend working for World Relief International, informing him of Sophie's situation and announcing our marriage. Since Mr. Richardson was a minister, we agreed to let him marry us. We were married three weeks later.

We were so happy, knowing that we were not alone as refugees. We loved our parents so much, but were thrilled to finally feel independent. We could do what we wanted, as far as sex was concerned; we could have moved in together. We also wanted to respect the community we lived in, though.

Sophie moved out from her place and stayed a few weeks with Kim until we were married. For the three weeks of our engagement, we did not make love, but we saw each other every day.

We were sitting in front of her unit one morning. Life in the refugee camp had become routine to us—the smoke coming from stoves in the morning when people cooked breakfast, the adults gathering in groups and talking, the children playing soccer and jump-rope in the courtyard, all of it. Often, we saw mothers breastfeeding their babies in public. We looked at the mothers and then at each other; then we burst out laughing and giggling. One afternoon, Sophie said to me out of the blue, "I didn't know why we made love the first time. I think you seduced me," Sophie said. I was silent. She spoke again, "No, you did not seduce me, we just fell in each other arms that evening. We went crazy then. We made love four times."

"It was the first day of our New Year. Your father kept us apart for three days before the New Year, remember?" I said.

"I missed you so much during those three days of captivity," Sophie replied, paused for a second, and continued, "Captivity is a little exaggerated, but… I never thought about sex then. I just wanted to be around you. The emotion built up inside me each day, stronger and stronger. I told Mom that I needed to see you for half an hour, and we ended up in your bed until seven in the evening."

"Those three days that you were not permitted to see me, I couldn't do anything, other than thinking of you and calling your name all the time," I said.

"Those strong emotions that built up during the days of our separation brought us together," Sophie said.

"Wasn't it wonderful?" I said.

"It was wonderful," she replied. "Same as two weeks ago, when we made love in the hotel. That was even crazier. What got into you?" she said with a mischievous smile.

"No, you started it," I said.

"Oh put the blame on me. You moaned like a… ha!" she replied, searching for the right word to finish her sentence.

"Would you do that again?" I asked her with a smile.

"No, never…" she returned, giggling.

"Every time your parents put a leash on you to separate us, we ended up making love when we met. Wasn't it strange? I asked.

"Yes…" she replied. "The more he kept us apart, the more he pushed us together. I miss him."

"Don't worry. We're going to find him," I said.

"We will…?"

"Absolutely, can you come to my place tonight, or I can come to yours? It's been a month since we last made love, darling. This engagement is driving me crazy."

"No, we cannot make love until we marry next week. Then I will find out how desperate you are,"

"I see…." I looked at her with a smile.

"After we marry, what're we going to do?" Sophie asked.

"Make love every day," I replied.

"No, not that, let's be serious. What's next in our life?" Sophie's tone became serious.

I looked at her with a smile, and said, "Going to America."

"Really…?" she replied.

"Absolutely…" I said sincerely.

"Oh Savy, I have complete trust in you. We're going to visit Mom and Dad in San Francisco." I pulled her close to me and kissed her forehead.

Sophie raised her eyes and said, "I have a surprise for you…"

"What is that?" I asked. She pulled a jewelry box out from her purse, opened it, and said, "These are our wedding bands. Do you like them?"

"Oh, they're so beautiful," I said and grabbed her head with my hands, pulled it toward me, and pressed my lips against hers. I kissed her as long as I could. Then I said, "Where did you get the money to buy these beautiful bands?"

"Your dowry necklace was a little long for me, so I cut a piece from it and added my own gold necklace to it. Now we have two wedding bands, each weighing two and half ounces," she said, and added, "You don't mind if I shortened up your necklace a little, right?"

"It's a wonderful idea. Do you have more surprises?"

"Do you want more surprises?" she said with a smile.

"Do you…?" I repeated, looking her in the eye, searching for a surprise.

"Not yet, we need more practice," she replied, giggling.

She leaned in to kiss me. Life couldn't have been more perfect.

Minister Gene Richardson married us a week later. Our friends in the camp came to witness our marriage, and we had ice cream, hot tea, and coffee afterward. It was a wonderful day. After the wedding, I moved Sophie to my unit.

We made love the night after our wedding, but it was not as fun as when we did it in the hotel a month ago, for we had no privacy. Next to us was another family, with no wall separating us; just curtains. They could hear every breath we took. Sophie kept her hand on my mouth, reminding me not to moan too loud. She did not want people to know we made love. I told her that people knew anyway; there was no man who could resist a sexy woman like her. Hearing that, she pulled my ear just to hurt me.

One evening, I was up until midnight hanging out with some guys in the camp. When I returned to our place, Sophie was already in the mosquito net, lying on the thin bed on the floor. I crawled inside the mosquito net and kissed her cheeks.

"Hi, Sarah, are you awake, waiting for me? It is Abraham, your husband." I paused and added, "This camp is terrible. When God gives us a baby, we will move to a nicer camp."

Sophie looked at me and said, "It's not funny. Good night." And she turned away from me, closing her eyes to sleep.

She was so beautiful. I looked at her awhile and then started to peel her clothes off little by little until nothing was left. I took a light blanket to cover both of us and kissed every part of her body under the blanket, hoping no one would see what we were doing. She did not moan, but her body writhed a little under me. I moved on top of her and pressed my lips against hers.

As we came together, the mosquito net dropped on us. We finished our lovemaking, and I held her in my arms without bothering to get out and put our mosquito net back together. I was lost in her smell and her essence.

She said dreamily, "It's embarrassing."

I replied, "Don't worry. They know we're married." I waited a moment and then said, "Honey...?"

"What, honey?" she murmured in my ears.

"Who should be sacrificed to God, Ismail or Isaac?" I asked, kissing her earlobe.

"Please put the mosquito net back together, I cannot sleep like this," she replied.

The day after our wedding, we decided to spend quality time on the ocean shore, which was part of our refugee camp. This was our little honeymoon, given the fact that we had no money and limited freedom. Besides, Sophie loved the vast sea, the immense body of water stretching to the horizon as our eyes could see. It was hot at the beach and the sea in the area was deep.

We found a spot on a big rock, big enough for the two of us to lie down. We spread towels on the rock. Sophie took off her t-shirt and her sarong; underneath was the swimsuit she was wearing. She lay down on her stomach, and I lay next to her. We both looked at the horizon and the vast blue sea. After ten minutes, I stood up, got the suntan lotion from our bag, and spread the cream on my wife's back, rubbing it all over her back and into her neck as well. Sophie rested her head on the towel, her eyes closed.

She murmured, "I feel good, my dear."

Next, I spread the cream along her legs, rubbing it in. Then she turned around, lay on her back, extending her hands to me and said, "Put the cream on my arms and the rest of my body, my husband." I obeyed; I did what she told.

After a while she said, "It's my turn to put the lotion on you. I don't want you to get burned."

We lay next to each other silently. Then she stood up, looking at the sea below, and jumped in the water. She yelled from below, "Come on, the water's warm!"

I couldn't leave her alone, so I jumped in after her. We swam back and forth, joyfully, for a while. We climbed back to our rock, drying each other off, and then kissed for some time. I glanced at my wristwatch. It was one-thirty.

"I'm tired and hungry. What do we have for lunch?" Sophie said.

"Sit down. Please allow me to serve you," I said.

"Ok, what do we have?"

I brought out two chicken sandwiches, handing one to her and keeping one for myself, and I said, "We should celebrate our marriage with champagne, just the two of us."

"Champagne! Where is it from?" Sophie asked.

"This is one of the presents from our American friend," I said and showed her the bottle.

"How nice!" Sophie replied.

"I don't want to go back into the water after the champagne," I said.

"Pop the cork and pour me a glass," Sophie demanded.

I poured the champagne into two glasses, handing her one and keeping the other for myself.

"A toast to our marriage!" We touched the glasses together.

"It's nice that Pastor Richardson speaks Cambodian," Sophie said.

"He worked in Cambodia for twenty years until last April."

"Was he trapped in the French Embassy?"

"I don't think so. I think he got out just before the Communists took over."

"He was lucky," Sophie replied. "What's the plan to get out of here? We can't just take a boat or a canoe from here to the 7th fleet."

"We'll take the bus to Bangkok and then we'll go to the American Embassy," I said.

"And what?"

"No, we won't go directly to the American Embassy, but to Pastor Richardson's office first. He can bring us to the Embassy. He could help us in telling our story to the immigration officer at the Embassy," I added.

"Your plan may work," Sophie said. "When will we leave?"

"Next week, at the latest," I said.

"Why not sooner?"

"We just got married. There are some people who pay attention to us here. Besides, there will be a big holiday in town, some kind of religious holiday. There'll be a big ceremony at the pagoda. I've heard that we will be allowed to participate in this holiday. They'll show a movie at the pagoda at night. I'd rather let things settle a little, and then we can leave the camp."

"Are you sure we should leave next week?" Sophie asked again.

"This plan should be very secret; no one should know about it, even Kim, our best friend. The day we leave, everything we have should be left the way it is. We have to leave with what we have on us, no travel bags, nothing."

"Right. Kim would be devastated when she found out we were disappeared," my wife said.

"I know, but we will let her know where we will be if our plan works."

"Maybe we'll have to put some extra clothes in a shopping bag, pretending that we're going shopping in town."

"Yes. We have to make sure no one knows our plan, or we'll get caught before the bus leaves the city. The bus leaves the station at seven in the evening and arrives in Bangkok in the morning. When we get to Bangkok, we'll look for Pastor Richardson."

"Pastor Richardson won't leave us out in the cold," Sophie repeated dreamily.

"Absolutely not. He's our friend," I assured her.

"We've got three hundred baht in cash from wedding presents from our friends," Sophie said.

"It's nice. It's enough for the trip to Bangkok next week," I said.

"When we get to America, we'll go to San Francisco, looking for Mom and Dad. I really miss them," Sophie said, looking a bit tearful.

"Absolutely, we'll find them,"

"Oh, I love you, Savy," she replied softly.

Our little honeymoon ended at four in the evening. After lunch, we did nothing, just lay in the sun, relaxing and reading a book that I had brought with me. I read Sophie a short story until she fell asleep.

Chapter Twenty-One

We folded up our mosquito net and blanket and put them neatly in the corner. Our suitcase was next to them and our shoes lay at the door, as though nothing was out of the ordinary. We walked out of the refugee camp at six in the evening of August 23, 1975.

We told the guards we needed permission to go to the market to exchange clothes we had just bought and which were too big. After they thoroughly inspected us, we walked through the gate, Sophie carrying a small shopping bag with three dresses and two blouses inside. It was the last time we saw the camp.

As usual, the market was busy. We giggled as we walked past the hotel we stayed in for three hours, making love and ignoring our favorite TV show, *Little House on the Prairie*; it was just two months earlier.

We entered the market from the south end, walked through it, and made it through to the other side. I stood waiting on the corner while my wife went to the bus station to buy the tickets. Less than five minutes later, she came back with two tickets in hand and we walked briskly to the bus station. Seeing the bus, we climbed the stairs, walked inside, and took our seats. It was sad to leave our best friend Kim and others behind without saying goodbye.

The bus was crowded and left the station at seven in the evening. As we headed north on the highway, my wife closed her eyes, pretending to sleep. I looked at her once in a while and realized how lucky I was to marry a beautiful woman like her. We had come a long way in just five months.

We had good times in Koh Kong, shed a lot of tears in the refugee camp, and still managed to have some sweet moments together. It was love. We were risking going to jail if we got caught escaping from the refugee camp; we risked our lives for freedom. My wife knew that and she had complete faith in me. We both put our life in God's hands, trusting in Him. Love couldn't be sweeter without danger.

We were risking our lives, hoping America would bring us happiness and freedom and deliver us from poverty. Poverty is a social disease that has to be treated as any other sickness, I thought to myself, as we rolled down the highway. Sophie was still asleep, and my mind drifted far away.

For the last four months in the refugee camp, I had given most of my attention to Sophie because she meant so much to me. But thoughts of my family at home had also been in my mind because I loved them very much; they were a part of me, my blood. My love for Sophie was completely different. It was a love coming from emotion and my heart, a different kind of love.

The image of Sophie running out of the bus, yelling goodbye to her mother in the refugee camp two months ago, was vivid on my mind. Later, she had told me that she missed her parents. We both were children who had so much love for our parents, and yet we needed to make a choice for our happiness. In spite of all that, our love for our parents was unshakable.

It was dark in the bus. I lost track of time as I thought of our future. Suddenly, the bus stopped at a station for a routine inspection. A police officer climbed in with a flashlight in hand. He pointed the flashlight at each passenger, row by row, as my heart pounded. I felt the light running over my face as I closed my eyes, pretending to sleep. I heard the officer talking to the driver. I glanced over at Sophie and saw that her eyes were closed and she was in a deep sleep.

Then the door of the bus closed and the bus moved down the highway. Breathing a sigh of relief, I put my arms around my wife and fell asleep. In my sleep, I had a strange dream.

My wife and I are in a strange, beautiful town, with light snow falling from the sky. We are not sure whether it is day or night, because the sky is bright, but there is no sun. People walk on the sidewalks on both sides of the street, in both directions. They seem very unhappy. Houses are big and beautiful, some with white fences around them and beautiful, light snow covering the lawns. Mysteriously, at least two or three houses on each street in this town have "For Sale" signs, posted on their beautiful lawns. Why are they are leaving such beautiful homes and a beautiful town?

We walk into a restaurant and sit in a corner by the window. We order two glasses of wine. The wine tastes all right, but the atmosphere seems gloomy. Soon a man comes over and shakes our hands.

"I own this place. Welcome, my good man and my good lady," he says.

Nobody talks like that; it must be in the old days, I say to myself. The man continues, "Are you passing through this beautiful town?"

"Yes, sir. You own such a beautiful restaurant, but you seem to be very unhappy. The town seems very sad and quiet," I say. "You mind telling us why you are so sad?"

"We have been at war for almost six years. Most of the citizens of this country believe that this war is wrong and not in the interest of our nation. Our King spent billions of dollars for a war that we do not understand. Our children are dying for nothing."

"Tell the King to stop the war," my wife says proudly.

"The King lied to us about the cause of the war. Later, we found out that the war is wrong. The people of this great nation have asked the King to stop the war and to bring our kids home. He does not listen to us. He has spent our national treasury on the war. He does not listen to us."

"It's not unusual. A King owns everything in the country he rules. He can do whatever he wants. The King in my country has done the same thing. We were taught that everything in the country a King rules is the King's possession, including our lives. It's normal," I say. "I've noticed that people in your town are moving out. Are they selling their beautiful homes?"

"No, my good man and good lady, the truth is that people do not have the money to meet their obligations. They have to sell their houses," the man pauses for a second and continues, "Our financial system is falling apart now. My bank is withholding my credit line, but not because I am a bad creditor. I paid my loan on time and with handsome interest for the money I borrowed. The bank's president is my best friend. He is sorry about it, but he told me that the bank does not have money to lend."

"It doesn't make any sense," I say. "How come the financial system collapsed? How come the bank doesn't have money—unless the money stopped flowing in the financial system? Where is the money?" I ask a lot of questions, given the fact that I had only two years of college education from Cambodia.

"That's what we don't understand," the man says and smiles faintly at us with tears in his eyes. "May I ask: where are you heading to?" Then he stands straight, looking at us curiously.

"We are going to America," my wife says proudly.

"We always wanted to go to America, ever since we were kids. People are nice there, and there is no King or Queen in America. People created the government and the government is for the people. Isn't it wonderful?" I say.

"My good man and my good lady, I have to go, but I'll be back to continue our conversation later," the man says, bowing his head a little. "Enjoy your stay in our town."

My wife and I sit silently, sipping our wine, looking at each other sadly.

"Where are we?" my wife asks.

"I don't know," I say. "It's a strange country. The town seems like it used to be a rich town, but it's not anymore. The bad King ruined everything."

Two men walk into the restaurant and sit at the table next to us. They order two bottles of beer. They seem very cheerful, in fact; they're the only two happy people in the entire town. One is white and the other a little darker, but not altogether black. I hear them speak and signal for my wife to listen carefully to their conversation.

"The King is on our side," the white man says.

"Good," the dark man says.

"Ok, what's the plan, buddy?" the white man asks.

"We'll finish it up," the darker man says. "You ship the cash to us, out of this fucking country as much and as fast as you can, understand? Believe me! They are going to die without money."

"How do I do that?" the white man says.

"You idiot, figure something out. Talk to someone who knows the business," the darker man says.

"If we take all the money out of the country, what's the King going to say?" the white man asks the darker man.

"The King has more money than anyone in this world can imagine. He's a smart King, he knows how to take good care of himself. Don't worry about him. You just take the money out of this country, and we'll be set," the darker man says.

"Money, money, money…" I cried out as I slept.

"Honey, wake up," my wife said.

I woke up.

"What was it? You were talking in your sleep."

"Oh, honey, I had a nightmare," I said.

"Tell me what you saw, honey," my wife said. "Was I in your dream too?"

"Yes, you were in it, but the dream was not about you or about us," I said.

"Can you tell me about it?"

"In my dream, I saw a rich country become poor because the bad King brought the country to war and did not listen to his people's voices. The bad guys, who must've been the enemies of the good country, came and took all money from the good country. The bad King did nothing to protect the treasure of his country from being stolen.

"What country, honey?"

"I don't know. It was a very bad dream," I said and kissed her on her forehead sadly. We stopped talking and went back to sleep.

At four in the morning, the bus pulled slowly into a station and parked neatly by the sidewalk for a forty-five-minute rest. Most of the passengers descended from the bus, some stretching out their arms and legs to relax their muscles after the long ride in crammed seats, and some walking back and forth on the sidewalks. Others stopped by the lavatories, and still others browsed in the shops at the station. Only a few remained in their seats, sleeping.

We got out of the bus along with the others and mingled with the crowd to avoid any suspicion. It was my wife's idea to mingle with the crowd rather than to sleep in our seats, regardless of how tired we were.

We kept to ourselves with smiles on our faces, avoiding eye contact with anyone in the crowd. We picked up a Thai magazine and some morning papers at the stand, then got on the bus with the other passengers and took our seats.

The bus left the station at four-forty-five, heading toward its final destination, Bangkok. We closed our eyes to sleep once more, regardless of the sun rising and daylight breaking all around us.

When we arrived at the outskirts of the city of Bangkok, two hours later, it was impossible to pretend we were sleeping. We read the newspapers and the magazine we had bought. From time to time, we looked each other in the eye. There was no need for words; we understood one another through eye contact.

The bus drove through the streets of Bangkok in the early morning. Bangkok was much bigger and more modern than Phnom Penh. We arrived at our final destination, the bus station in Bangkok, at seven-thirty. The passengers filed off, one after the other. We stood by the door of the bus for a few seconds before we stepped down. My mind was racing a million miles, wondering what would happen next.

I looked around but ignored the passengers behind me, who rushed to get off the bus. We stood before a passage with metal barricades on both sides that led directly to an exit ramp. On our left, though, there was a small space leading to the other side of the street. I glanced through and saw a taxicab parked on a corner. Instinctively, I held my wife's hand and guided her through the small space, instead going all the way to the exit like the others. Once at the cab, we jumped in and asked the driver to take us to the World Relief International headquarters (WRI).

The cab made a U-turn, heading to WRI. Through the window, I saw three guards at the bus exit checking the IDs of every passenger who'd been on the bus we had just taken. I shuddered, realizing we would have been caught and thrown in jail if we had walked out through the main exit. What made me walk through the space between the metal barricades was a miracle, surely an invisible hand guiding me. I glanced at my wife, and she smiled to me to confirm that we were indeed lucky.

The cab stopped in front of the WRI in a nice section of Bangkok.

We went inside to the front desk and asked the receptionist if we could talk to Mr. Gene Richardson for a minute. The receptionist picked up the receiver and called Mr. Richardson. She hung up the phone and told us to wait in the reception room. Five minutes later, Mr. Richardson walked in as we sat quietly, waiting anxiously for him.

"My friends! My friends! How is married life?" Mr. Richardson greeted us and extended his hands toward us. We shook hands and embraced one another with excitement. He was our first American friend, whom we loved and trusted with our lives. "What are you doing here, my friends?"

"We're on the way to the American Embassy, and we thought to stop by to say hello," I said.

"Do you know someone in the Embassy?"

"No, we'll just go over there and hope they'll bring us to America."

"You two just got married two weeks ago, you left the camp illegally, and now you plan to walk into the Embassy and ask them to take you to America?" Mr. Richardson exclaimed.

"You forgot: I left Cambodia illegally too," I replied with a smile.

"I'm sorry, Mr. Richardson; my husband is trying to be funny. I don't think it's funny," my wife said and looked at me with disappointment.

"It's ok. It's kind of funny, actually. Since you're here, let me introduce you to my boss, and then you can go on your way," Mr. Richardson said and walked back inside the office, letting us wait in the reception room.

Ten minutes later, Mr. Bishop, whom Mr. Richardson introduced as his boss, came and shook our hands. He was tall, with blond hair and blue eyes. He's handsome, I thought. Then the two Americans whom I considered my only friends in the world talked to each other quietly for a few minutes.

After, Mr. Bishop walked inside and Mr. Richardson came to us and said, "You two stay here for a while. Don't go anywhere yet. He's going to make a call to the Embassy. He wants to know more about immigration law and about your options. He has a lot of friends who could sponsor you two. Just wait here until we come back."

An hour later, Mr. Richardson walked toward us from the other door of the waiting room.

"You know what you've done is very dangerous," Mr. Richardson said. "If you had been caught on your way here, they would have put you in jail."

"We know that, but we took a risk. Life in the camp is uncertain. Americans have been picking up millions of Vietnamese in the China Sea since the fall of Saigon. All these Vietnamese have to do is sail a boat off into the sea. If they make it, they go to America. They're risking their lives for freedom. What Sophie and I are doing now is the same; we're risking our lives for freedom," I said, tears in my eyes.

Mr. Richardson tapped my shoulder and said, "We know, my friend." He turned to Sophie and said, "We wish we could help everyone in the camps, but we cannot. We are not the government and we don't want to interfere with the government's work. They have laws to follow. Mr. Bishop is on the phone with the Embassy as we speak."

"Thanks. Why are you so nice to us?" Sophie asked.

Mr. Richardson smiled at us but said nothing. He rose and walked back inside, motioning for us to sit down and relax. Half an hour later, Mr. Bishop and Mr. Richardson walked out toward us with grins on their faces.

"Mr. Bishop just talked to the Embassy and it looks like everything will work out. I am going to take you to the Embassy to process the paperwork, and they will send you to the base and then fly you to Illinois. A family from Wheaton, Illinois, will pick you up at the airport. Dr. Henry Waterman of Wheaton, Illinois, will be your sponsor," Mr. Richardson explained to us.

"Wheaton, Illinois?" I exclaimed.

"Why do you seem so surprised, honey?" Sophie said.

"Nothing. It's just that I read about Wheaton, Illinois, two years ago. I always wanted to live there. Now we are going to Wheaton, Illinois. Isn't it strange?"

Mr. Richardson looked at me with a smile.

"Are there other wishes that have come true?" Sophie asked.

"You, honey! The first time I laid my eyes on you, I knew that I would marry you."

"You're too confident. Don't you think he's too confident, Mr. Richardson?"

Mr. Richardson smiled at us with joy in his eyes.

"Thank you, Mr. Richardson, and you, Mr. Bishop, for your help. We owe you our lives," I said.

"No, you do not owe us anything. God works in your life and He has a great plan for you two," replied Mr. Bishop.

"Thanks," I said. We shook hands with Mr. Bishop to thank him again. He gave us a smile, a smile that showed that he cared.

We left the WRI building with Mr. Richardson and headed to the American Embassy. At the Embassy, we were interviewed by the immigration officer and had to fill out some more paperwork. After that, we were transferred to the U-Tapao Air Force base that same afternoon. It all worked out. Everyone was willing to help us—Mr. Richardson, Mr. Bishop, and the officer at the immigration office in the Embassy.

Later that afternoon, we were in a U.S. Marine Corps Jeep, travelling from the Embassy compound to the U.S. Air Force base on the gulf, 90 miles south of Bangkok. We stepped out of the Jeep and down onto the base grounds with joy in our hearts. My wife looked at me, grasped my hand, and led me to the Coke machine standing by the entrance of the base. She pulled out a quarter from her small purse.

"This is the last quarter we have, honey," she said and showed me the coin. She slipped the coin in the machine and pushed the red button. A can of Coca-Cola dropped to the bottom of the machine. I took the can, looking at my wife with a smile, and shook it several times. Slowly, I drew my ballpoint pen from my shirt pocket and used it to punch the top of the can, hard. A sharp sound issued, and bubbles flowed fiercely from the inside.

Handing the can to my wife, I said, "Cheers! These are bubbles of the only champagne we can get for a quarter. Cheers to freedom! Our dream is coming true!"

She sipped the Coke, and gave the can back with a smile. I sipped it. It was the sweet taste of our adventure just beginning.

We walked toward our new apartment at the base. It was a miracle. "I love you honey, always," I said to my wife.

Sophie

Chapter Twenty-Two

U-Tapao is a U.S. military base in Thailand, set on the gulf, 90 miles south of Bangkok. It was a strategically important base during the Vietnam War. There were more than 7,000 U.S. military personnel on duty, as well as three recreational clubs and a beach, hospital, chapel, library, theater, several shops and an airfield,which is the best airfield in all of Thailand. From this base, giant B-52 bombers took off and dropped bombs in the enemy territories in Vietnam and Cambodia, each carrying 100 to 108 bombs with 500 pounds of high explosions each. KC-135 Tankers, a different type of bomber, also set off from this base for missions in Southeast Asia. During the collapse of Indochina, the Americans used the base to shelter refugees, Cambodians and Vietnamese, before transporting them to the States.

The refugee camp in the base was huge. There were approximately 5,000 refugees and most of them were Vietnamese who had left their country by boats and were picked up by the Americans in the open sea. Some were Cambodians, but they were far fewer. The majority of Cambodians in the camp were servicemen serving in the Gulf of Thailand before the fall. They had escaped with their family in the war-ships and then handed the warships back over to the U.S. government went they arrived at U-Tapao.

Refugees in the camp had complete privacy in their tents. Meals were provided three times a day, served in huge tents assigned as dining areas in the camp. Movies were showed outdoors every night under the vast sky. There was also a nice beach within walking distance. My wife and I spent a lot of time on the beach, swimming and burying ourselves in the sand. Life was good at the base.

In early 1975, the U.S. military began to move out of Indochina; the war against the Communists was not a defeat, but a setback. For nine years, B-52s and KC-135 Tankers had taken off from this base for missions to stop Communist expansion in Southeast Asia. They were missions comparable to a fight against the spreading of a cancer.

Wounded American servicemen were transported from Saigon to this base for treatment and then returned home to join their families in the United States. The war was bad, they said. The truth was, the Communists who took away people's rights and freedoms were bad, not the war. The American men and women in the military sacrificed their lives to protect the freedom and liberty of the human race, regardless of nationality or religion.

The U-Tapao base became a sanctuary for thousands of Vietnamese and Cambodians who escaped from their homelands, seeking freedom and liberty. Most of these refugees left behind friends and families.

We owe our life to you, Americans, I thought. My mother had good instincts and saw the danger coming ahead. She saved my life with the limited resources she had by encouraging me to leave Phnom Penh. Her love was immeasurable. I missed her so much. I didn't know how I could repay her. My tears came when I thought of her, my brothers, and my sister.

"Honey, what's wrong? You're crying," Sophie asked as she sat next to me and put her hand on my shoulder, wiping the tears from my cheeks with her other hand.

"I miss my mother, brothers, and sister."

Sophie was quiet for a moment. Then she said as she put her hand on mine, "I'm sorry, honey, you've gone through so much in your life. The ocean's so vast and so calm. Koh Kong is on the other side, if I am not mistaken," she added.

"You're right, honey." I replied and looked at her with a smile.

"It has been five months of happiness and ordeals at the same time."

"We're crazy, don't you think?" I said.

"You started the whole thing," she said and smiled at me.

"Ok, you can blame me for your misery. If you didn't come looking for me in the restaurant that morning, our whole venture together wouldn't have happened." I paused, looked at her and said, "I'm the luckiest man in the world. You're everything in my life."

She rested her head on my shoulders and our eyes gazed ahead to the horizon, where the sky and sea met.

"Honey, we may face a major problem when we arrive in America," I said, looking at her.

"Why do you say that?" she straightened up and looked me in the eye.

"English is a very difficult language to learn."

"Everyone in the world speaks English, so how can it be difficult?" Sophie replied.

"Everyone speaks English, but very few speak it properly. Learning a language requires both writing and speaking. I assume that we'll put a lot of time into learning written rules and grammar. It may not seem like that big of a deal, because English grammar and French are some-what similar. Since we know French, it won't be a big deal, right? Wrong.

"English grammar has so many exceptions. In the end, we'll have no idea what the rules are and what the exceptions are. According to the general rule, a noun requires an article—a, an, or the—in front of it in a sentence. Nouns cannot stand without articles, but the article is not needed if a sentence is used in the right context, like mass transporta-tion, for example, 'I came by train' is grammatically correct, not 'I came by the train.'

"You'll see by the time we finish the chapter about articles that we have no idea when we need an article in front of a noun or not. You want more examples?" I asked.

"You worry too much, and you're starting to talk nonsense."

"English pronunciation is even worse. We were taught that the sounds of a vowel and consonant in each word should be pronounced distinctly. Honey, I spent all day yesterday repeating the word 'column,' trying to pronounce each vowel and consonant in it distinctly. You know how hard it is to put 'M' and 'N' together? The English sounds of 'M' and 'N' are stronger than our 'M' and 'N' sounds. I thought I did all right, but last night our teacher said the 'N' is silent in the word 'column.' It turns out that the word 'column' is easier to pronounce than I thought."

"Oh, my poor husband; you work too hard for nothing. Do you have some more words to cheer me up with?" Sophie said with a smile.

"Oh, you want some more," I smiled, "The letter 'S' turned out to be a very difficult sound to make. It's impossible! It's a sound like a hissing snake. I can't do it, honey. Don't get me wrong: the English language is a beautiful language, but it is hard to learn. I don't think I can learn it."

"They say French is a romantic language, not English," Sophie said.

"I don't know what they say. I just don't want to sound romantic with every single word I say to you."

Hearing this, Sophie did not say anything. She just looked at me, amused.

"Since you have a hard time speaking English, what're you going to do?" Sophie asked.

"We'll find out. America is a very big country. I heard they speak Spanish in America. I may learn Spanish instead," I said.

She put her hand on my head, brushed my hair, and said, "You're a real genius, you know that?" I said nothing, just smiled at her.

We were silent for a moment, looking to the horizon, and Sophie said, "Honey, I sent a letter to Kim at the camp, telling her that we are here and on our way to America."

"It is very nice of you. She must be thrilled to know that we are free," I replied, brushing my wife's hair gently.

"I wish she were with us now."

"I want to help her, but I don't know how."

"I believe that sooner or later she will end up in the U.S., for the American government wouldn't leave the refugees in the camps, in the cold," Sophie said, looking me in the eye.

"You are probably right."

At seven o'clock in the morning of September 8, 1975, my wife and I walked in a line among more than a hundred Cambodian refugees toward the airfield. A huge green airplane stood before us. I'd never seen an airplane that big; it was approximately 100 feet in length and the two wings spread out about 130 feet. Attached beneath each wing were two big, metallic cylinders in which two propellers would generate high air pressure to make the plane fly. The machine's tail was high in the sky, about forty feet from the ground.

The cockpit there was a large epigraph reading, "U.S. AIR FORCE," and on the middle of the tail was the emblem of the United States, the Star-Spangled Banner. We walked from the front and under the wing toward the rear, where we entered the plane.

Standing at the door, my arm around my wife's shoulder, I looked into the airplane. It was spacious, with dim lights on the ceiling. There were four rows of hammock seats—any of which we were free to choose—stretching from the front of the plane to the back. We looked at each other, walked inside the plane, and took our seats in one of the two middle rows, in the center, facing the windows. We had only one small shopping bag, which we brought with us when we left the refugee camp; I lay it in front of me.

Sophie rested her head on my shoulder, looked at me, and said, "We are going to America now."

I smiled at her and said, "Yes, America: our new home and new country."

As soon as everyone in the plane was aboard, the door closed. At the door of the cockpit, a very handsome American soldier in a neatly pressed combat uniform stood straight, guarding the door, preventing anyone from passing through it. His hair was cut short and his shoes were shined. Instead of a helmet, he wore a regular hat, which matched with his uniform in color and style. There was a pistol in the holster hanging from his right hip.

Before the plane took off, there was an announcement informing us of the safety procedures and rules on the airplane. Meals would be served at the appropriate time. The announcement was in Cambodian, for there was a Cambodian translator on the plane. I held my wife in my arms, kissing her forehead, as the plane took us to a new continent, a new world.

I wondered whether I could ever go back to Cambodia and when I would see my mother and siblings again. Sophie looked at me, tears rolling down her cheeks; she probably had the same emotions as I did. Good thing the trip would bring her closer to her father, mother, brother, and sister after three months of separation. We looked at each other, weeping, unsure whether we were happy or sad. It was very difficult to leave the country of our birth, even though we knew that our lives would be better in America.

God, you are merciful to us, you are our Protector, I said in my mind.

The airplane C-130 Hercules hummed and flew through the sky, over the China Sea and the Pacific Ocean, heading toward Guam, where the plane was scheduled to land on another U.S. military base in eight hours.

A half hour after the flight took off, breakfast was served. Since there was no service on the plane, boxes of breakfast were passed to us from the front. In them there were orange juice, milk, water, a piece of bread, jelly, butter, scrambled eggs, and plastic silverware. When breakfast was done, we passed the boxes back to the front row, where someone collected the garbage and disposed of it.

This procedure was repeated for lunch and dinner. For lunch and dinner, everyone had the same food. The lights on the ceiling were turned low, except during mealtimes, and a dim light was spread inside the airplane. Much of the time, Sophie rested her head on my shoulder and slept. I, too, leaned against the back of my seat, sleeping.

As I dozed, her scent hit my nose; it was a special fragrance, natural and sweet. I glanced at her from time to time as she lay there, eyes closed, lips slightly apart. She was beautiful, an angel in my arms.

People walked past us once in a while to use the lavatory at the back of the plane. We did the same when we had the opportunity. The dim light in the airplane made us feel like it was night, and we lost track of time. We slept most of the time. When we were awake, we talked to each other in whispers so as not to interrupt others who were asleep.

"Had enough sleep, honey?" Sophie asked me, brushing her hand against my cheek.

"Yes," I replied with a smile and asked, "What do you think about the food?"

"Actually it was very good—better than the food served on Air France."

"Really…?"

"Yes. There's no service here, though," Sophie said with a smile.

"Oh, honey. It's a military company, you know that," I replied. Sophie smiled; she understood.

"In our country, the military dictates to civilians. In America, unlike in our country, the military is the instrument of the civilians. It's how it should be," Sophie said.

"Cambodians have a long way to go in organizing the country, the government, and laws," I said. I looked at her and leaned to kiss her on her lips, saying, "You are my blessing from Heaven."

"I love you too," she whispered in my ear and then fell asleep in my arms. I looked at her beautiful face. At that moment, my mind drifted back to when I was younger.

I remembered my cousin Sarah; we used to play together almost every day. I remembered our conversation on the boat we took along the Mekong River. We dreamed of going to America, and here I was on a C-130 Hercules of the U.S. Air Force. I was on an airplane heading to America, but without Sarah. I really missed her. Was I lucky? Or was I in the invisible hands of God, who protected me from danger?

When I left home six months earlier, I had only fifty dollars in my wallet. I spent the last quarter in the Coke machine at U-Tapao. Without a doubt, my life for the last six months was in the invisible hands of God, who created me and everything else in this universe.

I missed my mother, my brothers, and sister very much, but I knew that the same God who saved my life would spare their lives as well. Someday I will see them again, I thought to myself.

I thought of Chantal, my best friend in this world and my lover. She died in vain, blown up by a bomb, the day she brought me home after we spent precious moments in each other's arms the night before.

She meant everything to me and then she died. I thought life was so cruel and merciless back then, but I was not so sure any more now.

Is it true that God has a unique plan for each one of us, I wondered? It seemed that He had one for me. The presence of God in my heart was personal, but it was hard to make others believe what I believed.

Then I heard an announcement: the plane was landing in fifteen minutes. Sophie opened her eyes and said, "We're landing soon, honey, aren't we?"

I nodded.

"You miss her, don't you?" Sophie asked.

"Who?" I asked and stroked her hair.

"Chantal."

"Why'd you say that?"

"I can see it in your eyes," Sophie replied.

I paused, smiled at her, and said, "She died a year ago in a bomb blast. I was wondering whether it was painful, or if she died instantly."

Sophie caressed my cheek with her hand and said, "If she was alive, you wouldn't leave the country, and we wouldn't have met either. Am I right?"

"You are always right, darling. You know that I love you more than anything in this world. You know that, right?" I said and leaned to kiss her. She returned my kiss with a smile. Life was wonderful.

The C-130 Hercules landed at a military base in Guam. When we descended from the airplane, buses took us to an empty building resembling a warehouse, where we rested for five hours. At first, the building was completely empty, but after a while we were given chairs and bunk beds so we could rest comfortably. We were also provided with some juice and snacks before the trip continued.

Our next stop was the Honolulu International Airport, where we were on the plane for two hours before our journey continued. We could see the airport from the window as the plane refueled. I was so excited to see the United States for the first time. We wished we could get out so that we could have a good view of the airport and the landscape around it, but for some reason we were not allowed to get out of the plane.

Our final stop was Camp Pendleton, the United States Government Marine Base in San Diego, California. The refugee camp in Camp Pendleton was huge, ten times bigger than the camp at U-Tapao. In this camp, our immigration paperwork was processed. We had the option of going to Canada if we wanted to, since we spoke French. We opted to stay in the United States, our home, our new country.

Before we left the camp, I became ill and was admitted to a hospital at the base for two weeks. It was nothing, just a sudden change in my metabolism, I figured, since the doctor never really gave me a diagnosis, and I have been very healthy since the day I was released from the hospital.

I was well taken care of during my stay. The nurses came to check my pulse two or three times a day and wrote it down on a chart hanging from the foot of my bed. I remember that I did not talk much and mainly lay in bed, enjoying movies on TV. Popeye the Sailor Man was my favorite show and the first comedy cartoon show I ever saw.

Khemerin was right. American women are beautiful with their blonde hair and blue eyes, I thought to myself, though I never shared the thought with Sophie.

My wife came over to visit me almost every day during my stay in the hospital. It was comfortable there, but my mind was restless, since I was leaving my wife in the camp, alone. I knew then that I loved her even more than I had thought. I couldn't live without her.

Two weeks after I was released from the hospital, we were processed out of the camp, starting the departure to our sponsor's residence in Wheaton, Illinois.

Chapter Twenty-Three

We left Camp Pendleton on October 15, 1975, at nine in the morning on an American Red Cross bus with other refugees, all of them from Vietnam. Earlier that morning, an officer at the camp's processing center handed us I-94s, permits of permanent residence in the United States, along with social security cards and a check for three hundred dollars.

On the bus, my wife sat next to me by a window, looking out and ignoring the din of conversation in the bus. It was a beautiful morning. On the way to the Los Angeles International Airport, the bus went up the mountains, offering us a wonderful view of the forest below, thick with green trees and birds skimming the tree tops along the mountains. We wound through valleys with high mountains on both sides of the roads and beautiful houses built on the mountains here and there.

The bus had left San Diego, heading toward Los Angeles at fifty to sixty miles an hour on the smooth, broad highway. We did not drive through downtown Los Angeles, but I could see the tall, beautiful buildings from the distance. There were so many cars, large and small, going both directions on the highway, some racing past us.

"America is very beautiful, honey," I said to my wife.

The bus stopped in front of the American Airlines departure gate, and a lady in a American Red Cross uniforms stepped in as soon as the door opened. She stood by the door and called on the names on her list, one by one. When she called Sophie and me, we stepped out of the bus and got in line with the other refugees. She told us to wait in the hall as she went to the check-in counter, and the moments seemed like hours.

Five minutes later she came back and handed us two tickets, one for me and another for my wife. She dropped us off at the gate and left us with an airline employee, who escorted us to the right plane to Chicago. Our flight left the Los Angeles airport at noon.

On the plane, we did not talk much. Sophie rested her head on my shoulder most of the time, tears rolling down her cheeks.

"Are you all right?" I asked her. She nodded, yes.

"Why are you crying?" I asked her again.

"We made it. But I miss Mom and Dad," she said, holding my hand tight. She continued, "We'll find them. They know we're coming because I sent my uncle a letter when we were at U-Tapao."

"That was a good idea," I said with a smile.

"Who are these people, the family sponsoring us?" Sophie asked.

"What do you mean?"

"Hope they're good people," Sophie replied softly.

"I'm sure they are," I said without confidence.

"What if they keep us as their slaves?" Sophie asked.

"It won't be too bad then, we won't have to worry about looking for jobs," I replied with a smile. I paused and looked at her. I could tell she was not happy with my reply, so I added, "You know, I was kidding. First, you worry too much, and secondly, I believe that they are good people. They will help us to find jobs and a place to live. Then we'll go to English classes to learn English, and later we will become Americans." I paused and added, "Besides, slavery is illegal in America. You know that!"

"How does the government know that they won't keep us as their slaves?" Sophie asked.

"You're right, the government will never know, but we have to trust the system," I said vaguely.

"Honey, we used to live in a country where the government lied to us every day," Sophie said, looking me in the eye, and continued, "Do you think the U.S. government could lie to her people?"

"Everyone can lie, but honesty is important. It is essential for success in life. Besides, the president and law-makers are elected to their jobs for a period of time, not guaranteed them for life, like in our country."

"Don't underestimate what human minds can do. The leader of a country usually has so much power. He could destroy his own country to serve his self interests, one way or another. You have seen what happened in our country."

I leaned to kiss her on her forehead and said, "You're right, but why do you care? We are in America now."

"No, I don't."

As we carried on our conversation, a flight attendant came to offer us some drinks. We both ordered Cokes. Later, we had chicken, pasta, coffee and ice cream for lunch.

Our plane landed at the O'Hare Airport at six o'clock in the evening. It was a four-hour flight, but the time in Chicago is two hours ahead of Los Angeles. As we walked out of the plane, we took our name tags from our bags and hung them on our necks as we had been instructed before we left Camp Pendleton that morning.

Dr. Waterman, his wife, and their friend were waiting for us at the gate, where they came to greet us as soon as they spotted us walking aimlessly. They hugged us as if we were family members who just came back from a long vacation. They brought us to their home in Wheaton, Illinois.

In the car, we sat in the back seat with the lady who was their friend. On the way to Wheaton from the airport, I was thinking, "Who are these people? They are so nice to us. We're hungry and they'll give us food. They'll give us clothes when we are cold. They're welcoming us to their home when we have no place to live. They're treating us like family members."

The Watermans lived in a big, beautiful home. There were four bedrooms, one of which served as a library, with books from floor to ceiling. The living room, kitchen, and dining room were very large. A thick brown carpet covered the floor from the front door to the back door and throughout the house, except in the kitchen area. It was impressive; I'd never seen a house covered with beautiful carpeting like that.

They also had a two-door garage where two cars were parked.

Americans are rich, so much richer than I imagined, I thought.

Mrs. Waterman showed us to our room. It was beautiful and spacious with classic Americana-style decorations. We put our small bags in a corner and sat on the firm bed, looking at each other with smiles.

"Welcome to our home! This is your room," Mrs. Waterman said, and peeled back the duvet on our bed to reveal layers and layers of sheets, blankets and spreads. We had never known such luxury.

We stayed with Dr. and Mrs. Waterman for a few months until they found us jobs washing dishes in the dining hall of Wheaton College. They also found us a one-room apartment in the east side of town, on Roosevelt Road, a big road leading to downtown Chicago. Even though we had our own place, we kept close to our sponsors; they were our new best friends.

Wheaton is a suburb of Chicago and just a forty-minute drive from the city. The population is approximately 55,000 and a commuter train runs through town all the way to Chicago. In downtown Wheaton, there is a U.S. post office, a small shopping center, restaurants, and a movie theater. The oldest restaurant in town is called Round the Clock; it is located next to the movie theater, on the corner of West Wesley St. and North Hale St. The restaurant is open twenty-four hours a day and seven days a week.

Two blocks east of the downtown area is the public library, the only library in town. Wheaton has two public high schools and one private college, Wheaton College. Wheaton is probably the city with the most churches in America. They're everywhere in town, and you'll find one on nearly every corner and block of the center of town.

Our life was good in Wheaton, Illinois. We both made eight hundred dollars a month. Paying four hundred dollars for rent, we had enough left for food and utilities. We were happy because we had each other. Sometimes we went to Pizza Hut for a romantic dinner.

At work in the kitchen at Wheaton College, we lifted big heavy pots and pans and put dishes in the dishwashing machine, watching them rolling inside the machine, where they were washed and dried. It was fascinating to us. On one occasion, a big pan accidentally dropped from where it hung on the ceiling, making a loud noise. Immediately, I crawled under a table, subconsciously thinking it was a bomb dropping. Everyone burst out loud laughing, seeing me hiding under the table. I was so embarrassed.

I walked over to my wife, and said, "I'm sorry, honey, I don't know what got into me. It's an instant reflex."

She said, "I know, we haven't gotten over the nightmare of the war back home yet."

One day in early November, after a long day at work, we walked out from the Wheaton College dining hall at four-thirty in the afternoon. When we got outside, we were so surprised at what we saw. We stood frozen still, with our palms up, feeling tiny snowflakes dropping in our hands. It was the first time that we had ever seen snow, white and beautiful.

"Honey, it's so beautiful," I said to my wife.

We walked to our apartment while the snow kept coming down, heavier and heavier, covering the ground in a blanket of white. We walked and ran back home, making snow balls and throwing them at each other as we had seen people do in the movies. It was the most joyful experience in our lives, the first time we saw snow.

"America is beautiful," I yelled out to my wife. "Like in my dream, we're walking in the snow. It's like my dream on the bus when we left the refugee camp." I ran toward her, lifting her up, and we both fell in the thick snow.

"I love America," Sophie said loudly.

That evening when we got to our apartment, I rushed my wife to our sofa, instead of our bedroom, took her clothes off, and made love to her passionately. We laughed out loud after we were through, for the sofa was broken. In spite of the mild mishap, I felt great. Our love was a love from heaven, like Adam and Eve in the Garden of Eden.

Six months later, we had saved enough money to buy an old car. We paid eight hundred dollars to our friend who worked with us. We learned how to drive and became independent of our sponsors.

One Saturday morning, my wife and I went to a grocery store in town to buy food for the coming week. I was amazed by the size of grocery stores in America. They seemed so large and organized, with all kinds of clean, fresh, neatly stacked fruits and vegetables in tidy sections. I always bought apples and grapes, for they were rare and very expensive back home in Cambodia.

The other section that attracted my attention was the meat and poultry section, where beef and chicken cuts were sliced and laid on the meat counter. I'd never seen such a vast array of meat before I came to the United States. I quickly learned that food was cheap compared to other products sold in America, which made sense to me, for food is indispensible. What a great country, I thought to myself, pushing the cart from aisle to aisle, my wife next to me.

Suddenly, she grasped my hand and stopped me.

"Look! That couple at the meat counter," she said, "They look like us; they must be Cambodians."

"Should we go and find out?" I asked.

"Yes, we should."

We walked toward them.

"Hi!" my wife said in Cambodian, "I just wondered if you were one of us. We are from Cambodia and got here approximately six months ago."

The woman turned to my wife and said, "Oh my God! We're so glad to meet you. I'm Savvana and this is my husband Narith. We live in West Chicago. We moved to the U.S. about the same time you did."

We exchanged names, phone numbers, and addresses. Narith and Savvana were the first Cambodian immigrants we met in America. We were so happy to meet people from our country who we could talk and relate to—for we were lonely for lack of friends. Later, we met more Cambodian families in the area. Day by day, we grew detached from our sponsors and began to associate mainly with our Cambodian friends.

Every weekend, we spent time with our Cambodian friends in the community, drinking, dancing, spending hours and hours watching TV, and attending parties. Our lives started to spin out of control.

"Savy! I really like Channary, you know, Mrs. Sok? She is very sweet and knows how to throw a party," my wife said as we lay in bed in one evening.

I said nothing and stared at the ceiling without blinking my eyes. I had a million things on my mind.

"We went shopping and she bought me the blouse I wore this evening. Do you like it?" My wife asked.

"Yes, it was nice of her," I replied softly, "Do you think you spend too much time with her and her family?"

"What do you mean?" she said, turning to face me, "I like her and everyone in her family. They are my family."

"Honey, tomorrow night I have to work at Denny's. We do not make much money. You work and I work two jobs, just to pay the bills. The apartment is too expensive; half of my pay check goes to rent."

"Savvana's husband makes a lot of money," my wife said, turning her back toward me. "He works in a factory in Addison. He makes seven dollars an hour. Savvana said her husband can find you a job at his place, for he is very close to the manager."

"We have English class this Thursday night, from seven to nine," I said softly and put my arms around her.

"We were invited for dinner at Mrs. Sok. It's rude to turn down her invitation," Sophie said and brushed my hands away. "I'm not feeling well and I don't want to be bothered. Good night!" It was our first argument. We argued more each day as time went by.

Savvana's husband found me a job at the plastic factory, where I got paid six dollars an hour. It was more than twice what I made while working at Wheaton College. Our finances improved a little but not that much.

I worked in the factory for almost six months; it was a miserable time of my life. At work, everyone spoke Spanish and I spoke Cambodian only at home. I hardly heard any English spoken, except when I was watching TV. I also drifted away from my English class at the College of Dupage; it seemed that I just couldn't find time to attend classes. I foresaw that the situation was a detriment to me, for I lived in America but could not speak English. I decided to quit my job at the factory and work at Central Dupage Hospital in the housekeeping department, just to be around more English-speaking people. I went back to work at Denny's restaurant part-time. This decision displeased my wife greatly, for she thought I was insulting her friend. I did everything I could to make her happy, but things went more and more sour each day.

One Saturday evening, when I returned from work at Denny's, Sophie was not home. At first I thought she went to an ice-cream store across the street. I checked for her over there, but she was nowhere in sight. She couldn't have gone shopping for groceries or to the mall, because we had only one car, and I had driven it to work that day.

I picked up the phone and called our Cambodian friends. None of them were willing to tell me where my wife was. I called Mrs. Channary Sok, asking her whether she knew Sophie's whereabouts. She refused to tell me where my wife was and I knew then she was hiding Sophie.

Emotionally, I was falling apart, trying to stand strong and face the situation. I went to the police station in downtown Wheaton and declared my wife missing. The police took the matter lightly. One officer came to me, patted my shoulder, and told me that my wife was not missing, she had run away. He told me to go home and get some sleep.

That night I couldn't sleep.

How you could do this to me, I thought to myself? Without you my life is over; nothing in this world has meaning to me. I fought back the tears.

For several weeks, I could not eat and hardly did anything other than work. Every day, I asked fellow Cambodians about the whereabouts of my wife. None of them were willing to tell me. I realized they were not true friends after all.

What was wrong with me? I asked myself the question over and over again but could not answer it. A month after Sophie left home, I received a court order to annul our marriage. It was not easy for me. I needed a lawyer to represent me in court. I was scared, given the fact that coming from Cambodia, seeking a new life in America, I would have to present myself in front of a judge in an American court. The Public Aid Office of Dupage County provided me with legal protection, free of charge. I saw Sophie for the last time in court, and I've never seen her since.

After my wife left me, I kept her picture in my wallet for a long

Sophie

time. Sometimes I took it out and stared at it for hours, hoping and praying for her return. Her dark brown hair rested on her shoulders and sat in a fringe above her eyebrows. Her beautiful, white teeth shone as she smiled for the picture, and her pointed nose and lush lips were more inviting than ever. Her green eyes sparkled like diamonds, and her perfect, long eyelashes showed even in the picture.

I felt pretty dysfunctional until around the summer of 1979. One day, I strolled north along the shore of Lake Michigan, toward the main pier of Chicago. Hundreds of people were at the beach enjoying themselves—some with friends and families, some playing in the water, and others lying on the beach under the hot sun with thick suntan lotion on their bodies. Children chased one another with delighted shrieks.

On my right, the vast lake extended as far as my eyes could see, and on my left was Highway 41, Lake Shore Drive, running along the lake and tall beautiful buildings, perfectly arranged on each block, stretching into the sky. The Standard Oil building stood majestically tall among the other buildings. I'd love to work there in that building and I will one day, I thought to myself.

Once at the pier, I walked to the end and sat on the edge, dangling my feet just above the water and looking to the horizon. I sat there in deep thought, tracing back in my mind to the day I first met my ex-wife, the day we got married, and all the adventures in between that led me to America. I took out Sophie's picture from my wallet and stared at it for a long time. Then, slowly, I tore it apart with my hands trembling, tears spilling down my cheeks. I tore the photograph in four pieces, and then eight, and then sixteen, and then thirty-two, and I threw them in the lake, watching them alternately floating and sinking in the waters of Lake Michigan. "Goodbye, Sophie," I murmured softly.

About the Authors

William Wheaton (born Savy Yeb) was born in Cambodia and immigrated to the United States of America in 1975, during the Communist revolution known as Pol Pot Regime. He has been completely assimilated into his new country, becoming a US citizen in 1980.

William Wheaton, educated in Illinois, has a passion for literature, devoting his life for the last 30 years to learning and embracing the English language. He lives with his family in Bethesda, Maryland.

Paul Armstrong grew up in the United States and Poland. He is fluent in Polish, and is currently a student at the University of St. Thomas, triple majoring in history, philosophy, and economics.

Paul is fascinated with art in all of its forms, particularly literature. Active in his community, Paul has previously been published in publications on campus, as well as *The Concord Review*.

Sophie

See 1stWorld Books at:

www.1stWorldPublishing.com

See our classic collection at:

www.1stWorldLibrary.com